She knew better seductive lure of longing or want—in the end the longing would go unfulfilled, and the want would remain nothing more than a teasing trick the mind played.

This man may have reawakened longings best left buried, but he was more dangerous than Jonathon or her husband ever could be. She shivered. If he decided to harm her, she could easily be killed with one swipe of his muscular arm. Worse, if she allowed herself to fall prey to the longings teasing at her, he could easily crush her heart and her spirit. Gillian took a deep shaking breath. She needed to be exceedingly careful if she wished to survive.

No. This was not supposed to have happened. She had no hopes of ever having a husband to care for her, to desire her. Dreams of an idyllic life of love and children were not meant for her. She'd set those aspirations aside long ago. This marriage was nothing more than a means to an end.

She was supposed to have calmly and reasonably offered what she had hoped would be considered a fair exchange.

Rockskill Keep desperately needed protection. And so did she.

Author Note

Welcome to the twelfth century, Denise Lynn style. Take one damaged, hurt, albeit determined, heroine and pair her up with the youngest of the four Roul brothers. Toss in a medieval keep situated at the edge of a rocky seaside cliff and a few really bad guys, and mix lightly. Sprinkle it with a little murder and mayhem. Knead well. Bake for a few hundred pages, and what do you get? A partnership forged out of necessity and a romance borne from mutual need.

At least, that's what I intended to create. But as we all know, sometimes recipes flop and we get brittle, crunchy chocolate chip cookies instead of soft, fluffy ones. Either way, they still taste good.

Grab a beverage of your choice, relax for a few and come join me on this jaunt into my version of the twelfth century, where men have muscles of banded steel and squishy hearts that need a little TLC from heroines unafraid to go toe-to-toe with their bluster.

I do hope you enjoy Rory and Gillian's trials and tribulations even half as much as I enjoyed writing them.

THE WARRIOR'S BRIDE ALLIANCE

DENISE LYNN

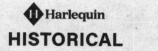

Harlequin

HISTORICAL

ISBN-13: 978-1-335-54002-7

The Warrior's Bride Alliance

Harlequin Enterprises ULC
22 Adelaide St. West, 41st Floor
Toronto, Ontario M5H 4E3, Canada
www.Harlequin.com

Printed in U.S.A.

Award-winning author **Denise Lynn** lives in the USA with her husband, son and numerous four-legged "kids." Between the pages of romance novels she has travelled to lands and times filled with brave knights, courageous ladies and never-ending love. Now she can share with others her dream of telling tales of adventure and romance. You can contact her through her website: denise-lynn.com.

Books by Denise Lynn

Harlequin Historical

Falcon's Honor
Falcon's Love
Falcon's Heart
Commanded to His Bed
Bedded by Her Lord
Bedded by the Warrior
The Warrior's Runaway Wife

Warehaven Warriors

"Wedding at Warehaven"
in *Hallowe'en Husbands*
Pregnant by the Warrior
The Warrior's Winter Bride
At the Warrior's Mercy

Visit the Author Profile page
at Harlequin.com for more titles.

Dedicated with a big, huge, grateful Thank You
to my editor and with love always to Tom.

Chapter One

Rockskill Keep, Scotland—
Spring 1146

'I have need of a husband.'

Rory of Roul shook his head to clear the thick fog muddling his mind and making his head pound. *Where was he?* He tried desperately to dredge up his last memory, but failed. Was it fog clouding his memory, or was it smoke from the fires set after the battle to lay waste to the land? Land now covered by dead bodies. Bodies not of men, but of smooth-faced boys who'd only recently sparred with wooden swords in mock battles. His stomach rolled at the horrors he'd committed.

No. The battle was over. Without his liege's permission or knowledge, he'd gathered his men and left. He was no longer in Normandy. He'd run like a traitorous dog with his tail between his legs back to King David begging for a mission—a wolf's mission—any mission.

He shook his head again. Slowly clearing the murkiness of his mind. He and two of his men had been heading for Rockskill Keep on the King's orders. Rory jerked his head back, only to wince at the contact with the stone wall behind him. *She needed a what?*

The bite of iron manacles securing his wrists and ankles to the cold wall at his naked back kept him from laughing at her statement. Why was there a woman on the battlefield? He blinked, then stared at the woman standing before him, not on a field of battle, but in a dimly lit cell, and asked, 'Where are my men?'

'They are secure.'

'Secure?'

'In a better state than you.' She shrugged, adding, 'For now.'

She stepped closer. The top of her head barely reached his shoulder. 'You worry about your men for naught. You should be concerned for your own well-being.'

He snorted. His well-being had been forfeited the moment he'd deserted his post and walked off the battlefield. The penalty for desertion—treason—would be death. The best he could hope for was that his liege the Count of Roul—his brother Elrik—would use a sharp blade and make it a quick, clean end. 'Where am I?'

'Rockskill Keep.'

At least he'd arrived at the location of his mission for King David. 'I demand an audience with the Lord of this Keep.'

'That would be impossible, as he is dead.'

A piece of information King David either didn't know or had forgot to mention when he sent him here to bring the shipwrecks, smuggling, murders and other happenings at Rockskill to heel. 'Then who is in charge here?'

'I am.'

'And you are?'

'The Lady of Rockskill.'

Rory wrenched hard against the restraints, angry at the knowledge that he was at this vixen's mercy. He pulled harder on the chains, his chest nearly hitting her nose.

She didn't move, didn't as much as flinch, simply looked

up at him, warning, 'If you harm me, you will die. But if you hurt yourself, I will send in the midwife. Trust me when I say you will not like her attention. She enjoys making her charges cry.'

He ignored her threat to send a woman's healer instead of a surgeon to attend him. The slanted tilt of her lips and arching of her brows let him know she'd insulted him on purpose. And while he highly doubted a woman could make him cry, he was in no position to test that theory.

She reached out, stopping just before her palm touched his chest. Her hand was so close that a breeze would not have passed between them. He looked down, wondering if her touch would burn, and suddenly was grateful that he only lacked clothing from the waist up.

The woman paused, frowning. As if uncertain of her next move. Rory lifted a brow. If he didn't know better, he would guess this woman had never been alone with a man before. Yet she had just claimed her husband had died.

He watched the play of emotions cross her face as she stared at his chest, as if the sight was unfamiliar. Her curiosity while studying his shoulders, chest, then stomach blinked to hesitancy before she quickly flashed her gaze back up. But the raising of her finely arched brows and the slight widening of those blue eyes silently spoke of interest.

She jerked her hand away, produced a dagger from behind her back and held the tip towards the tie of his braies. 'It would be an easy thing to strip you completely. Perhaps I should see if the rest of you will suffice as husband material.'

Was she that witless, or truly that bold?

Rory doubted if she'd be bold enough to do so, but he had no desire to discover the answer, at least not while chained to a wall. 'Do you know who I am?'

She tucked the dagger back behind her. 'You are Rory of Roul, the youngest of King David's wolves.'

She knew who he was and yet still saw fit to capture him? He frowned, unable to remember how this had happened.

'You appear confused.'

'How did I get here?'

'As I said, I have need of a husband, someone well able to defend my Keep, and you were drinking at the inn near the village—Rockskill's village.'

'What a fortunate coincidence.'

She laughed. 'No such thing, my love.'

'I am not your love.'

She ignored him and continued. 'Nobody comes or goes from Rockskill without my knowledge. Nothing happens that I do not know about. My men are everywhere and, like my people, they are very loyal.'

It was the same on Roul Isle. However, neither he, nor his brothers, had ever captured and held anyone in a cell without a valid reason. Needing a husband was far from valid.

Now that the fog had somewhat cleared, he remembered the inn—little more than a large, thatched cottage set along the road, it had looked like a safe place to stop for a meal and a drink before crossing on to Rockskill land. He'd not realised they had already done so.

King David had been vague about the border, saying only that it had been a moving line of late due to the constant fighting between Rockskill and the neighbouring lords. The King had been confident the current border lay after the second of the two narrow streams.

Since the inn was located between the trickling waters, Rory had been certain they'd yet to cross on to Rockskill land. He and his men, Adam and Daniel, had struck up a conversation with the owner of the inn. Not halfway through the first tankard of ale, he'd become light-headed and his vision had blurred. Well able to hold his drink, his odd reaction had given him a clue too late that something was dangerously wrong. He vaguely remembered trying to question the owner—right before he'd slid off the stool.

'The inn between the streams—'

She cut him off to say, 'Is on Rockskill land…for now.'

'You had the innkeeper drug me.'

'Along with your men.'

The woman had to be desperate to have taken such drastic measures. 'Why do you have such a need for a husband?'

'Not just a husband. But one who is strong.' She reached out as if to touch him, but instead slowly skimmed her gaze over one of his shoulders, then along the muscle of his upper arm. 'There is no doubt that you are built for strength.'

He fought to ignore the heat caused by her pointed look, noting that her hand, still suspended in the air between them, trembled. He'd been correct—she wasn't as experienced, or unaffected, as she tried to appear. Did she have any idea how appealing her naivety was to men? If he were not chained to the wall, he would likely run as far and as fast away from her as possible—after stealing a taste of her lips. This lovely young woman was walking, talking danger to any male who wished to remain wifeless.

When he'd been younger, he had abhorred the idea of taking a wife—until he'd watched his two older brothers with their unwanted wives. Their forced marriages hadn't been easy at first, but after a few rough months of getting to know each other, and more than a few rather rousing shouting matches, along with the unnerving female tears, Gregor and Elrik both seemed…happier and well satisfied with their lives. They were slower to anger and, for the first time Rory could remember, they laughed, an odd sight and sound, but one that had been missing from their lives for a long time.

Sometimes he wondered what it would be like to have a ready woman to share his bed nightly, a gentle touch, a soft voice, someone to share meals or a laugh with, someone to dream of the future with, and children. But a condemned man, even one still walking about freely, had no right to consider those things.

Rory drew his attention back to the woman before him. 'There are many men built for strength.'

'Ah, but I need one with a reputation of being not just able, but also willing to use that strength.' She briefly touched the silver-tipped hair at his temples. 'Who better than one of King David's fearsome wolves?'

He saw the look in her eyes. They had darkened slightly as her pupils had enlarged. Yet her forehead had creased with uncertainty. She was as nervous and skittish as a kitten without its mother. While she might have been wed, she had little experience with men. So, this teasing brashness was an act—one she did not excel at performing.

After quickly putting both hands behind her, she continued, 'The man also needs a measure of wealth.' The woman waved towards a jumbled pile at the far corner of the cell. 'Your double-linked mail and finely made weapons are worth a small fortune.'

He silently cursed at the ill treatment of his armour. However, she was right. Elrik had paid dearly for the mail and the sword. 'You still haven't answered my question. Why are you in such need of a husband?'

'Is not every woman in need of a husband for one reason or another?'

That might be true, but it was highly unusual for a woman

to take men captive in pursuit of one. 'You seem in a particularly desperate need for a husband.'

'My reasons are my own.'

'I would think you might share those reasons with the man you are threatening with marriage.'

'Threatening? You make it sound as though you are being tortured with the mere mention of marriage.'

He tugged at the irons round his wrists. 'Is that not what this is?'

She grasped his shoulders and pushed them against the stone wall. 'Stop before you injure yourself.'

Her slight movement brought her closer. The warm softness of her body pressed against him.

Rory closed his eyes and breathed deeply. Lavender and some seductively feminine scent invaded his senses. He dragged his chin across the top of her head, groaning as the dark blonde hair brushed soft against his skin, making him long to bury his face in the silken tresses.

As if realising just how close they were, she jumped back as if burned, nearly stumbling in her haste to put some distance between them. Once steady on her feet, she narrowed her eyes. Staring at his chest, she asked, 'What has the wolf's heart beating so fast and hard?'

Rory cleared his throat. 'Were I not chained like an animal, I would show you just how fast and hard your own heart could beat.'

Her frown deepened. 'What makes you think I would permit such liberties?'

He smiled at the ragged breathlessness of her voice that only lent more strength to his thoughts of her inexperience and to his thoughts of escaping her siren-like call. Chained to a wall like a dog would make escape difficult, but perhaps going out of his way to insult her might cause her to find him less…interesting. 'Permit them? You have done much to encourage them. The boldness you have shown thus far does not speak of a woman who would hide behind a veil of shyness.'

Her blue eyes widened. 'What are you saying?'

'That you have intentionally beckoned me to take such liberties. Come, release me from these chains, I will gladly provide what you seek.'

Even with the dim, flickering torch light barely illuminating the cell, he saw a flush of colour darken her cheeks and a shimmer spark to life in her glare. 'I am not a strumpet who freely gives away favours.'

'Perhaps not. I have no way of knowing. But at this moment, the only difference I can see is that, instead of coin, you expect marriage as payment.'

'Oh!' She gasped, then grabbed the skirt of her gown with both hands, spun round and rushed from the cell, slamming the door behind her.

Rory shook his head and sighed bitterly. What had she expected him to think, or say? She'd been the one to put on an act of boldness by capturing him, chaining him to a wall, then coming so close that he could inhale her scent. Whether the mummery was good or bad meant little as it had left him with an uncomfortable longing he'd rather not have and a less than favourable opinion of her.

He once again tugged against the irons.

King David had sent him here to bring Rockskill's Lord to heel—permanently ending the nefarious deeds taking place along the coast—in any manner possible. Since the Lord was dead, if this woman was to be believed, either the man had perished recently, or someone had stepped in to lead the ongoing criminal acts. Regardless, Rory still had that task and others to complete before he surrendered to Elrik. While he *had* gained entry to the Keep, this wasn't the method he'd had in mind.

All he could do now was wait and hope that she didn't intend to keep him chained here for long.

Lady Gillian of Rockskill paced the length of her bedchamber. Shame, rage and utter confusion fired her steps and she found herself covering the distance from the door to the long narrow windows on the other side of the room quickly—too quickly. Her current mood would be better suited for a tromp through the forest or scrambling over the rocks to stomp along the narrow strip of shore.

What was wrong with her? How could she have been so foolish? Her intention had been to simply speak to her prisoner.

What devil had possessed her to be so bold, so brash, and thoughtless enough to get so close that she could almost stroke his flesh and smell the lingering scent of rosemary that mingled with leather and sweat? Something about that purely male combination on him stole her normally good sense and left her wanting something she couldn't quite identify.

She was no longer some young untried girl who anxiously awaited her marriage, longing for love and dreaming of the joy she'd find in her marriage bed. She'd been wed and knew those dreams were simply that—dreams—and that the love she'd sought didn't exist. But, oh, how she'd longed for them to be true a long time ago.

At night she used to lie in bed and wonder what it would be like to be kissed and touched by a man. She would close her eyes and imagine some strong, brave, dark-haired man would kiss her until she swooned in his arms. His touch would be tender, inviting, encouraging her to want more.

More of what, she'd had no idea, but her body had pulsed with what she could only assume was need…want.

Instead, she'd thought to practise kissing her friend Jonathon. Once. They sneaked off into the stables to take their friendship to another level—at least that's what he'd claimed they would do. But the look in his eye right before he'd kissed her had frightened her and, when she'd thought to back away, he'd held her in place. His kiss had started as a gentle and welcome touch, but something had flickered in her mind, telling her what they were doing was wrong. This boy was more her brother than lover. When he'd tried to push his tongue past her lips, she had pulled free at the unwanted intrusion.

She'd tried to explain that she cared for him as a brother, but nothing more. He'd laughed at her and forcefully pulled her back against him, claiming that no brother would ever kiss her like this. Then he'd ground his lips against hers, leaving them bruised and swollen.

That kiss had cured her of wanting any man to handle her in such a manner. The bruises on her arms where he'd held her far too tightly had taken days to fade. But the memory had never left her. She'd tried since then to keep their relationship as just that of friends. Usually it wasn't a problem, but sometimes, usually after a bout of drinking, Jonathon would get that look on his face, the one that made her uneasy. She made certain to leave his presence before he could act on whatever was urging him to be cruel.

After their one shared kiss in the barn, she'd run crying back to the Keep, hoping to hide in her chamber until the bruises faded. But her father had seen her and questioned her swollen, bleeding lip. She had protected Jonathon out of deference to their long friendship, but her dear cousin Albert had whispered in her father's ear and when her sire had removed his wide leather belt, she'd known she was in for the beating of her life. No amount of begging and crying on her part had stayed his arm. His reasoning was that he wasn't going to have a whore for a daughter, even if he had to beat her ungodly appetites from her. She hadn't understood what he'd been screaming about, not then.

Within a week she had found herself married off to the first man he could find. Unfortunately, that man had been one of his friends, Sir Robert—a man just as old, just as cruel, just as demanding. Her dreams of having a husband to care for her had withered the moment her sire had announced the betrothal.

Then, on their wedding night, Robert had effectively killed whatever sliver had remained of her dreams and any hope of finding someone kind to love her. Those dreams and hopes had stayed buried ever since.

Until today.

Somehow, just the glimmer in Rory's gold-flecked, forest-green eyes, the muscles covering his chest and arms, the deepness of his voice and a trace of his half-cocked smile had reawakened those dreams and the longings that went with them. She didn't understand how. Nor could she fathom why now of all times such a thing would happen.

She gritted her teeth and clenched her hands at the horrible realisation that, somehow, he had recognised the odd longings that had beset her.

All her careful planning had vanished the moment she'd entered the cell to find that her men had stripped him of his mailed armour, tunic and shirt.

The surprise at seeing such a muscular bare chest and arms had caught her off guard. Her surprise had so quickly turned to interest that she'd been unable to hide her riotous emotions.

While she'd seen many a handsome man—some of them

possessing a fine warrior's form, although not quite as splendid as his—she'd never been alone with them, or so close. At least not close enough to inhale their scent or see the play of flesh as it moved over their well-defined hard muscles.

Never before had she had the opportunity to come so close to a man without suffering the consequences of her *filthy* curiosity. Rory had been shackled, unable to correct her baseness with his hand, and he had not even shouted at her for the rough treatment he'd suffered at her instigation, so she'd been overly bold with a man who could not offer her harm. How did that make her any different than Jonathon?

Not counting her father, or her cousin, Rory was only the third man she'd ever been alone with in her entire life. Her husband had seen her as more of a bother than anything else. When his cold gaze came to rest on her it had left her trembling in dread. Even Jonathon, her lifelong friend, leered at her in a way that made her feel ill and afraid at times. Rory, a stranger held prisoner in her Keep, secured in chains, had looked at her and she'd been overcome with the desire to drown in his gaze.

She closed her eyes against the shiver rippling down her spine at the recent memory. Even though he'd insulted her, insinuated she was little more than a whore, he had obviously desired her. When she'd pushed his shoulders against the wall to keep him from harming himself, she had noticed the rapid beating of his heart at their accidental closeness. His response made her wonder if his kiss would be cruel, or kind? Would his touch leave her bruised, or longing for more? She wanted to imagine he would be different from Robert and Jonathon, but knew well the dangers of dreaming and wishing.

'Cease.' Gillian's hoarse whisper did little to stop the images from racing through her mind. She knew better than to fall prey to the seductive lure of longing or want—in the end the longing would go unfulfilled, and the want would remain nothing more than a teasing trick the mind played.

This man might have reawakened longings best left buried, but he was more dangerous than Jonathon or her husband ever could be. She shivered. If he decided to harm her, she could easily be killed with one swipe of his muscular arm. Worse, if she allowed herself to fall prey to the longings teasing at her, he could easily crush her heart and her spirit. Gillian took a deep, shaking breath. She needed to be exceedingly careful if she wished to survive.

No. This was not supposed to have happened. She had no hopes of ever having a husband to care for her, to desire her. Dreams of an idyllic life of love and children were not meant for her. She'd set those aspirations aside long ago. This marriage was nothing more than a means to an end.

She was supposed to have calmly and reasonably offered what she had hoped would be considered a fair exchange.

Rockskill Keep desperately needed protection. And so did she.

Chapter Two

A frantic knock at her bedchamber door tore her attention away from her thoughts. She retrieved the short sword hidden beneath her bed.

Her maid called out through the door, 'My Lady. I have news.'

With a sigh of relief, Gillian slid the wood bar free of the iron holders that held it against the door for her protection and ushered her older nursemaid inside her chamber.

Her eyes wide, and voice shaking nearly as much as her wrinkled hands, Catherine warned, 'A messenger arrived. Your cousin sent word to his men that he is beginning his journey back to Rockskill. I overheard them say that he hopes to arrive within a month or so at most. A priest rides in his company.'

Gillian cursed. Albert was to have been gone at least another two months or longer. He despised the bitter cold winter brought to Rockskill. Vowing not to spend another winter in this *godforsaken* Keep, he had fled south until warm weather arrived, leaving most of his men behind to keep a close eye on her. His early return threatened to bring a sudden end to her plans. And the presence of a priest in his company did not bode well for her current marital status.

Catherine asked, 'Did he accept your offer?'

Since she'd never made the offer, he'd had no chance to accept it or turn it down.

At her silence, Catherine reminded her, 'You know how important this is for yourself and the Keep. More so now than before.'

'Yes, I know.' Gillian slid the sword back beneath the bed.

'So, did you speak to him of your plans?'

'No. The men had stripped him of his armour and clothing.' With a huffed sigh of disgust at herself, Gillian added, 'So, I was caught off guard when I first set my gaze upon him.'

'Not surprising, since the only man you've been in close contact with was either your father, or that worthless old sod he wed you to.'

Catherine had never made her intense dislike of Robert a secret. 'Do not speak so ill of the dead.'

'I'll not apologise, my Lady. That man was as useless a husband as a three-legged mule would be if hitched to a loaded cart.'

'Oh, Catherine, your rage at Robert is only because I never bore a child with him.'

The woman rolled her eyes while making a dismissive snort. 'At his age, he would have needed divine intervention for that to have happened.'

'Perhaps the vessel was at fault.' Not certain if her late husband's claims of her barren state were true, she could only repeat the words of blame he'd shouted into her face when each of her monthly times proved once again that she was not with child. 'Either way, it is done. Robert is gone.'

Gillian swung around to cross the chamber and stare out the narrow window opening. 'I can do nothing about anything that happened before this day. Somehow, I must find the courage to see my way through to protect our future.'

'He is chained to the wall, is he not?'

'Yes.'

'Then, my Lady, the absolute worst he can do is turn down your offer. He cannot harm you.'

'And that is what I fear.' Now that Albert was returning so soon, what would she do if this man did turn down her offer? Rory's unexpected appearance was a fortuitous god-send she could not ignore. Men of his stature did not often travel to Rockskill. There was not enough time to find another one as strong or wealthy enough to suit.

'Lady Gillian, I know that sweetness is something you rarely apply, but is this not the time to try a taste of both sweet and bitter?'

'What do you suggest I do? Whisper softly while threatening him with a blade?' She'd tried that and had gained little more than an amused look from him.

'No, you need not threaten *him* at all. Not when you have two of his men confined in another cell.'

Gillian spun away from the window. 'Catherine!'

Her maid quickly reminded her, 'The times be dire, my Lady.'

'Yes. But threatening to harm his men? That seems a bit...' She let her response trail off. Who was she to quail at doing something underhanded? Isn't that what she'd done by taking the three of them hostage to begin with? Gillian took a deep breath. She'd been the one to devise this plan because she'd been out of options. It was too late to appeal once again to King David—by the time he would reply to any plea for help, she could find herself wed to whichever beast Albert found most objectionable to her.

While this wolf of David's did not seem afraid for his life—as if he didn't care whether he lived or died—he had asked about his men first. Was their welfare more important than his own?

She headed for the chamber door.

'My Lady?'

'Since Albert will soon arrive at our gates, I seem to be out of time to decide my next move. Summon our priest and have him wait in the guard room above the cells.' Before leaving the bedchamber, she added, 'Bring the leather satchel from my chest and wait with him.'

If she couldn't convince the King's wolf to wed her, perhaps a bit of despicable prompting would make him more willing to agree.

Halfway across the great hall, Jonathon put a hand on her shoulder, stopping her. 'A word?'

Gillian looked towards the heavy door leading to the cells below, then up at Jonathon to gauge his mood before she nodded. 'A brief one.'

He waved her towards the small chamber at the rear of the hall. Closing the door behind them, he leaned against it. As he looked at her, that heavy-lidded gaze fell over his face and made her stomach roll.

His leer made her aware he had been drinking either ale or wine. She took a deep breath as she walked behind the table covered in notes, accounts and missives she'd been working on earlier. 'You wanted to talk?'

He nodded. 'The goods in the caves are ready for your inspection.'

'Goods?' She knew of no recent activity. 'From?'

'The ship we gained almost three, maybe four weeks or so ago.'

Since Jonathon would never make the decision to take a ship on his own, apparently Albert had issued orders before he'd left, without making her aware of them. She stared at Jonathon. 'A ship?'

'And a fine one it was, too. Between the gold on the ship and what we can gain from the armour and weapons—'

Gillian raised a hand to stop him. 'Gold, armour and weapons?' She swallowed the urge to be sick. Few ships would carry that type of cargo. 'Whose ship?'

He swaggered towards the table, leaned over to rest his hands atop it and smiled. 'Come, Gillian, you should be pleased.'

She backed away from the heavy smell of ale on his breath, wondering why she hadn't noticed it before agreeing to this discussion. The only thing that could have explained that lapse in judgement was Rory. She turned her attention back to Jonathon. 'That doesn't answer my question.'

He straightened and shrugged. 'It was a royal ship. And the soldiers aboard died like frightened whining puppies when they mistakenly made it to shore.'

'Jonathon! Tell me you didn't murder them.'

'I put them out of their misery, just as Lord Albert always ordered.'

Gillian fell on to the chair behind her. 'What have you done? Are you trying to bring King David's troops to Rockskill?' Never mind that she had one of his wolves chained to a wall below.

Jonathon frowned. 'I thought you would be pleased.'

'Pleased?' How could such an event make her glad? She studied his face. Something shimmering in his gaze made her wonder if Jonathon had done this on his own thinking to help her feed the people of Rockskill? No. Surely he wouldn't have been that foolish.

'It will do much to fill our coffers.'

While that might be true, how could they barter or sell the goods with the King's wolf here?

Jonathon leaned across the narrow table to grasp her arms and pull her from the chair. 'Come, Gillian, we should celebrate and not worry about what might, or might not, happen.'

He leaned closer to kiss her. When she jerked away from his touch, he grabbed her head to hold her in place as he lowered his mouth over hers.

Trying not to gag at the smell and taste of the ale, she fought off his hold, but not before he left her lip bleeding.

She wiped a hand across her mouth, then shouted, 'Get out of here!' She pointed a shaking hand towards the door. 'Go! Get something to eat and then take yourself to bed, Jonathon.'

'I didn't mean to hurt you. I only—'

He did truly look sorry. Gillian sighed and lowered her arm. 'I know. Please, just go and sleep it off until you clear your mind.'

When he left, she dropped back into the chair and held her head in her hands, fighting the need to cry.

What was she going to do now?

She took a couple of deep breaths and wiped the tears from her eyes.

Someone would pay—likely with their life. As angry as Jonathon made her at times, she couldn't forget their past and what they'd shared as children, or the times he'd come between her and Albert.

She could never be what Jonathon wanted, could never share his bed, or be his wife.

But he was her only friend and she would always do all in her power to keep him safe. She owed him that much, even though right now she was so angry with him that she wanted to punch him.

* * *

The silence of his cell was broken by the sound of approaching footsteps. Rory listened to the exchange of voices outside the door, before it slowly creaked open to reveal the woman's return.

She stood in the doorway and stared at him a few moments. The lit torch in the wall sconce bathed her form in a soft halo of light, making her appear nearly angelic.

He failed to bite back a chortle at the fanciful thought. This Lady of Rockskill was no angel and, even if she were, he most certainly wasn't deserving of one.

'You find something amusing?' She stepped inside the cell, closing the door behind her.

'No, not in the least.'

He looked closer at her. The redness of her eyes spoke of recent tears. Her lower lip was swollen. Who would be low enough to harm a lady in her own Keep?

'I am in desperate need of a husband.'

Obviously. Or least a champion to protect her from whoever was hurting her.

'As you've already stated.'

'I have your men.'

'Yes, you do.'

What was she planning?

'Do you care for them?'

Was she the type of person who would stoop so low as to harm innocent men to get what she wanted? Rory studied her. Within the space of a breath, she dropped her gaze to stare at the floor. Her hands, clasped before her, tightened until her knuckles turned white. She lowered her shoulders as if in defeat.

While she'd been sly enough to take him captive, and was just brazen enough to tease him earlier, he didn't think she had the stomach to harm his men. Yet he found that her suddenly submissive stance bothered him in a way he didn't understand. He didn't like it. But Rory drew in a slow breath to keep from ordering her to straighten her spine.

'Adam has a wife and a young daughter.' Perhaps if he could appeal to her motherly instincts, providing she had them, she would set aside her thoughts. 'Daniel's wife recently died. His two boys are living at Roul Keep in his absence. You would threaten either of them with harm?'

Her chest rose with the heaviness of her breath. She lifted her head to meet his stare and squared her shoulders in what he feared was determination. 'If I must.'

Rory felt his lips twitch at the shakiness of her voice. No, his momentary worry was for naught. She might threaten them, but it was doubtful she would carry out the threats.

'Why do you so desperately need a husband?'

She worried her lower lip between her teeth, flinched and then frowned. Finally, she explained, 'When my husband, the Lord of Rockskill, died, my cousin immediately seized control and now seeks to rid himself of me by wedding me to the most beastly man he can find.'

All of this was over nothing more than a betrothal disagreement? Rory wanted to rage at the absurdity of the situation. Instead, he asked, 'And which *beastly* man has he suggested?'

'Suggested?' Her voice rose. She shook her head and in a milder tone explained, 'He has done more than suggest. He has moved three of them into my Keep. One is Sir Cranwell.'

Rory snorted. If her cousin was looking for beastly, Cranwell would more than suffice as the man's appetite for women, willing or not, was legendary. Perhaps she did have a good reason to be overly concerned. 'Did Cranwell bring his women along, or is he terrorising the ones here?'

'Both, I fear.'

'Who else?'

'Smithfield.'

Had someone wanted to threaten a woman into submission, Smithfield would be the man. His appetite for women had nothing to do with the bedchamber. Far too many young women had perished under his not so tender attention. Their bruised bodies and broken bones had testified to the manner of their deaths.

He couldn't imagine who the last man would be. 'And?'

She gasped softly and took a step back. Her reaction made him narrow his eyes. Who, besides David's wolves, would frighten a woman so much that she was reluctant to even speak his name?

Rory cursed. Only one man could make Smithfield's gruesome treatment of women look almost kind in comparison. Where Smithfield's brand of torture ended in the woman's death—a blessing to be sure—this fiend denied such an escape. His victims, be they men or women, endured a lingering terror that usually ended only when they took their own life. 'Blackshore?'

The colour left her cheeks. 'Yes.' She nodded, her answer a choked, hushed whisper.

With the choice of men her cousin had placed before her, it was no wonder she'd taken such drastic measures to secure herself a husband. Still, being forced into this position was unacceptable. He was not the husband for her.

He did not know for certain what penalty Elrik would impose on him. Likely, it would be his death, as that would be the expected payment for desertion. If his brother did demand his life, the last thing Rory wanted was to burden a wife in such a manner. She would not only suffer loss at his death, but her future would be marred by his act of treason. While

he would be gone—consumed by the fires of hell—her reputation would be tarnished for ever, leaving her alone with
no hope for a future marriage.

No. He couldn't help her.

'You claimed your guards were loyal. Why have they not
ousted these men?'

'Not all my men are guards. They are but villagers who
cannot stand against armed guards. Besides, Albert has in-
stalled enough of his own men to easily control what force
I do command. A precious few have already learned that
the penalty for going against Albert is death. I will risk no
more of their lives.'

He wondered if these villagers she likely used as spies,
since they weren't trained in weapons, were also involved
with the smuggling. That was something he'd discover later.
For now, he turned his focus to her guards. Their duty was
to protect their Lord or Lady, even at the cost of their own
lives. How could she not know this? 'You will not let them
do their duty even to save you?'

'No.'

Her tender heart concerning her men could eventually
prove her demise. 'Why have you not requested help from
King David?'

'I tried that once.' She looked away for a moment. 'King
David sent one of his men to see to the matter and I was
portrayed as nothing but a halfwit by my father and Albert.
Why would I try again?'

'Giving up shouldn't have been an option.' Considering
he had done the same thing—given up and walked away—
his comment left a sour taste on his tongue.

'You wouldn't understand. I doubt if King David's wolf
has ever been in the position of being without options.'

He held back a bark of laughter at her statement. Did she

truly think he and his brothers freely chose to serve as David's wolves? They did so to pay for their father's act of treason. Serving at the King's whim was the only way to retain possession of Roul Isle and to save their father's life. Twice now they'd been released from duty, only to have been called back into service. Each of them realised this duty would last for life. Rory swallowed at the knowledge that he was no better than his sire—perhaps worse, since his treason had not been committed against his King, but against his own brother.

Instead of correcting her misconception, he asked, 'What will you do if I refuse your proposal?'

She held his gaze and straightened her spine, giving Rory the impression she might possess less of a tender heart than he'd first thought.

'Eventually you will accept. Or you will watch your men die.' When he remained silent, she opened the door and called to a guard, 'Bring me the man called Daniel.'

When the guard left to do her bidding, she stepped closer. 'You think me weak. And while it is true that I do not possess the physical strength, experience or bravery to deal with your men on my own, I am quite capable of ordering the deed be done.'

Rory willed his body not to betray his rage. Once certain his breathing would remain steady, and his heart would beat evenly, with every ounce of outward calm he possessed, he asked, 'You think that will convince me to take you as my wife?'

She shrugged. 'I know little about you other than what everyone has heard of the King's wolves, but I am not foolish enough to believe everything I hear. You may be as violent and heartless as the tales tell, but I think, when it comes to those under your command, you are honourable. So, yes, I do believe you will go to any length to protect your men.'

From the commotion in the corridor, it was apparent her guard was having some difficulty retrieving Daniel. His man's curses were punctuated by the repeated thuds of something, or someone, being shoved forcefully against the stone wall—most likely her guard.

She glared at him. 'It will be worse for him if my guard is injured.'

'Daniel, cease!' Rory shouted.

The thudding stopped and, within moments, the guard pushed Daniel inside the cell, where he landed on the floor at her feet. His arms were bound behind him, his ankles held fast by manacles. He struggled to his knees, snarled at her, then turned his attention to Rory. 'My Lord?'

Before he could say anything, Rockskill's Lady turned to her guard. 'Leave us.'

Once the man pulled the door shut, she addressed Daniel. 'Your Lord has a decision to make. He will either wed me, or watch you die.'

Daniel's eyes narrowed briefly as he glanced up at her. But he returned his focus to Rory. Not a trace of fear, or regret, showed on his man's face. 'As you will.'

Rory groaned. The man was too loyal. He knew that both his men would die for him without question. But hearing the surety from his man's lips made him ill at the thought of being responsible for so needless a death. Now who possessed too much of a tender heart? He wasn't much better than she when it came to the safety of his men.

Unfortunately, from the self-satisfied look on her face, she'd already guessed at his answer.

A sudden thought gave him pause. This unexpected snag in his plans could prove beneficial in more ways than one.

He'd been sent here to deal with the difficulties at Rockskill and being the Lord of the area might make accomplishing that task easier and quicker. The sooner he could restore order to the land, the sooner he could face his brother's decision.

From what he had heard, King David had a soft spot for women. Once all his tasks were accomplished to the King's satisfaction, surely the King would assist him in ending this marriage before rumours of his traitorous deed came to rest at Rockskill. Then everyone's needs could be satisfied without undue lingering harm to her. Perhaps the King might go as far as to find her a suitable husband.

In the meantime, before his life was forfeited for his act of treason, he would have the opportunity to have a taste of what a marriage might have provided him were it possible. While he wouldn't experience everything he had once hoped for, would it truly be so bad to have a soft woman to hold, or someone with a gentle voice to talk to? What harm could there be in being her champion even for just a short time? He glanced at her lip. She certainly could use a protector. Maybe he could try to prove that all men weren't beasts if she'd let him.

'Agreed. I want them released.'

She studied him a moment, then sighed heavily. From the way her shoulders relaxed, he could only assume she was relieved. 'Of course. They are your men and you will have need of them.'

Daniel gasped, before saying, 'My Lord, you are not—'

'Yes.' Rory fought not to choke on his words. 'I will wed our captor.'

He ignored Daniel's vehement argument against the idea to warn her, 'There are terms.'

'Once the ceremony is completed, Rockskill lands, Keep

and all in it are at your disposal. Anything you want will be yours.'

'Anything?'

Once again, she folded her hands and glanced down at the floor before meeting his gaze. 'Yes. Anything Rockskill has to offer.'

He kept his reply to nothing more than a nod. To do otherwise would only let the harsh laugh building in his throat escape. Her nervousness had returned. As well it should.

'I'll not go to this marriage ceremony in chains or half-dressed.'

She frowned a moment, but finally nodded and called her guard back to the cell. 'Release him. See that he has his garments, but not his weapons.'

She remained silent while her man saw to her orders. When Rockskill's guard once again left the cell, Rory asked, 'My men?'

On her way towards the door, she said, 'They will be released and seen to as soon as the ceremony is completed.'

He understood her reasoning, but he wasn't about to enter this union without someone from Roul present to witness the event. He wasn't a freeman who could simply choose his bride and wed her. His eldest brother was not just his liege, but the Lord of Roul Isle and the Count of Roul. There was protocol to be followed. It was bad enough he was marrying her without a betrothal agreement or his brother's approval—something that would likely provide more heat to Elrik's anger. 'They stand for me.'

She stopped and turned around. 'Anything else?'

Her clipped tone and arched brow let him know her question wasn't asked in earnest. He could list many things he'd like before this ceremony took place: a bath, clean clothes, food, a woman of his choosing, many more months if not years. Instead, he shrugged. 'If I think of something else, I will be certain to let you know.'

She turned once again to leave. Rory intentionally waited until she'd stepped through the opening and into the corridor before asking, 'What do I call the wife I will share a bed with this night?'

Chapter Three

*S*hare a bed with her? Gillian shook her head at the idea. He couldn't possibly be serious. Did he truly think her that witless? She would be risking her safety to do so after forcing him into this marriage the way she had.

She took two steps back to stand in the doorway, then turned to stare at him. 'Share a bed?'

A slow smile curved one corner of his mouth. 'We will be wed.'

His deep, steady tone combined with the seductive half-smile made her shiver. 'You can't possibly think—'

'I don't *think*. I *know* my wife will share my bed.'

'But…' The certainty in his command left her unsure how to respond without giving her fears a voice. She let her words trail off while her mind raced ahead.

She was *not* going to share his bed. This marriage placed too much power in his hands as it was—sharing his bed would leave her far too vulnerable. She was not about to let that happen regardless of what she had to do to ensure it never did.

An idea of how to prevent sharing his bed, at least this night, made her lips twitch. She quickly swallowed the smile teasing at her mouth. Knowing he waited for her response, she answered his question. 'Gillian. My name is Gillian.'

She left the cell and walked slowly down the corridor, fighting the urge to run like some frightened maiden, until she reached the stairs leading to the small guard room above.

Rockskill's chaplain and Catherine sat next to each other on a bench. Her maid rose and offered her the satchel she'd brought from the chest in the bedchamber.

Gillian reached inside to retrieve a document, untied the ribbon securing the scroll and handed it to the man. 'Will this suffice as a betrothal agreement for Roul?'

The chaplain's eyes widened as he read what she'd written earlier this day while her guards were bringing Rory and his men to the Keep. He looked up at her twice while going through the single page. Finally, he lowered the document to his lap. 'My Lady, are you certain of this?'

'Do you like your life here, Father?'

'Yes.'

'So, too, do I. Unless you can think of another solution to our current problem in less than two heartbeats, this is what will be done.'

'What about King David?'

'We have not the time to wait for the King to find someone suitable for me to wed. Albert is returning to Rockskill, with a priest in tow. This needs to be done before their arrival. Besides, Roul is one of King David's trusted men, I doubt the King will disagree with this union.'

Father Bartles looked back at the document, then asked, 'But, Lady Rockskill, everything?'

'Yes, everything. It is the least I can do considering the manner in which he has been forced to agree to this marriage.'

Groaning, the chaplain closed his eyes, then asked, 'What did you do?'

She'd become used to his exasperated, long-suffering tone many years past. Like the errant child she'd been then, she dropped to her knees before him to take his hands between hers. 'Drugged him and his companions. Took them captive. Chained him in a cell below and threatened to kill his men.'

'Lady Gillian!' The horror in his voice was echoed in his wide-eyed, nearly bloodless expression.

'Yes, I have broken many of man's and God's laws. You can assign me whatever penance you see fit—later. Right now, I need you to marry me to this man.'

'You said Roul?'

'Yes.'

'A wolf,' he whispered, then shivered before commenting, 'Well, he is loyal to King David.'

'Yes, that he is.'

'He should be more than capable of dealing with Albert and the cur he brought to Rockskill.'

'That is my hope, too.'

'And you think bringing the wolf to our door is the only way to save Rockskill?'

Since she could think of no other way, she answered, 'I do.'

'What about having faith?'

'I have faith that in answer to my fervent prayers, I was given a wolf for protection.'

Father Bartles shook his head. 'I would not repeat that explanation to anyone else, Lady Gillian, they might think you have lost the ability to reason.'

They would likely be correct. But she wasn't about to admit such a thing. Instead, she took back the document, asking, 'Will this suffice?'

'If he will sign it, yes.'

Gillian rose and shook out the skirt of her gown. 'Then, shall we?' She wanted to get this over with before she had time to consider the enormity of her actions.

Father Bartles and Catherine followed her below. Four of her guards stood outside the door to Rory's cell. She hadn't wanted any of her men to know what was going on ahead of time, other than they had captured a possible enemy at the inn. Now that it was too late for them to stop her next move, she needed a few of them to witness the marriage.

Rory sat on a stool in the far corner of the cell, pulling on his boots. He'd already donned his clothing, mail hauberk and a black surcoat with the identifying grey wolf on the front. The rest of his armour—mail chausses and coif, along with a helmet, padded tunic and what appeared to be metal-ring-studded leather gloves—had been piled on to the bench. His man Daniel leaned against the wall, his feet still confined by the manacles, but his arms now free.

Gillian looked over her shoulder at the guards. 'Bring the other prisoner.'

After two of her men left to fetch the one called Adam, she handed Rory the scroll. 'This will place all of Rockskill into your hands. I specify only that our oldest child, if we would somehow happen to have one, male or female, take possession upon your death.'

'And if I die before you conceive?'

Just the way he asked that question, the rapidly changing expressions on his face—from shock to a nearly smug certainty that they would be having a child—made her stomach feel as though it was filled with a bevy of trapped butterflies. She swallowed to clear the unease. 'To ensure it not fall into my cousin's hands, Rockskill will then go to your family to do with as they please.'

He shook his head. 'Which would leave you with nothing.'

Being left with nothing sounded much better than allowing her and Rockskill to fall back into Albert's care. 'To keep that from happening, I suggest you do not die too soon.'

'After what you have done this day, it is tempting to strip you of everything.' He waved the agreement in the air, reminding her just how easy she had made it for him. 'But I'll not sign.'

Gillian took a breath to keep from screaming. 'My cousin returns soon. There is not the time to rewrite this to your satisfaction.'

'You will take the time.'

'Roul.'

'Rory.' He stepped closer until they nearly touched. 'My name is Rory. I would have my wife use it.'

His breath brushed against her hair. She looked up at him and found herself drowning in his golden-flecked dark green gaze. For the briefest moment everything in the cell, but the two of them, vanished and the passing of time seemed to hang in the air.

She suddenly wished things could be different. That they had met under different circumstances and could have had the time to come to know each other. She had a feeling that the tales told of King David's wolves were just that—tales and nothing more.

When she stood this close, with him confidently towering over her, she had the impression that had things been different she would find he was not a cruel, dangerous beast she needed to fear. This man could fulfil every young girl's dream for a husband—even hers. He would protect the woman he called his, he would care for her, honour her and perhaps with the passing of time even come to cherish her.

What, she wondered, would he do to the woman he'd been forced to take as wife? Would she find any mercy, any understanding behind the glittering stare? And once he discovered the truth about Rockskill would there be any softness beneath the hard line of his lips? Any tenderness in his strong embrace?

Gillian felt the soft sigh escape her parted lips and jumped back. What was wrong with her to think such things? There would be no tenderness in this marriage. If the plan still growing in her mind failed, she would be lucky to escape the wedding night unscathed.

His mouth curved into that irritating half-smile she was coming to recognise. The lout had once again guessed at the direction of her wayward thoughts and found it amusing.

'The agreement.'

When she frowned in momentary confusion, he held up the document. 'We need to fix this.' With a pointed gaze at the others gathered in the cell, he added, 'Alone.'

'Oh, yes.' She turned to her maid to retrieve the satchel, only to find the older woman shooting her a glare of censure. Gillian ignored the silent reproach to order, 'Leave us.'

Once she and Rory were alone, she closed the door to the cell, then pulled a readied quill, ink horn and a small knife from the satchel. Handing the quill and horn to Rory, she hesitated, tightening her hold on the knife.

He held out his hand. 'I could do more damage to you with one bare hand than I could with that knife.'

She dropped the knife on to his palm.

Using the stool as a makeshift table, he set about scraping off some of the words she'd written, added his own and then handed the parchment back to her. 'It may seem a bit... unorthodox, but it is this, or nothing.'

The whole day had been unorthodox. What could he have demanded to make it any more so?

She scanned the agreement twice, then read it again for a third time before realising how wrong she'd been.

His changes were far more than unorthodox—they were outrageous.

She lowered the parchment and stared at him, not sure where to begin this conversation. There were so many points of contention that it was impossible to choose the first one to attack.

'Did you hit your head when you fell off the stool at the inn?'

'Not that I'm aware.'

'Is this a jest to you?'

He widened his stance and crossed his arms before him. 'Not in the least.'

Gillian shook the parchment in the air. 'This makes me nothing more than your whore.'

'How so?'

'You will remain here at Rockskill until your services are no longer required. Required? What does that mean? What happens when I no longer require your services?'

'It means that once I rid your land of the danger facing you now, I will leave Rockskill.'

'Leave? Permanently? As in you will no longer call this your home, or me your wife?'

'While I have not specifically stated so, yes, I will leave permanently. As for the wife part, that will be in King David's hands.'

'So, you will petition the King to dissolve our marriage?'

'Yes.'

She peered at him over the document. 'Do you have any set amount of time in mind?'

'I have hopes it will not take overlong. Perhaps four to six months at the most.'

'So, you will remain here for a few months and then we will part ways as if this marriage never happened?'

'If you do not carry my child, yes.'

'Your *child*?' She turned her attention to the document before continuing, 'I do not see that in this agreement, but from your comment, you expect me to perform all…all my… *wifely duties* in exchange for your protection during the period you are here and I will retain full possession of Rockskill when you leave?'

'The length of this marriage matters not. But it will be a true one, or nothing.'

Something in the deepness of his voice sent a warning rushing through her. She brushed it aside. 'I will be exchanging my *wifely duties* for your sword arm. The Church will never sanction this.'

'In the first place, I never mentioned any wifely duties, but exchanging them is the only way you can begin to afford my sword arm. And as for the Church—marriage is a civil matter. If anyone has an issue with these conditions, they are free to take it up with King David.'

'As if the King would side against his wolf!' Too agitated to remain in one place, Gillian paced the length of the cell. 'You…you…' She couldn't think of a vile enough word to describe what she thought of him at this moment.

'Beast? Monster? Animal? Whoreson of the devil?'

She stomped back across the cell and curled her lip at his unhelpful suggestions. 'All of those, yes.'

Before she knew what happened or how it happened, she found herself pinned against his chest, his arms tight around her, holding her fast.

'Release me.'

'No. You could have asked for my help. Instead, you saw fit to drug me and my men, hold us in cells and then threaten their lives. Now, we will do this my way, or not at all. Do you understand me?'

She struggled to free herself. 'Let me go.'

He only slid one hand up to the back of her head and tightened his hold. 'Answer me.'

She looked up at him and tried her best not to once again fall mindlessly into his gaze. 'Yes, I *understand* you…' She let her words trail off, suddenly uncertain how to put them together in a manner that would make any sense.

'But?'

Hating the way her heart pounded at this closeness almost as much as she hated the relentless fluttering of her stomach, she closed her eyes. 'I cannot—I *will not* agree to share your bed. You are openly stating this marriage will be nothing more than a temporary disruption in your life. I will *not* debase myself. Not even for your sword arm.'

With his lips nearly against hers, he ordered, 'Look at me.'

'No. I cannot think when I do so.'

A gentle chuckle wisped across her cheek at her unthinking reply. The heat of his breath warmed her ear before he said, 'The only thing I openly stated was that I will return to the King's service when my assistance here is no longer required. Besides, I would never use any woman so poorly, least of all one I called wife. Come, Gillian, every woman knows their duty once they wed.'

She opened her eyes to glare at him. 'And those women also expect their marriage to be until death—not for some set period of time.'

'Being wed to me until death is not what you want. We both know that. You need only suffer my attention for half of a year at most. After that, you will retain full control of Rockskill, with Roul providing any and all additional protection needed. You and your people will be safe, and you will be free to live your life peacefully, in any manner you see fit. Isn't that what you really wanted?'

In truth it was more than she had wanted or could even imagine. A marriage now to keep her safe and freedom later to do as she chose. However, it was so far outside of what was normally accepted that she found it impossible to believe this agreement could work in her favour.

'Accept these terms in exchange for your freedom.'

'What will people say after you leave and don't return?'

'I am one of the King's wolves. My service is for life. Nobody will question my leaving. What you tell people is up to you. Besides, many men leave never to return.'

'Yes, when they go off to battle. This is completely different.'

'No, it isn't. But do you truly care?'

No…yes. Confusion swirled about her. She shoved hard against his chest to free herself. Gillian had thought that she only cared about protecting Rockskill and its people from Albert and his companions. But now, faced with these conditions for their marriage, she realised that her dignity was important, too. While it didn't really matter what others thought of her, what she thought of herself mattered greatly.

'Well, do you?'

Staring down at the floor, she shook her head, 'No, I do not care what others think of me.' She lifted her gaze to meet his. 'But I do care greatly about what I think of myself.'

When he didn't respond with anything other than a surprised look, she asked, 'How do I retain my dignity if I agree to be forced to your bed, knowing full well this marriage is nothing more than a temporary sham?'

'Forced?' He shook his head. 'I mentioned nothing about using force.'

'It is force if I am not willing.'

A slow smile curved his lips and he narrowed his eyes. For half a heartbeat, she swore she could see a wolf circling its prey, anticipating the taste beforehand. She backed away from the unknown danger before her.

'We will be sharing a chamber and a bed. Otherwise, the events that led us to this union will be easily discovered. It would then become obvious some form of coercion was used to create this marriage. However, I swear that I will not *force myself on you*...' he paused and stepped closer, too close, making it nearly impossible for her to breathe '...until you are willing.'

Her pulse froze, then raced at what sounded like both a promise and a threat. She believed the promise that he would not force her. But the barely veiled threat was another matter—the tiny difference in his choice of words was enormous. He'd said *until*, instead of *unless*, as if certain the moment would come when she would be willing.

'What is wrong, Gillian? Do you fear you might enjoy my touch? Does the thought of my arms around you, or my lips on yours, make you shiver with desire instead of revulsion?'

Shock and uncertainty rippled to her toes. Did his self-assured smugness know any bounds?

Not waiting for her answer, he said, 'Agree to what is written and be done with it.'

Why did unease skitter along her spine? She'd already proven that she was unable to bear children, so even if she did somehow fall prey to his desires what was there to be worried about?

There was no time to find another man to wed. She needed him. Rockskill needed him. If sleeping next to him in a bed was the worst that would happen, what troubled her?

She could endure his presence for the length of time required to keep Rockskill safe and to rid herself of Albert. Then, she could live the rest of her life in peace.

'Fine.' She nodded. 'If you amend the agreement, I will sign.'

'I have sworn not to force you. Is my oath not enough?'

'Your oath? No.' She knew exactly what a man's oath was worth—nothing. 'Men make oaths all the time. And break them just as easily.'

He furrowed his brow and parted his lips. She thought for a moment he was about to say something, but instead he reached for the document.

Gillian started to hand him the document, then paused. If anything happened to him during their marriage, did she really want written proof that they had never consummated the union? How far would that go to invalidate the rest of their agreement? Would it go far enough to give Albert, as her closest male relative, the right to take back control of her and Rockskill?

Still clutching the scroll, she lowered her arm to her side. 'You swear by all that is holy you will not go back on your word?'

At his nod, she relinquished the document.

He added his signature, then handed it back to her, saying, 'There is one other thing. It is imperative that no one know the details of our agreement.'

She frowned. 'But you wrote them in there.'

'No. I only stated that once you and your people are safe, I will return to my duties for King David, leaving you in complete control of Rockskill in its entirety, and that my family will see to your safety when I am not in residence.'

Another read through his changes proved him right. He hadn't mentioned petitioning the King to dissolve their marriage.

'All must believe we are well and truly wed for eternity, else this will not work.'

'All?'

'All. Including our men, your priest and your woman. They could easily be tricked—or tortured—into giving away information that would put an end to this plan.'

She hadn't thought of that. It would likely prove easy to torture Catherine for information. The woman was old and would not suffer pain for long. She couldn't speak for his men, but other than one or two of her men, she wasn't certain any at Rockskill could be trusted to endure pain much longer than her maid.

'I can keep Catherine from discovering the truth, but Father Bartles must sign the agreement as witness. He will most likely read it first and have questions.'

'There is nothing written in there about dissolving this union. The most important thing is the statement that Rockskill will always be under Roul's protection no matter what happens in the future.' He shrugged, adding, 'He has no reason to do anything but attach his signature. This record of our marriage will go only to King David, with a request for a copy to be drafted and sent to my brother Elrik.'

'Ah.' He'd thought of everything so quickly. She twirled the quill between her fingers.

'You hesitate overlong. Other than your woman and the chaplain, who already knows the circumstances of this marriage?'

'No one.'

'Your men?'

'No.' She shook her head. 'They only know that I had them bring the strangers here. You and I exchanged no words with any of them in attendance.'

'Then why the uncertainty? For your people's safety, let them believe what everyone else will think—that this is a true marriage in every sense. Once the marriage is finished, you can tell them whatever you want.'

'Fine. Agreed.' She signed the document, then returned it to him. 'But I vow you will never find me willing. Do not be foolish enough to think otherwise.'

His lips quirked briefly, but he only said, 'Call the others back in so we can get this over with.'

She paused at a sudden twist in her chest at his words. *Get this over with.* Why would that cause such an odd pain? No matter that it was brief and gone instantly, she shouldn't have had any response to those words. Just a short time ago, hadn't she said the same thing to Father Bartles?

'Gillian?'

She shook off the strange distress and called the others back into the cell.

Once they were all gathered, Father Bartles performed the ceremony. When he asked if either of them had rings to exchange, Rory's man Daniel stepped forward, reached into a pouch hanging from his belt, dug around a moment, then pulled out two rings, which he placed in his Lord's hand. 'Fairly gained trinkets.'

Rory nodded and slipped the smaller gold band on to her finger, then handed the other one to her.

Gillian looked at his man to say, 'Thank you', before sliding the larger band on to Rory's finger.

The ceremony was completed with a light, chaste kiss of his lips barely against hers before he said, 'Remove my men's shackles and give me a few minutes.'

She motioned one of her guards to free the men, then ushered everyone from the cell.

Chapter Four

Once in the corridor, Catherine waited for the guards and Father Bartles to leave before she asked, 'What did you agree to?'

Her maid had been present when she'd written the original terms, so she knew what they were. There was no reason for her to know what changes she'd agreed to. Besides, the maid was simply in the mood to complain. Gillian shrugged. 'A marriage.'

'What does that mean?'

'It means Roul will be the Lord of Rockskill and will take care of those threatening us.'

'And once that is done, what about this marriage?'

Catherine had helped devise this plan—why did she now have to be so inquisitive? Gillian knew the woman wouldn't cease until she was satisfied with the answers to her questions and she could smell a lie. So, she would use half-truths and hope it would be enough.

'As with any arranged union, he will continue to serve his King and I will see to Rockskill.'

'Oh, yes, see to Rockskill and be free to bear and raise his child alone.'

'How is that any different than what many women wed to men in their King's service do?' Catherine already knew she couldn't conceive, but her maid didn't need to know she and this husband would never share their bed for anything more than sleeping.

'But will you still be wed? Or will you have borne him a bastard?'

'We are well and truly wed.' That much was the full truth, since if by some miracle she became pregnant, they would remain married. 'There would be no reason for anyone to consider the babe a bastard.'

Catherine leaned closer to ask, 'You do understand that this husband is neither elderly nor feeble, like your first one was?'

'That is fairly obvious.'

'Not just in looks, Lady Gillian. He is not going to be the same in your bed either.'

'Regardless of the man's age, the act is the same as far as I am aware.' Gillian laughed nervously, seeking words that wouldn't give away that this would be a temporary marriage in name only. 'I fail to see where I would experience anything different. It will still be as uneventful, unfulfilling and boring as usual.'

Although, she wondered…worried that it might possibly prove otherwise. He'd brought feelings to life that she'd thought long dead. With those feelings came the slightest glimmer of hope that perhaps all those childish dreams and wishes might find fulfilment. No. She needed to stop this. How many times did she have to discover the uselessness in dreams before she finally set them aside for ever?

Rory stood at the doorway, one hand on the door to close it. His new wife's comment took him by surprise. *Uneventful? Unfulfilling? Boring?*

If nothing else, this marriage could prove more challenging than he'd imagined.

She might not be a virgin physically, but as he'd already guessed, she apparently knew nothing. Women usually either enjoyed the act or dreaded it. He'd never overheard one call it boring, unfulfilling or uneventful. Perhaps that explained her adamant refusal to share a bed for anything more than sleeping.

Earlier, the thought of seducing her into becoming willing had flitted across his mind. But he had quickly brushed it aside, knowing that if he did so it might jeopardise any assistance from King David and he would be honour bound to stay at Rockskill should she conceive a child—a child who would be tainted with the sins of his father.

Unfortunately, now the thought did more than simply cross his mind, it lingered long enough to send out roots and fill him with the desire to prove her assumption wrong. He would need to ensure those roots died swiftly before they took hold and grew into something uncontrollable.

As much as he would like to stand there listening to the two women talk, he did need to speak with his men. With reluctance, he closed the door.

The moment he turned to face his men, Daniel asked, 'What were you thinking to have agreed to wed this woman?'

'I was thinking your life wasn't worth losing over something so minor.'

'Minor?'

'It is just a wife.'

Adam snorted. 'Spoken like a man who has never been wed.'

'What can happen in the few months we'll be here?'

'Few months?'

'Since I will be awaiting Elrik's decision, I have no intention of staying any longer than it takes to complete the

King's orders. I do not wish that confrontation to take place here at Rockskill.'

Both men frowned. Adam said, 'You don't know—'

'Enough.' Unwilling to listen to yet another argument that Elrik would never harm him, Rory cut off his man's words. Nobody knew what Elrik would or wouldn't do. This wasn't a matter of stealing apples from old man Seamus's trees or not hewing enough lumber for the shipyard. He refused to let himself believe his brother would ignore his actions. To do so was dangerous, it would make him complacent and weak when Elrik did summon him.

'She needs our help.'

Adam shook his head. 'And she couldn't simply ask?'

From her swollen lip, he doubted there were any men she'd counted on in the past, or currently. 'I get the impression she hasn't had much luck with asking men to help her and acted out of desperation.'

'You feel sorry for her? And that was reason enough to marry her?'

'Feel sorry for her? No. What I'd like to do is walk out of here, forget this last day ever happened and never look back. However, there is a mission to complete. This will make it easier to gain the control over Rockskill that the King wants.'

'So, you thought it prudent to wed the Lady of Rockskill knowing all of the turmoil happening here?' Adam glanced at Daniel, then asked, 'You do remember everything we need to investigate? Shipwrecks, smuggling, border battles, unwarranted and unexplained deaths?'

'Yes, I remember. I also know that as the Lady of Rockskill, she is involved. How could she not be? To what extent I've yet to determine.'

'That doesn't bother you?'

'Why would it?' It wasn't as if he had any feelings for the

woman, or she for him. As far as his men were concerned, this was nothing more than an arrangement that would benefit them both. 'Whether she's giving the orders or not doesn't matter, we will be successful.'

There were many reasons there was no option but success. He didn't have to remind his men how important the completion of this task was to him. Since they'd been with him on the battlefield, they knew he had walked away from the last order he'd been given. He wasn't about to do so again.

He couldn't. Not if he wanted to live with himself—even if that life might be cut short. Additionally, if he wasn't successful, it would be impossible to request the King's help with ending this marriage.

'Now stay together and discover what you can this night. After we find and reclaim our weapons.'

The two women were still outside in the corridor when he pulled open the door. They abruptly stopped their conversation and looked at him, frowning as if he'd interrupted something important. 'My weapons?'

Gillian whispered something to the older woman, who then scurried on her way. With a nod she led the men to the far end of the corridor. 'The rest of your armour and weapons are here.'

After sheathing his sword, he secured the scabbard to his sword belt, then asked, 'Our horses?'

'Were stabled and cared for. Your shields, saddles and bags are intact in the stables also.' She hesitated a few moments, then asked in a rush, 'Are you planning to leave Rockskill right now?'

Her question and the worry furrowing her brow caught him by surprise. The thought hadn't crossed his mind. She assumed the worst so easily. 'Why would I leave my bride on the night of our marriage?'

His question brought an easy blush to her cheeks. One she tried to hide by turning her face away.

Unable to resist teasing her further, he stepped closer to trace a finger along the line of her chin. 'Especially when I have not yet had the chance to bore her.'

Gillian jerked away from his touch and glared at him. Apparently, she was aware he'd overheard her talking with her maid.

'No. I will not go back on my word.' He handed his men their weapons. 'Rockskill is now under my protection. I'll not leave that responsibility—or you—to another's care.'

'Are you hungry?'

Rory glanced towards the larger of his two men. 'Fear not, I am positive Daniel will sniff out the kitchens before they go to check on the animals and retrieve the rest of my possessions.'

The men nodded and left them alone. Gillian clasped her hands before her, asking, 'Can I get anything for you?'

With a hand on the small of her back, he urged her towards the stairs. 'You can lead me to the hall.' He tipped his head to add, 'We will share a meal and feign undying devotion to each other before those present.'

Gillian stumbled against him, but quickly righted herself and stepped away. 'Would you rather not have a tour of the Keep first?'

Could she possibly be any more nervous?

'No. I would rather do that on my own.'

'Ah. Perhaps I should present you to my men.'

He opened the door at the top of the stairs and waved her through, suggesting, 'Perhaps you should stop trying to pro-long your worry.'

'Worry? What do I have to worry about?'

'Besides being bored this night?' When she didn't answer, he continued, 'You might consider being worried that you have not told me everything about why you so desperately needed to be wed.'

Her glare was almost comical. 'Did you stand there and listen to our entire conversation?'

'No. Although your question now makes me wish I had done so. And I suggest you lower your voice.'

Those gathered near the door stared at the two of them and Gillian nodded at his suggestion. She led him towards the table at the other end of the hall.

'There is one question you never asked me.'

She frowned. 'You aren't already wed, are you?'

Rory choked on his chuckle as he tried to restrain it. 'It might have been wiser of you to have asked before now. But, no, I am not. I would have mentioned that before agreeing to marry you.'

She paused to speak to a maid, then asked him as they continued across the hall, 'You aren't already betrothed?'

'Since women are not fighting each other over the chance to wed a wolf, there is nothing to worry about there.'

Her eyes widened as if in surprise. 'Are women that easily frightened of you?'

He shrugged. 'Most, yes.'

She shook her head. 'I find that hard to believe.'

Rory chuckled. 'Trust me, I can think of no other woman who would have considered forcing me to wed them. They wouldn't have dared act that brazen.'

Her face flushed. 'Then what question did I miss?'

'You might have asked why I was on Rockskill land to begin with.'

'Oh. I suppose I might have given that a thought.'

They stepped up on to the raised dais and he moved behind her to pull out a chair. 'Allow me.'

Once she was settled, he sat beside her and answered the

question she hadn't thought to ask. He closely watched her reaction as he said, 'King David sent me here to stop the battles over your borders.'

'That would be a blessing.'

She sounded relieved and hadn't as much as flinched. But her response didn't surprise him. Any woman would rather not have to deal with battles on her land. After taking a swallow of wine, he added, 'And to seal off that door to nothing but death.'

She shivered, thinking of Hell's door that opened to a long drop down sheer cliffs. 'I have no argument with that.'

He wondered at the shiver. Had she been threatened with that door herself? Considering the beasts her cousin had found for her to wed, the man threatening her with that door wouldn't be out of the question. He leaned closer and dropped his voice. 'And to put an end to the shipwrecks.'

Gillian knew he was watching her closely, trying to gauge her reaction to his words. She held herself as still as possible, fighting not to give away a response.

A few moments ago, she had suspected he'd listened to her conversation with Catherine, but it appeared he already knew what was happening on her land and coastline.

This could go one of two ways. His tasks for the King could end the horrible things happening on her coast, giving her and her people a measure of peace she'd not had in more years than she could remember. How many times had she pleaded with her father to do just that, to end the illegal activities? The loss of lives due to the actions of Rockskill's men haunted her in her sleep and when she was awake. Those deaths rested heavy on her soul, no matter how many times she tried to convince herself she wasn't directly responsible.

As the Lady of Rockskill, everything that happened here was due to either her orders, or her intentional ignorance.

Her father, then Robert, and now Albert might have given the orders, but looking the other way didn't relieve her of the guilt. Each soul lost left blood on her.

On the other hand, since she was the Lady of Rockskill, his presence here at the King's command could result in her losing everything. Worse, the people she cared for could lose their lives. Unless…perhaps if she accepted full responsibility and worked with Rory to stop these happenings, her people would remain safe.

She frowned. Would that be the better option? While she knew little about him, Rory didn't seem to be a cruel man. She'd handed him full possession of Rockskill Keep with this marriage. So, even if she were stripped of her Keep, he would still be responsible for its existence and future. Would he honour that responsibility and take care of the people?

At her silence, he added, 'Which should end the smuggling.'

He knew everything. What had begun as a desperate way to save herself from being wed to a beast and to keep Rockskill from falling into Albert's greedy hands had suddenly become a very dangerous game. One she was ill-equipped to play.

A game she didn't need to play. She turned to him, willing to disclose everything she knew if it would stop the evil from continuing or expanding, even if it would cost her everything.

He leaned even closer and said, 'But more importantly, to find those responsible for the deaths of the King's men and deliver them to King David for his judgement.'

Her breath hitched. This could cost her more than simply everything she possessed. It could cost her nothing less than her life. He wouldn't believe she had brandished a weapon and killed the King's men. She wasn't even certain he'd believe she had given the orders to do so. And right now, she couldn't be sure who had given the orders. Was it Albert as she'd assumed? Or a small part of her mind whispered—had Jonathon taken it upon himself? Even though she wanted desperately to believe it had all been Albert's doing, she wasn't sure.

Jonathon was her lifelong friend. They had known each other since they were six years old. Yes, he often made her uneasy, but how many times had he stepped between her and Albert? Or come to her aid when she'd desperately needed him?

Even if Albert had left orders to take any ship that appeared in the area, Jonathon had to have seen the King's flag. He should have called an immediate halt and let the ship pass.

In a way, it was as much her fault as it was his. Jonathon knew how much she counted on the gold gained from their smuggling to feed and care for the people of Rockskill. He had likely seen it as an opportunity to bring her the much-needed funds to stock their larder and other supplies.

If this husband discovered the whole truth, she had more to worry about than being handed over to King David for punishment. She had to worry about her friend's life and those of the men who had followed his orders. Somehow, she needed to learn how to avoid the wolf's fangs, otherwise she could find herself completely at his mercy—or worse, facing death for the things her father and previous husband had started. Terrible things that she'd failed to stop even after their deaths.

She needed time to think. Time to see if she could devise a plan that would enable Rory to stop what was happening here without giving away enough information to put Jonathon's or the men's lives at risk.

Feeling his stare, she realised he awaited a response. She swallowed, then asked, 'Is that why you finally agreed to this marriage? Your tasks from the King?'

He took his time pouring them both a portion of wine and handed one to her, pausing as their fingers brushed. 'What other reason would I have had?'

Unsettled by his lingering touch, she pulled her hand from the goblet. 'Your men's lives.'

'You heard Daniel. He was willing to die. Adam would have been, too.' He set the goblet on the table. 'What could you have done then except kill me?'

Gillian sighed with resignation. 'And had I ordered that done, King David would have eventually come seeking his wolf.'

'Not likely. But my brothers assuredly would have ensured that Rockskill suffered the fires of hell.'

A shiver rippled down her spine. That would have been a greater threat than the King as their revenge wouldn't have been quenched by simple death.

'Besides, had you killed my men and me, you would have had to deal with your cousin and your three suitors on your own.'

She stared at him, admitting, 'I would have died by my own hand first. Thankfully, since all has gone as I planned, that won't be necessary.'

He turned slightly towards her, one brow hiked and a half-smile curving his mouth. 'Not every woman would admit to planning a forced marriage. Most would find the thought... unseemly.'

And most women didn't have her troubles beating at their walls. She narrowed her gaze. 'Since—'

He cut off her reply with a shake of his head and leaned closer. 'Before you respond, be aware that we are being watched—closely.'

She started to scan those gathered in the hall only to be

stopped by the warmth of a palm against her cheek. 'Cast an adoring gaze upon your new husband.'

Gillian remembered that they were supposed to be acting like a besotted pair of newlyweds. She faced him and smiled. 'No matter the changes in my plan, I still ended this day married.'

'Yes, you did.'

Fluttering her eyelashes, she added, 'You can withdraw your hand.'

He stroked his thumb lightly across her lips.

From the return of his half-smile, she knew he'd seen, and probably felt, her tremor at his touch.

Once again, he ran his feathery touch across her lower lip. 'How did this happen?'

Gillian turned away from his touch. 'I walked into a doorway.'

'Of course you did.'

She turned her attention to her wine goblet. After taking a drink, she drew the conversation back to what they'd been discussing. 'You may have already noticed, but in the unlikely event you didn't, I am not *most women*. And since we will be sharing a bed only for sleeping, there is nothing *unseemly* about this arrangement.'

He made what sounded to her like a strangled snort, but thankfully said nothing further on the topic. Instead, he tapped her shoulder and waved towards an approaching group of men. 'Ours?'

She nodded, bidding the men to come closer. 'Mine.'

'Ours.'

The deepening of his tone surprised her. He was most certainly falling into the role of husband quickly. She ignored his obvious correction and rose to address the two men at the head of the small group. 'Sir Thomas, Sir Richard, let me introduce you to Rory of Roul, now the Lord of Rockskill.' She waved towards her husband and regained her seat.

Both men's gazes flew from the gold band on her hand to the man seated beside her. 'Husband, these are five of Rockskill's loyal guards.' She didn't bother to add that he had already met two of them. He wouldn't remember since he'd been unconscious at the time.

Thomas frowned. 'My Lady?'

Of course, Thomas and Richard were going to remember. Gillian barely shook her head, but her wordless signal was enough to stop her men's questions.

'They seem confused. Did you not inform them of our upcoming marriage before sending them to gather me and my men from the inn?'

How could he have known that?

She could only stare at him in confusion.

He leaned forward and motioned towards Thomas and Richard. 'These two were seated at a corner table at the inn.'

'Ah.'

'Gillian, my love.' He covered her hand with one of his own and squeezed none too gently, before easing, but not removing, his grasp. 'Do not ever mistake me for a lackwit.'

'I hadn't thought to do so.'

'No? Then what was that look you passed to the men? The little shake of your head that stopped them from asking any questions. Did you think I wouldn't see it, or that I was unable to understand your silent order to say nothing?'

Gillian knew she was about to tread across very thin ice, especially considering what she had planned for this evening, but she forged ahead. 'Do you not pass the same type of orders to your men?'

'Of course. But you seem to have forgotten one small detail.'

'And what might that be?'

'These are no longer your men. They are mine.'

'This is my Keep.'

'I distinctly remember signing an agreement that makes me the Lord of Rockskill as long as I am in residence.'

She opened her mouth, then snapped it closed.

He leaned back in his chair. 'You were going to say something to refute my right to rule?'

'No.' As much as it galled her, she *had* given him that right in exchange for this marriage.

'Good. Now, explain to these men who is in charge.'

She took a deep breath and met their narrowed, accusing gazes. Neither Thomas nor Richard was pleased with her. Not that it mattered, they would still do as ordered, but she felt some explanation was required to retain their loyalty to her.

With a nod towards Rory, she said, 'He is my husband and as such is the Lord of Rockskill.'

'My Lady, how did this come about so quickly?' Richard broke his silence first.

'Were we not in desperate need of a lord to keep Albert and his companions in hand?'

Both men nodded.

'And should we not consider ourselves blessed that my request to King David for a husband was answered so quickly?'

There was no reason for them to know that she lied about sending any such request to the King. What was done was done, they didn't need to know the how of it all.

'Then why did you have him drugged and brought here to a cell?' Thomas looked more confused than before.

She owed them no answer, but to keep any further questions at bay, she explained, 'I didn't know this was the man King David sent as my husband. I only knew that well-armed strangers were here and I wanted to ensure our safety.' She leaned forward, shrugged and gave them a crooked smile before softly adding, 'As soon as I knew who he was, I released him. Father Bartles performed the ceremony immediately before Albert could arrive and put a stop to it.' She was amazed at the way the lies slipped so easily from her lips.

All five men turned to face their new Lord. Thomas asked, 'My Lord, can you forgive us for the harsh treatment earlier?'

'No forgiveness is required, since you only did as your Lady commanded for the safety of Rockskill.'

'Thank you. Do you have any orders for us?'

'Yes. Find Lady Gillian's maid and have her move the Lady's things into the Lord's chamber.'

'The Lord's chamber?'

'Yes.'

'Anything else, My Lord?'

'Pass the word about this marriage and...'

When his words trailed off, she carefully studied his face, noting a slight, barely perceptible tightening of his jaw, a tic in his cheek and the sudden, deadly glitter of his narrowed gaze. All were clear tell-tale signs of anger. She'd learned long ago to stay at least an arm's length from her father, previous husband and cousin when they'd displayed such signs.

What had the wolf so on edge?

She watched as his focus shifted from her to the double doors at the entrance to the hall, then back to her.

Gillian followed his line of sight and gasped softly. The hold on her hand tightened again as at least a dozen armed men entered the Keep.

Chapter Five

Gillian couldn't breathe. She hadn't seen this monster since Albert had left. She'd assumed that Blackshore had gone with Albert.

Apparently, her assumption had been horribly wrong.

Rory cursed softly. Before releasing her hand, he whispered, 'Breathe, Gillian. You are not alone.'

He then told the men, 'Watch them. They go no further than this hall.'

Once the five guards left to do his bidding, a smile Gillian could only describe as feral curved his lips.

'Blackshore, what do you want here at Rockskill?' he called out.

Gillian pressed back against her chair and did her best not to tremble as the worst of her potential suitors approached. The man's shock was evident by the sudden widening, then narrowing of his eyes.

'Roul, I didn't expect to find you here, thought you were still in Normandy.'

Rory draped an arm along the back of her chair. 'Duty called me back.'

'Duty? At Rockskill?'

'Ah, yes, a waiting marriage.' He possessively lowered his arm across her shoulders and stroked the side of her neck with his thumb in an all too intimate manner. 'I am sure you already know my wife, Lady Gillian.'

She tried to focus on the man standing before their table, but the unbidden urge to lean into Rory's touch threatened to steal her ability to think, let alone to focus. Certain no one could see her movement beneath the table, she placed one hand on his thigh and pressed her fingers hard into the mail covering his leg. He must have felt the pressure, because while he didn't remove his arm, he did at least stop the teasing strokes.

Blackshore turned his narrowed stare on her as he addressed his questions to Rory. 'Marriage? You came to your unannounced wedding in armour?'

'I was late and, instead of delaying the ceremony any longer, we wed immediately upon my arrival.'

'Does Lord Albert know of this?'

Before she could answer, Rory asked, 'Why would he? King David saw no reason to consult him on this, or any other arrangements pertaining to Rockskill.'

'He has taken on the duties of guardianship here.'

Rory withdrew his arm, making her shiver as his warmth was replaced by a cool draught. He leaned forward slightly, picked up a knife from the table and toyed with it a moment before saying, 'Not by any royal decree he hasn't. Now that Rockskill has a lord, he is free to return to his own lands unburdened by any responsibility with mine.'

Blackshore curled his fingers tightly around the hilt of his sword. 'Do you have a writ proving lordship of Rockskill?'

If the man had thought to intimidate her husband, he'd failed. Rory casually leaned back against his chair as if he had not a care in the world. He slipped his hand beneath hers, lacing their fingers together before drawing it up to place a kiss on the back of her hand. Gillian closed her eyes at the shiver running down her spine from the small act. He had to have felt her tremor, but he continued as if he wasn't going out of his way to distract her.

'I need prove nothing to you. The only people involved in this arrangement are the King, Lady Gillian and me. You have no say in this matter.'

Eyes blazing, Blackshore nearly shouted, 'I stand for Lord Albert.'

'You need to do so on his land, not mine.' Rory's tone remained calm. She felt his tension in the slight tightening of his fingers still entwined with hers, but he showed nothing of his mood.

'We shall see about that, Roul. This isn't over.'

Rory warned, 'If you value your life, it is.'

Blackshore shouted for his men, turned and stormed from the hall.

When the doors slammed closed behind them, Gillian's breath escaped in a rush of air. Rory released his hold, asking, 'You don't think that's the end of him, do you? He isn't about to gather his men and leave without a fight.'

'Had you dealt with him in the manner I had expected, any fight he might offer in the future would no longer be an issue.'

'What, exactly, was the manner you had expected?'

His curt tone chafed. She grabbed a hunk of bread and tore it apart. 'More than idle talking and veiled threats.'

Rory lifted his goblet and took a long drink of his wine before he set the vessel down and turned to pierce her with a cold stare. 'Our agreement was that I protect you and Rockskill from your cousin and his companions and that I see to it they leave your land.'

'No.' She tore the last piece of bread into bits and tossed them on the trencher. 'Our agreement was that you deal with them.'

'*Deal* with them?'

She wanted them not just gone, but dead. Her wishes were far from ladylike or charitable. But Albert and his companions weren't worth any measure of kindness. 'Yes, *deal* with them.'

'You need speak plainly, my Lady, because you can't possibly mean that you want me to kill them.'

She stared at him, incredulous that he would think she meant anything else. 'That is exactly what I mean.'

He parted his lips, then closed them and glanced around the hall before turning his attention back to her. 'We apparently need to have a discussion. But not here.'

'Would you care to do so back in the cell?'

His narrowed glare warned her that he was not amused by her threat. Gillian leaned away and quickly motioned towards the far side of the hall. 'There is a private alcove.'

He arched a brow, but when she thought he would reject that suggestion, he nodded.

Gillian shoved back her chair and rose, certain he would follow.

Nearly reaching the alcove, Rory grasped her elbow and turned her towards the stairs. 'Our chamber will suit better.'

'But—' She came to a stop.

Before she could realise his intent, he swept one arm behind her knees, the other around her back, and then easily lifted her from her feet. 'I see my shy wife needs a little coaxing.'

The comment, spoken in a louder tone, gained a riotous round of cheers and applause from those in the hall, making it obvious that the men had quickly passed the word about this marriage as he'd instructed them.

'Put me down.' When she tried to push away, he only held her tighter against his chest.

'Am I hurting you?' Rory asked as he started to walk up the stairs.

'No.' She paused, realising her mistake, then said, 'Yes.'

'Since you are not crying in agony, the pain must be bearable.'

Gillian took a deep breath and then wailed as if he were killing her.

Rory stopped immediately as the cheers behind them ceased. At the distinct sound of swords being pulled free of wooden scabbards, he glared at her, warning, 'It would be a shame to have Rockskill's men put to death for drawing weapons against their Lord.'

He heard at least one of the men advance. The scraping of weapons being drawn had been unmistakable. As was the sound of booted feet walking purposely up the stairs behind them, announcing the man's approach.

Was he going to have to use his sword to assert his control of this Keep so soon?

'Gillian, I'll not warn you again.'

Just as he was about to put her down to defend himself, Gillian shifted in his arms to look over his shoulder. She said nothing, but from the brushing of her hair against the side of his face, she must have shaken her head vigorously.

The approaching man must have understood her silent warning, because Rory heard him step back down on to the floor of the hall and sheathe his weapon. By the shuffling of feet and the scraping of metal across wood, the other men followed his lead.

He turned his attention back to the woman still in his arms.

Before he could say a word, she said, 'I did not expect them to respond in that manner.'

He didn't believe that for a heartbeat. From what he'd witnessed of Gillian thus far, she planned every move she made.

'I am sure you thought they would take your pitiful cries as the jest you'd intended.'

'No. I thought they would take them as a *shy wife* afraid of what was to come.'

'Of course you did.' Since Rockskill's guards knew she'd been married before, that was unlikely.

She relaxed her glare and then shrugged slightly. 'I hadn't given their reaction as much as a thought. My only goal had been to cry as if in agony, so you would release me.'

Now that explanation he did believe. Without responding, he carried her up to the landing. Instead of putting her down, he asked, 'Which chamber?'

'To the left, at the end.'

Arriving where she'd directed him, Rory pushed open the door with his shoulder and stepped inside. A dim, flickering glow from lit candles illuminated the interior. The small chamber belonged to a woman. Everything—from the floral tapestry hanging on the wall, the ribbons and comb on a tiny side table, to the overwhelming scent of roses—attested to this not being the master bedchamber.

He stepped back out into the corridor. 'The Lord's chamber. Where is it?'

'This is my chamber.'

He only repeated his question. 'The Lord's chamber. Where is it?'

'Albert occupies that bedchamber.'

'He isn't the Lord here. His belongings will be moved elsewhere if they haven't been already.'

She seemed to contemplate that statement for a moment, then smiled as if the thought pleased her greatly. 'Straight ahead from the stairs to the far end.'

He followed her directions and opened the door to the

chamber at the end of the corridor. Once inside he lowered her to her feet, then closed the door behind them.

Just enough light came through the three narrow windows to barely illuminate the chamber. A quick study of the room let him know that, yes, this was the Lord's bedchamber.

A large bed dominated the room. The tapestries hanging on the walls were of hunting scenes and battles. Two sizeable cushioned chairs flanked a lit brazier. One clothes chest rested at the foot of the bed—from the clothing and personal items resting atop it, he surmised the maid had received word to move Gillian's items into this chamber. Near the door was another chest with a bench placed alongside.

The alcove on the far side of the chamber wasn't close enough to see, so he couldn't tell if it was like his on Roul Isle—empty, dark and dusty from seldom use, or clean and comfortable like his brother's alcove at Roul Keep in Normandy that Elrik and his wife used every day as their personal hideaway.

'How are you going to deal with Albert?'

Her back was to him as she leaned into the recess of a window. If nothing else, Gillian didn't waste time with niceties. 'I have yet to decide.'

'What about the men he has lodged here as my would-be suitors?'

'They will be sent on their way.'

'Alive? Like the way Blackshore left the hall?'

Ah, yes, the discussion he had planned to have with her. Although he did find it rather amazing that she broached the subject herself.

'How would you have dealt with him?'

She turned to face him. 'That is why I married you.'

He wasn't about to bring death to someone without proof

of their deeds. 'Have they done anything other than threaten you, or caused you to be afraid, or made you feel ill at ease?'

'No.' She quickly added, 'But they have harmed and killed others.'

'Unless there is proof of that, I can do nothing.'

'There is my word and others will tell you the same thing.'

'Did you witness the killing?'

'No. But I know they have done so.'

'Hearsay isn't enough for me to murder someone. I cannot. I *will not* kill a man because of something that was said, but not witnessed.' He'd had enough of that type of killing and he was not doing it again. King David had agreed to let Rory make the decision regarding those deemed guilty of anything save the deaths of the King's men. Other than that, if Rockskill was brought to heel, the King cared little how it came about.

'You *will* not?'

The arch of her brow and the censure in her tone made him clench his jaw. He was not explaining his reasoning to her. Finally, he relaxed his jaw enough to say, 'I am not a murderer.'

'But I thought—'

'What?' He cut off her reply. 'You thought what? That the King's wolves seek bloodshed wherever they go?'

She said nothing, simply shrugged one shoulder.

'If that were the case, you would not be standing here arguing with me.'

'Oh.'

'You hired me to do a job. I will do it my way. Without any interference.'

'Hired you?' Her voice rose.

Rory sat down on a bench to remove his boots. 'What

would you call it if not hired? Would you rather call it forced? Or perhaps coerced? Threatened? Blackmailed?'

He could feel the coldness of her glare and looked at her. Gillian's mouth moved, but she said nothing. At least nothing he could hear.

The door to the bedchamber creaked open. 'My Lord?'

Without taking his attention from her, he nearly shouted, 'What?'

Something heavy hit the floor inside the chamber, then the door quickly closed. He didn't need to look to know that Daniel had dropped his leather saddle bag in the room and then sought a hasty retreat.

But his man returned in a heartbeat to stick a lit torch in the wall sconce near the door and place an ewer along with two goblets on a table near the bed, muttering an explanation, 'From the Lady's maid', before once again making a fast exit, leaving the two of them alone.

The light flickered across her face, making her anger apparent. Between her narrowed glare and the tightness of her jaw, he couldn't have mistaken her current mood for anything else.

'You would not have captured King David's wolf if you hadn't been certain I could take care of your trouble. That has not changed.'

'Then do so!'

He was already less than pleased with this day's events—was she seeking to anger him on purpose? He resisted the urge to shout back. Instead, he swallowed and kept his tone calm. 'The difficulties here will be resolved. The guilty will be held accountable, in whatever manner *I* see fit. The how and when of it is *my* choice, not yours.' He paused to let that sink in. 'I am the Lord here now.'

She looked away. He rose to approach her, grasping her chin to turn her back to face him. 'Am I not?'

Thankfully her glittering blue eyes were not armed with weapons, otherwise he could have been fatally injured. She jerked free of his hold and answered, 'Yes. Yes, you are now the Lord of Rockskill.'

Somehow her response sounded more like a curse than anything else. 'Then stop this and get ready for bed.'

With a huff, she folded her hands before her and shook her head. 'I am not sleeping with you.'

'This has become tedious.' Rory nearly growled in frustration. 'We have already had this discussion. You will sleep in the bed with me. I am not arguing with you.'

'You can't—'

'I can't what?' He cut off her denial with a wave of one hand. 'Make you? I am certain you know full well that I can.'

When she failed to respond, he said, 'You can get into that bed yourself, or with my assistance. Those are your only choices.'

Since she made no move to do as he had bid, he lifted her in his arms and placed her on the bed. To stop her from scrambling from the bed, he harshly ordered, 'Stay there.'

He then returned to the small bench to finish removing his boots. He tossed them aside to land with a thud near the foot of the bed.

After pulling off his stockings, he stood to remove his sword belt and placed the weapon on the floor alongside the bed. Then he took the time to remove and hang up his surcoat. Since he'd known he wouldn't have either of his men to help him disrobe, he'd had Daniel leave the lacings loose on his hauberk. He leaned over, then shrugged and let the long, metal-ringed shirt slide over his head and pool heavily on to the floor.

As he stood upright, Rory saw her jump, then move slowly towards the edge of the bed.

'Stay put, Gillian.'

She stared at him a moment, before turning away.

The heavy sound of mail landing on the wood floor reminded her that she'd captured and wed a warrior. He had no reason to act the caring husband. Gillian's breath caught. The rapid, hard pounding of her heart did nothing to lessen the nervousness setting her limbs to tremble. What was wrong with her? She'd been with a man before. She'd been a wife. Why now was she as skittish as a virgin bride? Especially since he'd promised they would do nothing more than sleep in the bed.

He casually scooped the pile of mailed armour from the floor and draped it across the bench. The sound of the rings clinking seemed to echo through the chamber and her stomach lurched. She closed her eyes tightly. What sort of danger had she brought on herself? She struggled to breathe and fisted her hands to keep them from shaking.

Gillian did not need to see, to know that the dipping of the mattress was from the weight of his body. Or that the loud, heavy sigh came from the man now sitting a touch away.

He had left the rest of his clothing on, but she knew those garments could quickly be removed. Gillian took a deep breath, knowing now was the time to act before it was too late. She bolted upright, claiming, 'I am thirsty.'

Rory reached over to the side table, poured a goblet of the wine, handed it to her and then poured one for himself. He stretched his legs out on the bed, tugged at the pillow behind him, then rested his back against the head of the bed and lifted the goblet to his mouth.

Guilt that she'd already drugged him once this day and fear he could die if the maid hadn't followed her directions exactly, putting her once again under her cousin's thumb and bringing the wrath of his wolf brothers to Rockskill, prompted her to lunge towards him.

She shouted, 'Stop!' then knocked the goblet from his hand. Wine splattered down the side of the bed and puddled on the floor as the goblet flew across the chamber, slamming against the door with a thud.

Rory tipped his head, narrowed his eyes and captured her stare. 'What have you done?'

'Done?' She shook her head. 'I've done nothing.' As long as she denied having done anything, he couldn't prove it. Not unless he drank the wine himself.

He glanced at the wine stain on the bedcovers, then back to her. 'Nothing?' Taking her goblet from her now shaking hand, he firmly cupped the back of her head with his other hand. Holding the goblet to her lips, he said, 'You were thirsty. Here, drink.' Once again narrowing his eyes, he added, 'Finish it all.'

All of it?

One, or two swallows would have her falling into a deep sleep—one so deep she'd be physically at his mercy, with little or no memory of what happened. But if she took more than that, she might never awaken.

He was already angry, that much was obvious. She didn't know him well enough to know how he would react, but she'd rather suffer his rage than risk death.

'No.' She shoved the vessel away from her mouth. The dark red liquid splashed over the rim and trailed a stain along the bedcovers that ominously brought an image of spilled blood to her mind. 'Stop.'

Her goblet joined his on the floor with enough force to knock a couple of the inset gems free and dent the cup.

But it was his curse, snarled in a low, deadly tone against

her ear, that made her jump. An icy cold fear clutched at her belly.

'What is wrong with you? Do you think I suddenly became so dim-witted that I wouldn't notice your odd behaviour?'

Too focused on finding a way to escape, she didn't respond.

'You drugged me, held me captive in chains, blackmailed me into a marriage and now seek to kill me?'

'No.' His question snapped her out of her ponderings. 'No. I sought only to avoid sharing the bed with you.'

'My word holds so little value to you?' He released his hold on the back of her head and pushed away to rise from the bed.

'No... I...' Gillian fumbled for words. At a loss, she threw her hands up in self-defeat. 'How am I to trust your word when I know nothing about you?'

She flinched at his harsh laugh.

Standing alongside the bed, he seemed to loom over her. 'But I know plenty about you.' He raised one finger. 'You have no regard for anyone but yourself and will do anything—no matter how brazen or rash—to get your own way.'

She couldn't argue that point. She knew that was very likely the impression she'd given him.

He stuck up another finger. 'You lie when the whim strikes you.'

'I have never lied to you.'

'No?'

His certainty made her frown, trying to remember when she'd lied, other than about the wine. 'I can think of nothing I lied about.'

'Did you or did you not place Rockskill under my oversight?'

'Yes.'

'And how many times have you sought to thwart me by issuing silent orders to the men?'

'That was not a lie. I simply find it difficult to remember I am no longer issuing the orders here.'

'Now you think to split hairs?'

She rolled her eyes and looked away, unwilling to argue so minor an issue.

'Look at me.'

His softly spoken command set her heart beating faster than a shouted order. This deep, even timbre of his voice set the fear growing in her belly to slither menacingly along her spine.

She warily met his gaze.

'Do not think to dismiss me with a roll of your eyes, or by turning away. I am not one of your servants. Do you understand me?'

She nodded.

'Did you, or did you not, just try once again to drug me?'

Unwilling to admit her wrongdoing, she simply shrugged.

He clenched his jaw for a moment, took a deep breath and then held up a third finger. 'You are a fool.'

'How so?'

'For all your bravado, you foolishly fear what may or may not happen more than any danger right in front of you.'

Gillian felt the frown furrow her brow. She feared her cousin and his companions. She feared her husband discovering how involved she was with the happenings here at Rock-skill. Those things were not unknown to her.

Tearing her focus from the thoughts whirling through her mind to stare up at the man who was now alarmingly close, she tried to guess his intentions.

The hard line of his tightly clenched jaw attested to the danger right before her. Was that what he had alluded to—that he was far more dangerous than what she already feared?

What had she done?

Light from the wavering flame of the torch flickered across his face, to be reflected against the unyielding glint of his darkening eyes.

Ice seemed to form along her spine. Had she unknowingly placed herself and Rockskill in hands far more dangerous than any her cousin might have found?

'I am sorry.' Easing away from him, she whispered, 'Please. I am truly sorry.' After the things she'd done to him this day he would be within his rights to end her life. No one would fault him.

Before she could move out of his reach, he grasped her arm, halting her escape. 'Stop.' Leaning closer, he said, 'Save your useless apology for someone else. You are sorry only that you were caught.'

Her breath hitched as he knelt on the bed and grasped her other arm to push her down, pinning her to the mattress. He seemed intent on making her suffer for trying once again to drug him. She wasn't ready to die. Fear overtook her, wiping away rational thought and she struggled against his hold, determined not to submit to him without a fight.

Chapter Six

Rory stared down at this woman he'd taken as his wife. What was he going to do with her?

Had he even the slightest desire to bed her, the stark fear shimmering from her eyes would have changed any longing he felt to revulsion. This was not the way to begin any marriage—not even a chaste, temporary one. What had happened in her past to have made her this afraid?

Had she become this terrified from nothing more than a snarl? *No.* This woman had knowingly captured a wolf, had intentionally coerced him into a marriage and sought to drug him for the second time in one day. She was no shrinking skittish maid who quailed and quivered at a raised voice.

He had told her more than once he had no intention of doing anything except sleeping in this bed with her. Even if she didn't believe him, he could understand if she'd been nervous or even timid, since he was after all, a stranger. But this outright fear confused him.

He'd heard her tell her maid that she found sex boring. This thrashing and struggling was not the action of a woman who had experienced simple boredom in the bedchamber.

She bucked hard beneath him, nearly knocking him from his knees. If he didn't get control of her, she was going to hurt one of them.

Rory took a breath and tightened his hold on her arms. Before she could guess his next move, he dropped on top of her, wrapped both arms around her, hooked his feet against her ankles and rolled on to his back, dragging her along.

Holding her hard against his chest, he could only turn his head away when she tried to repeatedly ram her head into his. When she seemed to finally run out of fight, he unhooked his legs and let his arms fall to the mattress at his side.

'Gillian, do what you will. I have no intention of harming you.'

To his relief, she silently crumpled with a gasp atop him.

He brushed the hair from her damp face with one hand and brought his other arm across her back, to hold her lightly. 'What is this?'

'I thought…' She paused, then added, 'Nothing…it was nothing.'

This wouldn't do. He couldn't always walk on eggshells around her. He needed to know what set off this terror. 'Come, Gillian, tell me.' When she remained silent, he explained, 'I cannot begin to understand what I do not know. Tell me how I frightened you so.'

'I thought you were going to force me out of anger for what I'd done, or perhaps even kill me.'

He couldn't deny he had been outraged. But he hadn't considered hurting her. Snarling, perhaps, but off the battlefield he had never raised his hand to someone smaller and weaker. He wasn't about to start doing so now.

'I told you I wasn't going to force you. And you stopped me from drinking the wine, so I had no reason to seek your death.'

He felt her shrug in response. Even though they would only be living together a few short months, he didn't want those months to be spent at complete odds with each other.

Besides, if he succeeded in completing his tasks for King David and protecting her, he somehow needed to gain her trust enough to divulge her part in the ongoings at Rockskill.

Idly rubbing her back, he asked, 'Even though the thought never crossed my mind, nor will it ever, what if I had forced you? Were you not married before?'

She nodded against his chest.

'So, it would not have been the first time you had shared a bed with a man, correct?'

Again, she nodded.

'Do not lie to me. Did he hurt you?'

'Except for that first night, no. Not like that, not in our bed.'

Ah, at some point in time she had faced harm from a man. Rory frowned. From the current swelling of her lip, she'd faced harm from more than one man. How was he to help her overcome her distrust of men in an attempt to make her future better?

He would be leaving. Which would allow her to find someone else if she so wished. She would never do so if she didn't believe some men were trustworthy. And life would be extremely difficult for a woman alone. 'I need to know the reason my wife fears me so.'

She pushed up to straddle him and asked, 'Do you trust me?'

'Not in the least.'

'Then why would you expect me to have any trust in you?'

To Rory the answer was apparent—he hadn't killed her at his first opportunity. Instead, he'd wed her. But from the frown furrowing her brow, he knew it wasn't obvious to her. He rested his hands on her knees. 'Have I done anything to cause you such mistrust?'

'No. Not yet.'

He found it interesting that she fully expected him to do so at some point. It said much for her opinion of the men in her acquaintance. 'But, Gillian, have you not given me reason to suspect your every move?'

Her frown cleared and, eventually, she looked away. 'Ah.'

'I didn't think you'd forgotten this day's events.' Intentionally keeping his tone light, he added, 'But if you have, I can remind you.'

'No.' She glanced down at him and shook her head. 'No need. I wasn't thinking about what I'd done, only about what I expected you to do to me.'

Guessing at her expectations would be easy, but he'd rather hear her explanation. It would perhaps be a way to ease her mind. 'And what might that be?'

The frown returned as she tipped her head and, instead of answering his question, said, 'You are an odd man.'

She had no idea how badly he wanted to laugh at her assessment of him. Instead, he nodded in agreement. 'Yes. Something for which you should be thankful.'

'Why?'

Rory slid the palms of his hands along the length of her thighs. 'Because, my dear wife, were I the *boring* sort, instead of simply odd, I would not be the one who was flat on their back on this bed.'

She froze for one instant before seeking to bolt. Fully expecting her movement to escape, he wrapped his hands around her waist and held her in place. 'For one who was bold enough to capture a wolf, you certainly do seem to be skittish now.'

Trying to peel his fingers away, she admitted, 'I made a mistake.'

'You will get no argument from me on that, but what's done is done.'

He let her work at freeing herself a few moments, then yawned before saying, 'I don't know what you think that's going to accomplish, but you're wasting your time.'

With a glare and a huff, she stopped picking at his fingers to settle back down on his belly. From beneath the hair that had fallen over her face, she looked at him. 'Aren't you the least bit angry?'

'Very.' Rory swept one side of her hair behind her ear. The silken strands curled around his wrist.

'Then why are you not raging and shouting?'

He wound one long lock of hair around a finger, then released it to watch it spring into a coiled curl. 'You will discover I only rage when irritated. The middle of a battle is neither the place, nor time, for riotous emotions.'

'Is that what this is to you? A battle?'

Her cheek was smooth beneath his touch. He stroked his thumb across the softness of her lower lip. 'Is it not?'

He felt the slight shiver beneath his touch. Her eyes fluttered closed. 'Hmmm?'

She was too easily distracted for him to believe she would find nothing but boredom in their marriage bed. He brushed the back of his fingers along her chin before resting his palm against her neck. 'Are we not engaged in a battle?'

Gillian blinked her eyes open as if having momentarily forgotten where she was, but it was the tip of her tongue retracing his stroke along her lip that made him catch a smile before it escaped.

'I am not certain I would call this a battle, are you?'

Rory shrugged in reply.

'If so, what is the prize?'

'Prize?'

She nodded. 'Yes, isn't there always something to be gained from a battle?'

'No, not always.' He teased the tip of his thumb along the line of her jaw. 'But I was hoping to gain a little truthfulness from you.'

'That is why you are being kind?'

'Kind? It would be unwise to see me as kind.'

'We are married. You could drop me on to the bed and simply take me.'

'Yes, I could, but other than a few moments of pleasure, what would I gain from breaking my word to you? Your fear? Your anger? Your hatred? More distrust? The worry of a knife being plunged into my back? I have too many other matters to concentrate on to be constantly on alert for your revenge.'

'Nobody else has ever given a thought to my reaction.'

'I am not anyone else.'

She fisted her hands atop her knees and looked up at the ceiling before turning to stare down at him again. 'You are just a man like any other. How do I know you aren't seeking to trick me? When you tire of being nice, will you then resort to ordering me about and taking what you want whenever and however you want it, with no regard for my thoughts, desires or feelings?'

Had that added to what she'd been fighting so vehemently against? Not just fear of being physically harmed, but also of being used as nothing more than a faceless, nameless body who didn't matter in the least?

'You don't know.' He tugged gently, seeking to pull her down against his chest. At first, she resisted, holding herself stiff, but when he tugged again, she let him guide her against him. Sliding one arm round her, he said, 'Gillian, I have no need of a witless servant ready to jump and do my bidding on a whim.'

'Is that not all a wife is—a witless servant?'

He knew little about having a wife other than what he'd seen with his older brothers and their wives. 'The Lord of Roul and the Lord of Warehaven each wed the granddaughter of a king. I am certain the first time either of my brothers mindlessly ordered their wife about for no reason other than simple arrogance, they would find themselves talking to air and their wife gone.'

'They are nobility. I am not.'

Nobility? Somehow, he was certain Elrik and Gregor would both have a hearty laugh at that notion. 'No matter what anyone may have told you, always remember that you are the Lady of Rockskill. From what little I've seen, this Keep is far more than a hovel—otherwise, men would not be fighting for control.'

'If not Rockskill, they would find another reason to fight.'

'Perhaps. But never forget, while it may currently be under my command, Rockskill will always be yours, Gillian.'

Hers.

The steady beating of Rory's heart beneath her cheek and the easy gentleness in his light caress on her back lulled her into almost believing he meant the words. It was difficult to imagine that this wasn't some made-up kindness that would disappear the moment she relaxed her guard.

But what about her? She hadn't even pretended at kindness. She'd had him drugged, chained in a cell, coerced into a marriage and had just tried to drug him again. Gillian splayed her fingers against the thin linen shirt covering his chest. She'd wanted him unarmed, cold, uncomfortable and defenceless. Yet, she'd been the one left feeling uncomfortable.

She curled her fingers, asking, 'Are you seeking to make me feel bad?'

He had slid his fingers through her hair, but now he paused. 'Feel bad?'

'Guilty, for what I did to you.'

'Ah.' He resumed toying with her hair as he continued, 'If you are now feeling guilt, then you shouldn't have done it in the first place.'

'Maybe you are right.'

When she started to move away, he tightened the arm he had wrapped around her. 'Are you saying you suddenly want to wed a man of your cousin's choosing?'

'No.'

'Then you still feel that the plan you devised was your only option?'

She paused. In the limited time available to her, what else could she have done? 'Yes, I do.'

'Other than a dull throbbing at my temples, was anyone injured?'

'No, but—'

He covered her lips with his thumb. 'Just answer my questions.'

She shook her head. When he uncovered her lips, she said, 'No.'

'Other than some discomfort and threats, was anyone actually tortured?'

Did he truly think being chained to a wall had been nothing more than a discomfort? Had anyone done that to her, she would have considered it torture. At the slightest quirk of his brow, she answered, 'No.'

'Was anyone truly forced into anything?'

'Other than marrying me?'

'I don't remember anyone holding a sword to my back or a dagger to my throat. In fact, I remember changing the wording of the arrangement and freely speaking the vows.'

Gillian fought the urge to chortle at his comment. Freely speaking the vows? He almost made this whole day sound as if it were commonplace. 'You talk as if this had been some kind of mutually agreed marriage.'

'I wouldn't go quite that far. But neither was it completed by force. Both of our immediate needs are being met. You have protection. I have easier access to complete King David's orders.'

Yes, he did have easier access to Rockskill now, didn't he? Once he discovered everything happening here and her involvement, she was certain his current kindness would disappear.

What would he do to her then? Dare she ask?

No, Gillian, don't be a complete fool.

She needed to hold her tongue, at least until she could figure out what to do.

In the meantime, perhaps she needed to employ a small measure of what Catherine would call sweetness. Even Rockskill's cook knew that a pinch of sugar would balance out the bitterness of any dish.

Would an act of…kindness…or sweetness on her part help draw the wolf to her side in the future? If…no, more like when he discovered his wife's involvement in the happenings here, would he be more inclined to protect her if he felt there was some shared intimacy between them?

Gillian frowned. She was contemplating the seduction of her husband, after swearing never to let him touch her. How exactly was she to go about this task? The one time she'd tried to draw Robert to their bed he had backhanded her hard enough that she'd ended up on the floor, nursing a bloody lip, while he cursed his wife's wantonness. Would Rory feel the same?

She sighed. Her future and the future of her people were at stake, she needed to see this through and there was only one way to find out how he would respond. She gently stroked the side of his neck. 'Now that you have taken away my reason to feel guilty, I am obligated.'

His hand froze in her hair. 'Obligated?'

Gillian almost swallowed the words that were ready to come out of her mouth, but she'd often heard her father say that with risk came reward. Barging ahead, she said, 'It is our wedding night.'

Before she could draw in another breath, she found herself on her back with him propped up on his elbows over her. His gaze warned her he hadn't moved so quickly because he was eager to take his bride.

She had little doubt that the glimmer shooting from his stare was anger. Oh, yes, he had warned her not to see him as kind. It was too late now to shrink away; she had made the offer freely.

'What is this sudden change, Gillian?'

The tone of his voice was nearly the same. But a tiny something different—a hard, sharp edge—changed his voice from easy-going to downright threatening. It had nothing to do with the volume or the timbre, it was more…the pacing of his words.

'I was only trying to repay your kindness.'

'You are doing it again.'

There—that was it. Each word was fully spoken, fully pronounced. As if he wanted to make certain she couldn't possibly misunderstand him.

'Doing what? Rory, I am doing nothing.'

'No?'

Even someone who had just met him would have recognised the heavy sarcasm in his one-word question. Her pulse quickened. She needed to find a way out of this, to somehow take back her offer.

'I just thought…since you were being so kind, that there

was something I could do for you in return. But if that's only going to anger you, then—'

He covered her mouth with his, effectively cutting off her words. A single stroke of his tongue across hers stole any rational thought. Gillian felt her eyes widen in shock, right before her lids fluttered closed and she softened her lips beneath his. To still her fidgeting hands, she grasped the bedclothes beneath her.

Rory pulled away slightly, to whisper against her lips, 'I am not some unwitting youth who can be distracted by the offer of a woman's body no matter how lovely the woman or enticing the offer.'

'I—'

'Be quiet.'

She closed her lips tightly.

'Yes, you were seeking to distract me. Worse, you were looking for a way to gain something for yourself. *No*, I am *not* interested in collecting on any obligation you might fabricate. Nor am I interested in becoming a useful tool for you to employ for your ends.' When she didn't respond, he asked, 'Understood?'

Gillian nodded.

'Now, lace your fingers behind my neck.'

She frowned, uncertain she had heard him correctly.

He hiked a brow. 'While I am not an unwitting youth, neither am I an ancient warrior looking for an inexperienced bride who will lie beneath me and do nothing while I sweat, pant and rut atop her. Put your arms around my neck.'

'Why?' His request made no sense to her.

'I am going to kiss you, that is all.' He paused, frowning, then asked, 'Does your lip hurt?'

To her relief, it hadn't hurt when he'd kissed her. She shook her head. 'No.'

'Hmm.' He didn't appear to believe her. 'Since I have no interest in kissing a log, you are going to follow my lead.'

'I don't—'

Again, he caught her by surprise, but at least this time she knew what to do with her restless hands. The hair at the nape of his neck flowed through her fingers like a running stream. It was as silken as her own.

His lips against hers were soft, pliable, so unlike the rest of his muscular form. He trailed his tongue across hers, then paused, as if waiting for something.

Jonathon's kisses had been distasteful and Robert had never wanted her to respond in any way. So, she was not sure if there was a right, or wrong, way to do this. Hesitantly she followed his lead. He slid his body halfway off hers, cupped the back of her head to tilt it slightly and resumed his sweet assault of not just her mouth, but her senses.

She clung to his shoulder with one hand, the other curled around his upper arm. This kiss was nothing like the ones she'd experienced with Jonathon or Robert. With his tongue sliding along the edge of her lips, sending shivers down her spine, this was the type of kiss she'd once dreamed of. One that swept her away and whispered of promises and longings answered.

Robert had been much older than her and the thought of him bedding her had filled her with revulsion. Through will alone, she'd beaten down her aversion and had gone to their marriage bed filled with nervous worry. But she had assumed that was normal for a new wife, so she hadn't let it overwhelm her.

Since he had never been outright cruel to her, she'd been certain that Robert would be patient and guide her through the act. But when she'd voiced her thoughts, he had looked at her in horror and harshly told her that she needed only to lie still, spread her legs and be silent. Any woman could have satisfied his need and he wouldn't have cared who.

While it wasn't as if she'd had any tender feelings for him, his offhanded treatment had still hurt. He made her feel she was worth far less than nothing. Before long she'd begun to believe that was true.

Rory obviously wasn't of the same mind—instead of ordering her to do nothing, he'd told her to follow his lead with this kiss. She wasn't at all certain this could really be called a kiss. It was so much more.

She was thankful for the bed beneath her, it kept her from falling to the hard floor with the light-headed dizziness that left her wondering if maybe she'd been wrong. Perhaps all men were not the same when it came to the bedchamber.

If that was true, was it possible they could also be different outside the bedchamber? He'd told her Rockskill was hers—did he mean that, or had he falsely fed her a slender thread to appease her in the moment?

The warmth of his hand slid through her hair, against her scalp, his fingers tilting her head so he could better ravish her mouth. He did it in a way that made her hope, if she did ever change her mind about her wifely duties, that he responded with as much intensity, as targeted a focus, as he did with this kiss.

She leaned into him, tightening her fingers still clinging to his shoulder. With everything his kiss made her feel— giddy, curious, wanted, surprisingly alive—she couldn't help but wonder what it would be like if they... He broke their kiss. She was unable to stop the moan of loss from escaping her lips.

Thankfully he said nothing since her thoughts were too scattered for any response. Instead, he rolled on to his side, pushed her on to her side facing away from him and dragged her against his chest. With an arm slung across her waist, he rested his chin on her shoulder. 'I will bedevil you no more this night. Go to sleep.'

Bedevil her? Is that why he had kissed her? To bedevil her?

She reached to move his arm, but he only tightened his embrace, warning, 'You will be wasting your time. Go to sleep.'

Unwilling to argue, she rested her arm along his and closed her eyes.

The weight of his arm around her, the warmth of his breath against her neck and the wall of a hard, muscular chest against her back all served to keep her heart racing. This alertness to his presence would do nothing to help her find sleep.

'How many of the guards are completely trustworthy?'

Grateful for the chance to concentrate on something other than his nearness, Gillian quickly replied, 'Eight.'

'And how many of those do you trust with your life?'

'Two. Thomas and Richard. Why?'

'We both know that Blackshore is not gone for good. With him, Smithfield, Cranwell and soon your cousin lurking about, you need to be guarded when I am not at your side. Your two, along with Adam and Daniel, should be enough as long as you stay in the Keep.'

'So, I am to be a prisoner in my own Keep?'

'Until everything is settled with your cousin and his companions, yes.'

'But—'

'It isn't up for debate.'

Gillian sighed at his instant misunderstanding. 'I wasn't questioning your decision. You can't leave your men to guard me while you go unprotected.'

'Let me worry about my safety.'

'You don't know friend from foe.'

'When I decide to leave the Keep, I will take a couple of the men you do trust with me.'

Her trusting the men was one thing—trusting the men with him was another matter altogether. Other than Thomas and Richard, who could she trust to protect Rory's back while keeping their mouths shut?

Not James, Colin or Warren. While those three young guards were loyal to a fault, they liked to talk and often failed to think first. Any one of them could end up telling Rory everything they knew about the smuggling before they realised what they'd done.

That would not do. At least not before she had a chance to somehow put an end to the activities first. She hadn't figured out how to do that yet, but she would—soon.

The three older guards, Norbert, Walter and Peter, wouldn't come right out and tell Rory anything, but they would be so intent on withholding information that he would soon guess something wasn't right.

She needed to speak to Thomas or Richard before Rory did. They could warn the others to be careful…but not too careful.

Why hadn't she thought of these difficulties ahead of time?

That was an easy answer—because she'd been so focused on thwarting her cousin and his men that everything else had faded into the background.

Chapter Seven

Rory stared at the back of Gillian's head. She was worrying over something...or worse...plotting something.

Beneath his arm he could feel the unevenness of her breathing and the random tensing of her body. Sleep was not on her mind.

She had been relaxed—for the most part—until he'd mentioned taking a couple of Rockskill's men with him when he set out to investigate the area. If they were as loyal to her as she believed, it was doubtful they would try to kill him, nor was it likely they would divulge anything about Rockskill's criminal activities—at least not knowingly.

So, what about the idea of them accompanying him bothered her? It made sense to be in the company of men who knew not just the area, but the people, too.

Rory rolled his eyes at the odd sluggishness of his mind. *The people.* She worried about her people talking out of turn.

Earlier, Gillian had sounded relieved, perhaps grateful, when he'd explained that King David had sent him here to stop the battles over her borders and sealing off that door to death. But when he'd mentioned the shipwrecks, smuggling and the deaths of the King's men, she had been lost in contemplation. Had she been weighing the idea of telling him who was behind these activities?

There were few secrets in a Keep of any size, so she would be aware of the nefarious activities taking place here. And she was the Lady of Rockskill, so her involvement was likely more than simply knowing of them. But how far did that involvement go?

And what about her men—did they know what was happening at Rockskill, the people involved, or were they participants in the activities? Rory couldn't stop his lips from twitching. His future jaunt around the area should prove interesting in more ways than one.

Those here might think he was vulnerable because he only had two guards with him, but what they didn't know was that King David had immediately sent a messenger to Roul Isle with orders for the rest of his men to gather here at Rockskill. The message should have been delivered yesterday or the day before. The force likely departed Roul Isle this morning.

If his estimation was correct, they would be outside Rockskill's lands in a week, or so—seven to nine days at most. He need only keep a close eye on his back until then. As much as he wanted to explore the village and the cliffs, it would be foolish to put himself at such undue risk. He would be placing himself in jeopardy and Gillian's safety would be compromised if anything happened to him.

Until the men arrived, he would confine his exploring to the Keep and bailey.

Besides, it would also give him time to keep a close eye on his wife. Since he was here, in bed, with a wife, her plan to drug and capture him had been flawless. The marriage part of her plan had not gone quite as she'd expected, but in the end, she did have a husband. Gillian of Rockskill was not someone he could dismiss or consider lightly.

There was no way of fully knowing her part in the happenings at Rockskill. He would find out, but right now, even though he would like to believe she'd been caught up in circumstances beyond her control, he doubted that would prove true.

Time would tell. But time was pressing. He needed to get close to this wife of his quickly. The safer and more comfortable he could make her feel might encourage her to let down her guard and unknowingly provide him with the information he needed. The difficult part was not letting this physical closeness turn into anything more. He could not risk getting her with child.

The gentle evenness of her breathing let him know she'd finally ceased worrying enough to have fallen asleep. Rory sat up, watching to see if she roused or her breathing changed. When neither happened, he got off the bed and retrieved his bag.

Inside was a missive from King David to Elrik. The King had taken it upon himself to try to ease the way for Rory to make peace with Elrik. He'd yet to send it to Roul Keep in Normandy because it seemed a cowardly thing to do. Letting someone else make it easier for him didn't settle well. Facing Elrik was something he needed to do on his own. Once things at Rockskill were under control.

After placing his bag and armour near the door, he took the missive over to the lit brazier in the corner of the room and held the end to the glowing embers until it caught fire. He appreciated King David's assistance, but he would not take the coward's way out. With a quick flick of his fingers, he sent the scrolled document into the brazier and watched it burn until nothing was left but ashes.

Gillian curled on her side and shivered in her sleep. Rory crossed the short distance back to the bed and slipped off her soft shoes. He stared down at her. She looked so small and innocent in her sleep with her hands resting beneath her cheek and her hair spilling on to the mattress to curl about her face.

But she was far from innocent. She was conniving. Much too willing to plot and plan. And so brazen in her attempt to get her way that he couldn't help being drawn to her. From the moment she'd walked into the cell, he should have been overcome with rage. He should still be filled with anger at what she'd done.

However, intrigue and a hot spark of desire had overruled his rage and anger. If the enemy was knocking at his door, would he not have done anything to protect himself and his people? In her place, with a self-proclaimed guardian who so obviously cared little about her safety or well-being, what other choice did she have?

Under different circumstances, she was the sort of woman he would give a second look, but not approach. Gillian was pretty with her finely arched brows, small nose and slightly pointed chin. Her gown was tucked tightly beneath her, leaving her curves obvious, and making him wish for a moment that his honour was less important to him.

Had he passed her in court, or in public, his second look would have let him discover the innocence in her gaze. That would have been enough to keep the wolf from speaking to her. She was not the sort of woman one dallied with. She was the type one courted and married.

He reached down to lift her, chuckling at his absurd thought because, after all, he *had* married her. She didn't stir in his arms, obviously exhausted from her day filled with plotting and worrying. Still holding her, he leaned over and drew down the covers before placing her back on the bed.

She would be more comfortable without her gown and chemise, but he knew there was no possible way for him to remove them without waking her up and when she found him undressing her, she'd once again be nervous and combative— or worse, she might assume he was ready to accept her offer to repay what she'd called his kindness. That would not do. He wanted to gain her trust. Taking advantage of her naivety wasn't the way to build any trust. Unwilling to lose what ground he might have gained with their kiss, he pulled up the covers and tucked them beneath her chin.

After placing a quick kiss on her forehead, he retrieved his belt, weapon and boots before quietly opening the door to the bedchamber.

He knew that if he was seen, some might question why he had not spent his wedding night with his new wife, but he'd been in the chamber long enough for the questions to be answered with nothing more than an arrogant glare.

No one needed to know that he slept near no one, least of all an unexpected, unfamiliar woman—even if that woman was his wife. If she accidentally startled him while he was asleep, it could cost her nothing less than her life before he was fully awake and aware of his surroundings.

He wasn't willing to take that chance. Instead, he'd take his nightmares elsewhere and return long before she rose.

Gillian leaned into a crenel and rested a shoulder against the stone support. The cut-out in the wall provided some protection against the brisk wind as she watched Rory, Norbert and Warren make the rounds of the inner yard.

Worry and fear waged a battle in her mind—one as great as the other. *Worry* for her new husband—there were too many of Albert's men about for him to be out in the open with so few guards. If anything happened to him, she would be in more danger than before. *Fear* that he would discover just how involved his wife was with the smuggling.

If discovered, she could easily place all the blame at Albert's feet. After all, hadn't he been the one to badger her father and then her husband Robert into upping the attacks on both the ships and the neighbouring lands? Surely Rory would believe his wife's word over anything Albert said.

No. She drew in a long, slow breath of the cold air. He had declined her offer last night. While he had been interested in kissing her senseless, he'd had no desire to make her his wife in more than name. She held no sway over the man she'd married.

It was doubtful the men would back up any claim she made. For all they knew, she was the one in charge of planning the nefarious deeds. Not once had she told anyone that Albert was in charge. And *she* was the one who kept a close eye on the goods retrieved from the wrecks. *She* tallied the items and oversaw their dispersal.

With Jonathon's confirmation that they had indeed taken one of King David's ships and killed the survivors, she and her friend faced a very possible risk of dying for the crime.

While it might sound witless to anyone else, she wasn't overly concerned for her own life. Rory, or his family, would see to Rockskill. She hadn't been certain of that yesterday, but her gut instinct now told her that he would not let anything befall the Keep or harm its people.

But if anything happened to Jonathon, what would become of his mother and sisters? He was the only man of the family. It was true, he found far too much pleasure in drink, but as far as she knew, he had always managed to see to his family as best he could. She couldn't let anything happen to him.

Perhaps her idea of taking full responsibility for the ongoings here was the better option. Gillian sighed. She had given none of this any consideration when hunting a husband.

Was she ready to give up her life for the lives of her people? It wasn't as if she had anything, or anyone, that offered her a future worth living for. She had no children, or any hopes of ever having them. She had no loving, caring husband. In fact, the husband she had now would likely be the one who handed her over to the King.

Gillian shook her head at the pitiful direction of her thoughts. Feeling sorry for herself would get her nowhere.

Her mind drifted back to Rory's mind-robbing kiss. She had been so certain that he'd changed his mind about her offer. And to her surprise she had found herself wanting him to do so.

While that might have given him a reason to feel connected to her in some small way, it would have made it impossible for her not to get caught in a trap of her own making.

Even now her heartbeat quickened as she remembered the warmth of his body against hers and the way he'd so easily coaxed a response from her. How was she to protect herself, or her heart from this man, if she foolishly developed an attachment to him?

Oh, yes, she had found herself a husband. A man strong and wealthy enough to protect her and Rockskill. And she'd found far more than those simple things. Not once had she given any thought to the man himself—a rash misstep on her part.

The worst thing about this odd attraction she felt towards him was that, somehow, he knew it. She didn't doubt for one heartbeat that the King's wolf would use that knowledge to his advantage. After experiencing his kiss, her fear was that he would succeed far too easily.

She sighed, her breath visible in the chill of the air and shook her head. This was yet another situation she would have to find a way around. But right now wasn't the time, not after the way her morning had already gone. Unfortunately, she wasn't hopeful the rest of the day would go much better.

At some point during the night, she'd rolled over to find herself alone in the bed. But this morning when she awoke, Rory was there beside her.

Curious about his absence, she'd asked him where he'd gone. That had been a waste of her breath—he'd shrugged it off, claiming she had been dreaming because he'd been there all night. She didn't lack wits and knew the difference between a dream and what was real. What had he been up to in the middle of the night?

Then, after getting ready for the day, she'd hurried from the chamber and down to the hall, hoping to catch Thomas. Luck had failed her as he was already in a conversation with Rory and was in the process of summoning Norbert and Warren to join them.

'Lady Roul?'

The only bright spot had been watching Rory and the two men stay within the bailey. She would have worried more had he decided to mount up and leave the Keep, to explore the village with so few men to guard his back.

'My pardon, Lady Roul?'

Since he seemed intent on the smithy and stables, perhaps she would have the time to—

'Lady Roul!'

Gillian's plotting came to an abrupt halt. To Rory's men *she* was Lady Roul.

She straightened from her perch to look at Daniel. 'Yes?'

'Do you wish to break your fast?'

'No.' Food was the furthest thing from her mind.

'Perhaps you would like to see to the Keep's activities for the day?'

'No.' Was this man trying to tell her what her responsibilities were?

Rory's other guard Adam looked at Thomas and frowned. Her man rolled his eyes and said, 'I think the men are hungry.'

His explanation earned him scowls from both of Rory's guards.

Gillian realised this could provide the opportunity she needed. It would be easier to escape the guards if they were busy doing something besides watching her. With a wave towards the Keep she said, 'Then by all means, let us go inside.'

She waited until the men had started eating before attempting to part company. 'While you break your fast, I'm going to find Catherine to see that the rest of my belongings are moved into the master bedchamber.'

With a forlorn expression worthy of any hound unsuccessfully begging for scraps, Daniel put down his knife along with the bread he'd been about to stuff in his mouth. Addressing the other men, he said, 'I will accompany the Lady.'

When he rose, Gillian waved him back down on to his seat. 'No, stay and eat.'

'My Lady, we are responsible for your safety while your husband is absent.'

She made a point of gazing around the hall, then brought her attention back to him. 'I see none of Albert's men about, so there is no one present who would seek to harm me. If any of his companions enter the Keep, Thomas or Richard will warn you.'

Once again, she deliberately trailed her gaze around the hall, before slowly looking from the entry doors to the stairs. 'I am certain you could stop them before they could reach the stairwell.'

'But—'

She ignored Thomas's raised eyebrow. Of course, her man suspected that she was up to something. To try throwing him off the scent, she leaned forward slightly as if to share a great secret. 'I do not need any help moving the rest of my meagre belongings. And I most certainly do not need any men's ears about while I speak to my maid.'

To force a blush to her cheeks, she thought about Rory's kiss last night and when the warmth of that memory heated her face, she looked down shyly and added in a softer tone, 'I need to speak to her of…womanly things.'

Richard ignored her, he was too busy eating to pay her any mind. But from the way Rory's men were fidgeting, they had taken her lie for the truth—that she wanted to talk to her maid about something intimate. Thomas, however, hadn't fallen for her tale, that much was obvious by the way his brows were now deeply furrowed. Hopefully, he would take her intent stare as an unspoken hint that she needed him to keep the men here in the hall.

She nearly sighed aloud with relief at his slight nod.

Leaving the men, she did her best not to run up the stairs. She checked her old chamber first and found it empty. She found Catherine in the master bedchamber. As she'd thought, her personal items had been moved and were currently spread out atop the bed. She closed the door behind her.

'Lady Gillian?' Catherine held a broom in one hand and a dead mouse by the tail in her other hand. 'I can only assume the tainted wine ended up on the floor.'

Horrified to know the drugged wine had killed something, Gillian could only grimace. She might have died had she swallowed the liquid. Worse, she could have inadvertently made Rory ill, if not killed him. Finally, she said, 'Yes. Put that thing down. I need your help.'

The older woman let the deceased rodent fall on to a small pile of dust and debris on the floor, propped the broom against the wall and followed Gillian into the alcove. 'What would you be needing help with?'

Catherine had the same expression as Thomas—cocked brows and a hard glare. Gillian turned to push aside a tapestry depicting boats upon a storm-tossed sea. 'I need to warn the men at the caves about Rory's presence.'

'And you can't have one of the men do that?'

'No. It will be bad enough when my husband discovers my involvement. I am not about to put one of the guards in jeopardy, too.'

'But…' The maid's words were muffled as an upper corner of the tapestry came free and landed over her head.

'Sorry.' Gillian freed her maid. After they rehung the tapestry, she said, 'There isn't any time for delay. Rory just started investigating the lay of the inner bailey. By the time he is done there and heads to the outer yard, I should have a few hours at least. So, I need to go now.'

She flipped over the latch and slid a narrow panel to the side, giving her access to the hidden stairs that led down and then out to a small walled garden inside the bailey. From there it was a short walk to the far postern gate. During the day that section of the wall was patrolled by one guard—the rest of the wall behind the Keep was protected by a steep rocky cliff. Since she often used that gate, the man would think nothing of her slipping out of the Keep. More importantly, with her husband focused on the stables, he would have no reason to be in an unused section of the bailey.

Gillian plucked at the ties of her gown. 'I need to change into something I won't ruin.' She possessed only two good gowns and neither would survive the jaunt down the filthy tunnel or scrambling over rocks and boulders near the caves.

Catherine quickly helped her from the gown and retrieved a plain, oversized, wool one from the open chest at the foot of the bed. The garment was perfect for this task. Since it was far too large for her, the sleeves were already attached, which would save valuable time. A wide cloth belt double-wrapped about her waist was all it needed to keep the extra fabric in place.

'My boots?'

'Under the bench near the door. What about the men His Lordship set to guard you?'

'They are currently eating and I'm certain Thomas will see that they don't come looking for me too soon.'

'And on the off chance they do?'

Gillian shrugged. 'If I'm not back, have one of the maids bury herself beneath the covers on the bed and you can tell the men I didn't feel well after our talk and am sleeping.'

'Our talk?'

She laughed. 'Oh, yes, you are giving me advice about what happens between a man and woman in the bed.'

'You were wed before—'

Cutting the woman off with a glare, Gillian said, 'I know that. You know that. It was the first excuse I could devise. Hopefully, Roul's men weren't paying close attention to what I said.'

While handing Gillian a hooded cloak, Catherine shook her head. 'What if your husband changes his mind and returns before you do?'

Gillian flung the cloak about her, pulled up the hood and then paused to look over her shoulder. She had no immediate solution for that eventuality. Before stepping into the stairwell she said, 'We need pray that doesn't happen.'

At the bottom of the stairs, she placed her hand flat on the door and felt around in the dark for the latch. She paused. This door only opened from the inside—once she let it close, the latch would fall back into place. How was she going to get back into the Keep without being seen? If she propped it open, she chanced any number of surprises on her way back up the steps, be it from human or animal. Neither option was anything she wished to encounter in the darkness.

She would re-enter the Keep through the front. Warning the men was more important than the risk of being caught on her return. She closed the door behind her, heard the latch catch and then made her way through the concealing vines climbing the stonework.

Gillian followed the path through her pitiful herb beds, noting the already out-of-control mint pushing into the still-tender lavender shoots and the sadly trimmed roses with their spindly branches. Before everything became too wild, she needed to spend time pruning and weeding.

Just as she was about to reach for the door in the postern gate, the snap of a twig caught her attention.

'Going somewhere?'

Chapter Eight

Gillian swallowed her curse at the complete lack of luck she'd found this day and turned to ask, 'Are you finished with the stables?'

Rory shrugged as he sat on a stone bench beneath an ivy-covered arch. 'One stable is like another.' He patted the spot next to him. 'Join me.'

Since she couldn't simply go on about her business without him following her, she sat at the far end of the bench.

'You didn't answer my question. Are you going somewhere?'

'No.' Gillian made a show of studying the beds. 'I came out to see how much work needed to be done. I've ignored this garden for the most part this spring.'

'I didn't see you leave the Keep.'

Of course not, that had been the whole idea. 'I came out with a group of maids from the kitchens. Since I didn't see you, I assumed you were still with Norbert and Warren.'

He looked at her as if he'd witnessed some oddity, but instead of confronting her outright lie, he said, 'Seems I need to speak to Daniel and Thomas.'

'Why? Did you find something in the bailey that needs their attention?'

'Yes, I did.'

She couldn't think of a single thing that might need the attention of a guard. 'What might that be?'

'You.'

'Oh.' She looked down at her feet a moment before coming to their defence. 'I told them to finish their meal. There was no need for them to follow me out here.'

'And I told them not to leave your side if I wasn't near.'

'But you were right here.'

'You didn't know that when you came out…of the kitchens.'

His slight pause let her know that he didn't believe her lie. 'I don't need a group of armed nursemaids shadowing my every move.'

He moved closer, curling his fingers tightly over the edge of the bench—the only indication of his displeasure. 'Yesterday you were so desperate for protection that you took drastic measures to capture yourself a husband. And now you suddenly don't need guards? What has changed?'

Gillian had no answer since nothing had changed. She sighed. 'It isn't their fault. I lied to them, so I could have a few moments of peace.'

'Your petty reason matters little. Their sole responsibility was to guard you. Yet, out of four men, not one proved capable of doing his duty.'

'It isn't their fault,' she repeated.

'Don't think to protect them, Gillian. They all had their orders.'

'And I issued different orders.'

He turned slightly to face her. 'You can issue all the orders you want, but when it comes to the safety of Rockskill and you, the men know to ignore anything you say that is not aligned with my demands.'

'Thomas and Richard are still *my* men.'

'*Your* men swore allegiance to Roul this morning. They now answer to me.'

Shocked that her men would do such a thing, she sprang to her feet and glared at him. 'You—'

'Careful, Wife.' Rory grasped her wrist and pulled her back on to the bench. 'If you lose your wits over some imagined slight, you might not retain enough sense to control your lies.'

When she didn't respond, he relaxed his hold and leaned towards her. 'I may not know you well, Gillian, but I am not daft. You are a terrible liar.'

Perhaps. Although he was the only person who had ever said so to her face. If she stuck to her lies, he could only wonder. The trick would be remembering what lies she'd told, or to steel herself and tell him the truth, take responsibility and let fate decide all else. Until she could make up her mind, she had to be careful.

She sighed. 'I don't know what you think I may have lied about, but I do really need to see to the herb beds.'

'They've survived neglect this long, they can wait.' He rose and pulled her up, too. 'Right now, there are four men who need to be confronted.'

'Confronted?' Her question sounded more like a strangled squeak. She tried again. 'Why do they need to be confronted?'

'I am not about to let them think their mistaken lapse in following an order is acceptable when it's not.'

'But…' Facing the men while he berated them was not something she wished to do. She knew that Thomas and Richard would say nothing to place the blame at her feet. However, she had no way of knowing how Daniel and Adam would respond. What if they decided to tell Rory exactly how their *lapse* had come about?

'But what?'

'Nothing.' Gillian shook her head. The only thing she could do other than give away her lie was to forge ahead and hope for the best. 'You are correct, the herb and flower beds can wait a while longer.'

He hiked one eyebrow and for a moment she thought he was going to say something. To her relief he must have changed his mind because he only motioned her towards the narrow stairs that led up to the wall walk. 'After you.'

They traversed the wall in silence until they'd crossed the drawbridge. Before entering the Keep, Rory stopped and turned to ask, 'There's nothing else you need to tell me?'

And by doing so, admit she'd lied to him? 'No.'

Hesitating, he frowned. 'You are certain?'

'Very.'

With a shrug, he turned away. Her temples throbbed. She couldn't let the men be blamed for something she'd done. Gillian reached out and grasped his arm. 'Rory, wait.'

Thankfully, he faced her. 'Yes?'

She tugged him aside. 'You can't blame them because I was able to sneak away. It's not as if this was the first time I have managed to evade those who were supposed to be keeping an eye on me.' At his frown, she asked, 'Did you never escape an over-watchful nursemaid?'

'No.' He moved closer, pinning her against the wall with his body.

The deepness of his voice beckoned her to look up at him.

Dipping his head until his lips were nearly against hers, he added, 'I was ever the good and obedient child.'

Gillian laughed, giving him the chance to capture and lightly graze his teeth across her lower lip. A shiver of desire rippled down her spine, leaving her breathless and unsteady on her feet.

She placed her hands against his chest for support. Rory stepped back and took one of her hands in his. He brushed his thumb over her knuckles. 'I fully believe you managed to evade your guards. But I doubt it was to tend any garden beds.'

Before she could respond, he tugged her to his side, slid his arm across her shoulders and resumed their entry into the Keep. 'I suppose I should take you to task instead of them. The difficulty will be deciding what punishment fits the crime.'

Gillian's heart raced. She knew by his tone that he was teasing her, but that didn't stop her from stumbling slightly.

He tightened his hold, pulling her closer and looking down at her. 'I could send you to bed without supper.'

'Yes, you could. But you would feel terrible if I starved to death.'

'Yes, I would.' A truly frightening half-smile crossed his lips. 'I could take you to bed and kiss you senseless.'

Her still-racing heart seemed to trip over itself. His jesting threat made her uneasy and set her to tremble. To her confusion she couldn't tell if her nervousness was from fear, or something else. Gillian swallowed to fight back her nerves and said, 'I don't think my crime warrants anything that drastic.'

A guard opened the doors for them. Rory kept his arm around her and made a point to walk slowly past the table where the men were seated.

Thomas shot her a glare. Daniel nearly knocked the table over as he jumped to his feet, his eyes wide as he stared from her to Rory. 'My Lord, I—'

'Don't bore me with excuses.' Rory cut his man off with the wave of a hand. 'Obviously, I could never hire the four of you out as nursemaids. Your skills at the task are sadly lacking.'

He led her to the high table and released her to pull out a chair. 'Have you eaten yet today?'

'No.' She removed her cloak, then sat down, hoping her stomach would calm itself enough to accept food.

Rory requested food be brought to the table from a passing maid, then leaned over to ask, 'Do you think you can remain here, while I go speak to my men, or do I need to chain you to the chair?'

Something she couldn't quite pinpoint in his tone let her know that his seemingly light-hearted manner earlier had masked his anger. She frowned. He was less than pleased with her. His ability to disguise his moods didn't bode well for her in this cat-and-mouse game they were playing.

Her participation in this game was not by choice, she had lied to him for the sake of her men and her people. She hated it, the lying, the sneaking about. Rory didn't deserve this type of treatment from her, not after he'd agreed to wed and protect her, even after the underhanded way she had captured him. She needed to tell him what he had likely already guessed—that his wife was more than simply involved in the happenings here.

But before she could do that, she needed to warn the men at the caves. They had to stop the shipwrecks and smuggling. If they didn't and were caught, there would be little she could do to save them. And she needed to make certain they disposed of any goods taken from King David's ship. Quickly. Because once she admitted her guilt, Rory would send his men to the caves.

A warm rush of breath against her ear drew her wandering mind back to the man beside her.

'What are you plotting now, Gillian?'

His question, spoken in a low, rumbling near-whisper, set every nerve afire. 'Nothing. Nothing.' She leaned away, hoping that even the slightest distance between them might stop the trembling of her legs. 'Go.' Waving him away, she answered his earlier question, 'Your chains are not needed.'

'Such a pity.' He reached out to draw a fingertip along the edge of her ear, chuckling at her shiver. 'I won't be long.'

As much as she wanted to talk him out of speaking to the men about this, she knew it wouldn't sway him, so she held her tongue and watched him cross the hall.

Rory pulled a small stool up to the end of the table, placed a foot on it and leaned forward with one arm resting on his knee. She couldn't hear his words, so he hadn't raised his voice, but Daniel and Adam stared down at the table, giving the impression they were being soundly chastised and took it to heart.

Her men, however, turned their attention from Rory to her. She squirmed on her chair beneath Thomas and Richard's accusing stares. She knew they were outraged—not that she'd slipped away, but that she'd been foolish enough to have been caught. In her mind she could hear them asking if they hadn't taught her better than that.

She also knew that no matter how angry they were with her, neither man would say anything to Rory. For that she was more than grateful. Somehow, she would make it up to them.

From the edge of her vision Gillian noticed a group of maids gathered near the doorway that led to the kitchens. The young women were talking, nodding and giggling as they kept turning their attention to Rory.

It was hard to blame them considering her reaction upon seeing him chained to the wall in a cell below. However, by now everyone in Rockskill was aware that he was wed to the Lady of this Keep—and she was currently present in this hall.

One of the young women broke away from the group and headed towards Rory. She and Rory might not have done anything intimate in their marriage bed, nor would they. However, she was not willing to permit a third person into their bed—especially not one who currently resided on Rockskill land.

The half-lidded stare on the maid's face and the distinct sway to her hips as she approached the men made her intentions obvious. None of the young women from the village would act so provocatively with the Lord of the Keep. They would fear losing their position almost as much as they would fear the cook's wrath.

This woman was not from Rockskill. Gillian studied her. She was unfamiliar. It was possible the woman came with Cranwell. The man had arrived with half a dozen of his women in tow. If that were the case, she needed to warn Rory to watch his back.

Before she could find a way to gain his attention, something must have alerted him to the woman's presence. He stopped conversing with the men, stood up and briefly glanced at the woman before directing his stare towards her.

Gillian couldn't read his expressionless face. Was he silently asking her a question, or was he disappointed that she was here? Would he welcome the woman's attention if she weren't present?

No.

She took a deep breath to chase away her unfair thoughts. If she knew nothing else about him, she was certain he would do nothing to bring shame on this pretend marriage. Had he not made it a point to insist they sleep together to keep up the pretence?

She relaxed her glare, letting the furrows between her eyes ease, and was relieved to see his lips twitch before he nodded and then turned away to look down at the woman now standing before him with a hand on his arm.

Once again Gillian wished she were close enough to hear his words. He said something to the woman that effectively wiped the hungry look from her face as she removed her hand from his arm, then he offered her a seat on the bench.

Instead of taking a seat next to the woman, he turned away and came back to her. Standing behind her, he put his hands on her shoulders. 'You might want to have a word with your servants about the company they keep.'

With his thumb stroking the side of her neck, it was all Gillian could do not to jerk away from his disconcerting touch. Knowing that this public display of intimacy was for the benefit of those in the hall who were now watching them intently did little to stop the return of the nervousness that had beset her earlier. 'So, you knew?'

'It is rather doubtful a servant would approach the Lord of the Keep while the Lady was watching. And the frown on your face was a good indication she wasn't one of your kitchen maids. Unless you were worried about my reaction to a very lovely woman.'

His teasing comment caused a flash of unexpected anger. 'Why would I be concerned about your reaction to another?' To her surprise, the words coming out of her mouth sounded calm, but her body stiffened with each one.

'Ah, yes, this is how a relaxed, worry-free muscle feels.' Rory's gentle stroking deepened along the tightness of her neck and shoulders. 'Take a breath, Gillian, I meant not to start an argument over nothing.'

She drew in a long breath and leaned away from him, freeing herself from his touch. 'I admit, I did wonder for half a heartbeat, but then realised you would do nothing to bring this marriage into question.'

'Especially not with one of Cranwell's women.'

In payment for his teasing comment before, she replied with one of her own. 'Oh. But it would be acceptable with another?' He curled his fingers loosely around her neck and she relented, laughing. 'I couldn't resist.'

Releasing her, he patted her shoulder. 'I have a few things I need to attend. Go, talk to your servants. See to whatever needs to be done this day, but do not leave this Keep. I will meet you back here for the evening meal.'

Gillian nodded and watched him take two steps away before he returned to cup her chin and tip her head up to his. Leaning over, he whispered against her lips, 'It is hard enough work seducing my wife, why would I waste my efforts on another?'

His parting kiss was brief, but when he left, she found herself clutching the edge of the table. Once the unbidden flare of tremors waned, she released the table and wrung her hands. She paused...*seducing his wife*...that's what he'd said. Was that why he'd brushed aside her offer? Because he wanted to take the lead? Maybe she hadn't done anything wrong—other than prick his male pride. Gillian sighed. She'd been right in thinking she was completely unprepared for this game he played.

If she trusted her gut instinct, it warned her that he was going to work hard at seducing her. To what end? Certainly not for the normal reasons—creating a child, satisfying lust. No, it was more likely that his goal was to discover what was happening here at Rockskill. If she didn't act quickly, he would soon discover that his workload would be rather light. His teasing words, touches and heated kisses would soon have her babbling everything to him.

Once again, she had become nothing more than a useful tool.

Yes, she'd willingly placed herself in this position. But a part of her still longed for someone to want *her*, to desire her for herself, not for the property that came with marrying her, or, in this case, for a way to complete a king's order.

That was the part she needed to tamp down. Once things were put to rights at Rockskill and Rory had finished whatever orders he'd been given, he would leave. With his prisoner in tow—her. He was here on a mission. She didn't expect him to do anything to save her from the King's retribution. Nor did she expect him to keep this marriage intact even if by some miracle King David didn't have her put to death. Perhaps, when this marriage was over, she could find a way to fill this worthless longing to be loved, or at the very least wanted.

Gillian drew in a shaking breath and stiffened her spine. Until then, she needed to put on an act as well played as his. At least until she could get word to the men at the caves. Once all was in order there, she could safely let down her guard because there would truly be nothing to hide from this husband she'd taken.

She studied the guards still talking to the woman. It was doubtful they would let her out of their sight again. And it would be impossible to talk Thomas or Richard into helping her. She needed to devise another plan, quickly.

Chapter Nine

Wolves chased her into the woods. Running as fast as she could, Gillian knew she'd not escape their evil clutches. Already she could feel their hot breath as they nipped at her heels.

Four savage beasts lunged at her, drawing a scream of terror from her throat. Limbs from trees and thorny branches from the overgrown bramble lanced her face and body, leaving deep, stinging scratches. She knew the pain of those burning slices would be nothing compared to what the glinting fangs of the animals behind her would feel like once they caught her.

Unable to see clearly in the darkness of the forest, she stumbled over a root and rolled down into a deep gully. Frantically trying to get back on her feet, she tugged uselessly at the fabric bound around her legs, holding her captive for the danger drawing steadily closer.

They surrounded her, circling, their golden eyes shimmering with anticipation. Their growls mingling. One moved closer, his teeth bared as he lunged.

'No! Dear Lord, no!'

Still caught in the lingering tendrils of her nightmare, Gillian rolled on to her side and reached under the bed.

'Looking for this?'

The sound of metal tapping against the wood poster of the bed pulled her fully awake. She bolted upright on the bed, dragging the covers along for protection.

She glanced around, at first not realising where she was, or who was in her chamber until he came to stand by the side of the bed.

'Rory.' A sigh of relief escaped. They'd been wed three days now, but she still wasn't accustomed to a man in her bedchamber.

He held up the sword she always kept under the bed. 'Imagine my surprise when I discovered this under your side of the bed. Why was it there?'

The fear from her dream still teasing at her, Gillian scrambled away from him. 'When Catherine moved my belongings into this chamber, I guess she moved the sword, too.'

He fell silent and frowned for a moment. Then, finally asked, 'You sleep with a weapon at hand?'

She nodded. 'Is that unusual?'

His eyes widened for a brief heartbeat. 'For a woman? Yes, it is. Very.'

'And how do you know that?' Just how many women's chambers had he visited to know what was, or wasn't, usual? She opened her mouth to ask, then closed it, suddenly not wanting to know the answer to a question that was none of her concern. 'Don't you sleep with a weapon at hand?'

Rory dropped the sword on the bed before walking to the bench near the door. 'If I didn't before, I will now.'

She stared at the blade. 'You're giving this back to me?'

'It's not as if you could do me much injury.' His bark of laughter grated. 'You don't possess the strength to effectively use a weapon that dull.'

'It's all I had.' She picked up the sword and looked at the blade. 'I had hoped that if one of my cousin's chosen suitors for my hand made it into my chamber I could point it at them and give them second thoughts.'

'Doubtful.' Rory pulled his weapon from the scabbard on the bench and brought it to her. 'Take this.'

She placed hers back on the bed and took the offered blade. It was longer and heavier than the one she'd stolen from her father's chamber.

'Look at the edge of the blade.'

The shine of polished metal was evident, where hers was dull in comparison. Gillian extended the sword with both hands and swung it back and forth. The length and weight of the weapon made it hard to keep the blade steady.

'What are you doing?'

She lowered the sword. 'Seeing if I could use it.'

'For what purpose? Hacking away at the overgrown weeds in your garden?'

'No.'

Rory extended his hand and she returned his weapon. While he strapped on his belt and slid the sword into the scabbard, he said, 'Get up, get dressed, eat if you must and then meet me in the bailey.' He pointed at the sword by her side. 'And bring that with you.'

'For what?'

'Since your father obviously didn't teach you how to defend yourself, someone needs to see it done.'

The sound of swordplay in the bailey drifted into the chamber. 'But the men are practising.'

'Yes.'

'Are you seeking to make a fool of me in front of them?'

'Have you seen your men handle weapons before?'

'Some. But not so much that I have paid attention.'

'Then fear not, you won't look nearly as foolish as some

of them do.' He headed for the door. 'The training in this Keep has been sadly lacking.'

His words barely slid into her ears. She was too focused on the tightening of his thigh muscles beneath the thin trousers as he crossed the chamber. He wore nothing but a white shirt with rolled-up sleeves, a V in the neck that ended just below his collarbone, a rounded hem that stopped at his hips, crossed bindings to his knees, a pair of leather boots and his belt. Even though his clothing was well made from finely woven expensive cloth and very well fitted, he looked more like a labourer than Lord of the Keep.

To her amazement, it didn't matter. What did matter was that be he labourer or lord, the sight of him made her long to taste his kiss and feel his arms about her. Gillian cleared her throat and asked, 'You aren't going out into a yard full of armed men dressed like that, are you?'

Rory laughed. 'I've spent the morning watching Rockskill's men work with weapons. My lack of mail places me in no grave danger unless someone gets exceedingly lucky.'

When she didn't respond, or get up from the bed, he turned back to look at her. From the partial lowering of his eyelids and the half-smile playing at his lips, she knew he saw the desire on her face.

He didn't make mention of it. Instead he said, 'Get moving. Thomas and Daniel will be outside this door to escort you when you are ready.'

Once he left, she tried to fling off the blankets and swing her legs off the bed, only to find the sheet twisted about both legs. Gillian laughed. The nightmare had been no dire omen of the future. Just a twisted sheet and hearing Rory come back into the chamber while she slept.

Again, last night, just as the previous two, she'd rolled

over at some point to find his side of the bed empty. It was oddly vexing and a mystery to be solved.

But that was something that she could attend to later. Right now, she needed to make quick work of getting ready for a day of being in the company of a husband who would likely do his best to keep her off balance.

Since it appeared she was going to be active, she plaited her hair into one long braid, forgoing any ribbons that would have been impossible to manage without Catherine's help.

Gillian rooted through the chest to find a gown she usually reserved for working around the Keep. It was worn thin and in places the patches had patches. The gown was plain, so old and worn that the once lovely blue had faded to a pale shade of grey, which helped hide the dirt and grime between washings. More importantly, it was comfortable and serviceable since it didn't matter if the garment became torn.

Granted, it was a little short, because the hem had been torn and repaired more times than she could remember, but she wore a chemise beneath, so what did the length matter?

As long as she could patch even the patches, she would never give up this gown. It was the first one she'd made by herself, without Catherine's assistance. The fabric was garnered from an old gown of her mother's that she'd found in the bottom of a chest stowed away in an unused chamber above. As ridiculous as it might sound to another, wearing it made her feel not just proud of something she'd done for herself, but…connected. It was as if something of her mother still lingered in the fabric.

That had been the reason she'd stolen this old sword from her father's chamber—simply because it had been his. It was all she had left of him. As cruel as he'd been at times, he had still been her father. He'd been kind, even loving when she was young and her mother was still alive. But the loss of his wife had changed him, turning him into a cold and brutal man. Perhaps he had cherished his wife, and she had kept his temper in check. When she'd died, there had been no one who could soothe his rages.

Even at five years old, Gillian had quickly learned to stay away from her sire when his temper had overtaken him. Catherine, Jonathon and his mother, Rockskill's cook, had been the ones to offer her comfort and safety when her mother died and during those times her father was beside himself with uncontrollable anger. So how could she not take it upon herself to repay their steadfast kindness through the years? No matter the cost to herself.

She forced the melancholy thoughts aside and picked up the sword. Her father had rarely used it. He had preferred the longer weapon, the one Albert had taken possession of immediately upon her father's death. This shorter weapon had been discarded as useless. But it had been her grandsire's, and then her father's, so she'd snatched it from the pile of things to be melted down for other uses.

Gillian ran a fingertip along the blade, feeling every nick and small gouge. She couldn't help but wonder—how many men had been wounded, or killed with this weapon? A part of her, a most fanciful part surely, hoped the blade itself retained some sort of memory that would help her if she ever needed to use the weapon in defence of her life.

A quick tap on the door drew her from her musings. She set the sword down and called out, 'Yes?'

Thomas stuck his head into the chamber. 'Lady Gillian, are you about ready?'

Apparently, the men were tired of waiting for her. 'Yes, let me put on my boots and I'll be right there.'

When they stepped outside the Keep, Gillian squinted

against the glare of the bright sunshine. How was she to learn to defend herself if she couldn't see?

'Here.' Rory placed a hard helmet on to her head. 'This will shield your eyes from the sunlight.'

She blinked, thankful to discover that he was correct, and turned her head, only to have the helmet slip around to cover half of her face, making her sigh and him laugh.

He adjusted the helmet and strapped it in place beneath her chin. 'A little big, but that should hold it in place.' He took her hand to lead her on to the practice field, asking, 'Ready?'

With a wave towards Daniel, he said, 'You're with me.'

He gave her sword to Thomas. 'See that this is cleaned and sharpened as much as possible.'

Once at the practice area set up in the bailey, Rory beckoned to an older boy standing at the perimeter intently watching the others. 'You, come here.'

'My Lord?'

'Your name?'

The boy looked at Gillian. She raised an eyebrow. 'Your Lord asked you a question, not me.'

With his stare on the ground, he turned back to Rory. 'Silus, my Lord.'

'Silus, would you be interested in joining Rockskill's guards?'

Gillian smiled at the way the boy's entire face lit up.

'Oh, yes, my Lord.'

'Good. Then your training starts now. Go with Sir Daniel and do whatever he tells you to do.'

Once the two moved away, Gillian touched his arm. 'That was kind of you.'

'Kind?' Rory snorted. 'No. You need someone to spar with and I would prefer it be with someone at your own level of skill.'

Taken aback by his blunt response, she frowned at the quick jab of pain in her gut. His reasoning made sense, so how could so little a slight hurt her feelings? This was one of things she needed to fight against—his ability to unbalance her so easily.

Rory placed a finger beneath her chin and lifted her head. 'Don't let the nonsense of your nightmare affect your day, Gillian.'

'How—?'

'You were kicking, panting and crying out in your sleep. From what I could gather, wolves, or perhaps a lone wolf, were chasing you.'

Would she ever be able to keep another thought or feeling to herself while he was around?

She turned her head away only to have him grasp her chin and hold her firmly in place. 'You need to clear your mind of things that have never happened, nor will ever happen. It was a dream. Nothing more. And you need to stop letting words hurt you.'

He placed a wooden sword in her hand and closed her fingers around the grip. 'Do not hold a weapon when you cannot focus solely on what you are about to do.'

He released her and stepped back. 'Raise your weapon before you as if to fend off a blow.'

When she hesitated, uncertain what he meant, Rory raised his arm holding the blade and his forearm in front of his upper chest.

She imitated his stance and stared at him. A near-feral grin crossed his lips, showing his teeth. Her heart thumped. That was the expression the wolf who'd approached her in the dream had worn.

Before she knew what was happening, he lunged, slapping the flat of his blade against hers. The force of it jolted up her arm, burned her hand, knocked the weapon free and sent her backwards to the ground.

He stood over her with his arm extended, the point of his sword rested over her heart. 'Lesson number one. Focus only on the task at hand.'

Knowing he wasn't going to run her through before all of Rockskill, she batted the blade away. 'You did that on purpose.'

Helping her up, he nodded. 'Of course, I did. Your mind was so obviously on something else that you needed a fast diversion.'

'You thought attacking me was in order?' She brushed the dirt off her gown. 'I am not one of your men.'

He wrapped one arm around her, pulled her from her feet up against his chest and covered her lips with his own. One, slow, slide of his tongue sent her senses reeling. She grasped his shoulders for support. When he was done ravishing her mouth, he put her back on her feet and said, 'No, you most certainly aren't one of the men.'

Before she could form a coherent response, he handed her the wooden sword and ordered, 'Arms up.'

Her lips still tingling from his kiss and a bevy of small wings fluttering low in her belly, she raised her arms and once again found herself unarmed and flat on the ground. But this time, she scrambled to retrieve her weapon, pushed herself up to her feet and faced him, shouting, 'Stop it!'

'You are free to go back inside the Keep and see to the mending if you wish.'

The mending?

Gillian narrowed her eyes, turned the wooden sword in her hand and rushed towards him, intending to slap the weapon from his grasp.

He only spread his feet and swung his blade up, easily warding off her attack.

Not willing to give up so soon, she repeated the act. This time he yawned. 'When you are finished, let me know.'

Again, she rushed him. Instead of defending himself, he reached out and tore the wooden sword from her grasp. 'You are only going to tire yourself out.'

Panting, Gillian reached out for her weapon. He tossed it towards a pile and handed her his. 'Now that I have your full attention, let's get on with this, shall we?'

She followed him over to a stack of hay. Now what was he going to do?

He stood behind her and reached around to lift her arms. 'Hold the grip with both hands.'

She did as he instructed and fought to ignore the warmth of his breath against her ear. Oh, he was gaining her full attention, but likely not in the manner he meant and most definitely not in a manner she desired.

Rory swung her arms back and forth, side to side. The weapon quickly became nearly too heavy to hold. 'You have not the strength to use this sword for slashing. If forced into hand-to-hand combat with this sword you need to be quick to fell your opponent before you tire.'

He pulled her arms back and then thrust them out quickly. 'Use it to jab at someone attacking you.'

The shorter, more direct movement made her arms less tired.

'I want you to jam the tip of the blade into the hay, pull it free and jab again.'

She did as he instructed, again and again, until he grasped her hips and turned her slightly. 'Now stand at an angle to the bales. Lean into the jab, put your weight behind it and let the momentum carry the sword into the target.'

Following his instruction, she jabbed at the bale and leaned forward as she did so. More than just the tip of the weapon sliced through the hay.

'While aiming for his groin would certainly get his attention, that's not your objective. Don't pick up a weapon unless you intend to kill your opponent. Aim for his chest.'

Gillian raised her arms, but when she lunged at the target, the blade lowered.

'Stop.'

He stood behind her and reached around to grasp her arms. His thumb grazed the side of her breast, sending a jolt through her body and drawing a gasp from her lips.

Rory tipped his head down and nipped the rim of her ear. She jumped from the sharp pain that instantly washed away any thought of desire. 'Keep your mind on the task at hand, Gillian.'

He grasped her upper arms and raised them, bringing one elbow level with her shoulder. Then he stepped away. 'Feel the weapon as nothing more than an extension of your arm. Reach hard and fast for the target. Now, try again.'

Instead of a bale of hay, she envisaged him standing there. To her amazement this time her aim was true. The blade stayed level and slid in, then back out with ease. After she'd repeated the movement a few more times, he said, 'Now put your other hip facing the bale.'

Apparently, her left arm was weaker than her right, because while she could complete the move, it wasn't as easy. The first few times it felt clumsy and awkward.

She jabbed from the left, the right and front as ordered, over and over until her arms burned, sweat dripped down her nose and her legs shook.

Finally, knowing she couldn't jab one more time without stumbling or falling to her knees, she turned to him and dropped the sword. 'No more. I can't.'

He chuckled, unlaced and removed the helmet from her head, then drew her against his chest. 'You've done more and better than some of your men, Gillian.'

She stiffened for a second, then rested easy against him, thankful for the support. 'Perhaps, but I am certain none of them have such a patient teacher, nor such a nice place to rest.'

Her heart seemed to skip at the comment that slipped unbidden from her mouth. Before she could push away, he lowered his head to her ear and soothed the spot he'd nipped earlier with his tongue.

All thought of escaping his embrace vanished. Not all battles fought in a war needed to be won and she sighed in momentary surrender. 'Roul, you need to learn how to play fair.'

'You are a fine one to talk about playing fair.'

Gillian shrugged. She certainly couldn't argue that statement. 'Point taken.'

He stepped back, ignoring her moan at the loss of his support, and took her hand. 'Walk with me.'

Rory knew she'd been trying her hardest to ignore his overt attempts to seduce her. He also knew the moment she'd surrendered. He'd heard it in her sigh and in the way she relaxed against him.

This wife of his might have been wed before and she might have shared a marriage bed that entailed more than sleeping, but she was as naive as an untested virgin.

Did she truly think she could win this game?

Eventually she would slip, letting all her secrets fall into his waiting hands.

His only hope was for that to happen before he ensnared himself in the trap he'd set for her.

It had quickly become far too enjoyable to tease and tempt her into trusting him enough to tell him what he needed to know about the smuggling.

He'd leant over her while she'd been held in the icy grip of her nightmare and had to fight the need to gather her into his arms so he could chase away the fear. While that would have been a kindness to her, it would have plunged him into a nightmare of his own making. There would have been no turning back once he'd held her naked body against him.

He swallowed. Just the memory of seeing her thrashing about on the bed this morning was enough to blur the line between seducing her out of necessity and doing so for shared pleasure. That line was thin enough already.

Her fingers pressed against his. 'Something wrong?'

'No.' Rory shook off the threatening haze of desire. 'Just thinking.'

'About?'

'Nothing of any importance.'

Her hold on his hand lessened immediately. He knew he'd hurt her feelings and put a wedge between their tenuous closeness. But wasn't that part of this game—draw her close, push her away, then draw her close again? Gillian of Rockskill might be bold and brash, but she'd built no protecting walls around her heart and even though it would earn him a special place in hell, he was going to use that to his advantage.

He was going to have to figure out how to keep his guilt at bay—otherwise it would choke him to death before his brother Elrik had the chance.

Even though his circumstance was different, Rory wondered how his brothers did it with their wives. Did they feel guilty after arguing or fighting with them? Their women had been tasks assigned by the King, near enemies forced to wed who found a way to fight through their intense dislike for each other to find a shared sliver of happiness.

The arguments he'd witnessed between Elrik and Avelyn had at first made him afraid for the Lady's life. But Elrik had never raised a hand towards her in anger. Sometimes, Rory thought they argued just so they could lock themselves away in their chamber and make amends.

Their relationship made him wonder what it would be like to have a wife to come home to. One he could talk to, honestly, openly, about anything. A woman to care for and one who would care for him in return. Someone soft and warm to hold at night. Someone who feared King David's wolves so little that she wouldn't hesitate to speak her mind, or to argue when the need arose.

He glanced down at Gillian. What he had wondered about and what he had were two different things.

In the end, it didn't matter. Neither the type of wife he had dreamed of, nor the one he currently had made any difference. He had no future to offer them. His act of cowardice had seen to that.

He led her through the stable and out into the small orchard. The fruit trees did their best to grow in the rock-strewn ground. Rory paused to watch the workers in the field turn over the earth, before leading her on a rambling route through the orchard.

He waved a hand towards the field. 'What will be planted?'

'Potatoes, turnips, carrots, beets—just root vegetables.'

There was an entire Keep and the villagers to feed. Rory mentally sized up the plot and found it lacking. 'What if a large group of visitors arrive?'

His coming men, for example.

'There are other fields, Rory.'

'That's good to know, since this is rather small.' He

glanced up at the sky and changed the direction of their stroll to head back to the Keep. 'Come, it feels like rain and I've no desire to get wet and shiver with cold when there's a warm fire inside.'

Lost in her own thoughts, Gillian silently walked where he led.

He'd sounded mildly relieved when she'd told him this wasn't the only field for crops. Had he been concerned about feeding those in the Keep and in the village? She frowned. Until she told him about the activities here, it would be a little hard to explain that was the reason she took any coin Albert offered her from the shipwrecks—it was used to feed her people. It was the only way she could do so. As abhorrent as the shipwrecks were to her, she had always known that if she refused the money, they would all starve.

Rory came from a larger Keep, likely with more people to oversee. He would soon wonder how Rockskill survived. Which meant she needed desperately to get to the caves and see to things there before everything came crashing down around her.

Chapter Ten

Rory stopped to stare at the sky before urging his horse along the path leading to the village. It had rained nearly non-stop for the last four days—hopefully the sun was rising on a clear day. They'd crossed the open, rock-strewn field outside Rockskill's wall and entered a sparsely wooded area. The bend in the path led out to the small village. Maybe a dozen or so huts lined each side of the dirt road. Children played in the narrow lane while mothers kept an eye out through the open cottage doors.

There was one obvious lack—men. Other than small boys and elderly men, the absence of healthy adult males was plain.

Rory knew that there were few fields and very little live-stock to tend. He could see that much for himself. Other than the small valley that contained the village, the rest of the land was rocky with a few patches of wooded areas.

Warren's claim that they supported themselves fishing was believable. Except today the wind had the sea churning. A fishing boat could not withstand the angry white-capped waves that crashed against the rock cliffs. The men couldn't be out fishing. So, where were they?

He now understood the hard side glances Norbert kept shooting towards the younger guard. He'd been trying to warn the talkative man to shut his mouth.

This underhanded secrecy was to be expected. After all, he was a stranger. However, he was also the Lord here and they had to realise that sooner or later he was going to discover what was happening on Rockskill's land.

Their passage through the village drew little attention, which to him was odd. Were the villagers so used to strangers that they'd lost all curiosity? Had a stranger ridden through Rory's village, they'd have been stopped and questioned by everyone—including the children. But the children here at Rockskill moved quickly to their mothers' side. One young girl buried her face in her mother's skirt in a manner that made Rory wary. What was happening here?

He tipped his head towards the woman, only to see her look down at the ground in response.

Rory brought his horse to a halt. The guards stopped and looked at him. Norbert frowned. 'My Lord?'

Unclenching his jaw, Rory pinned the older guard with a glare. 'Have they always been like this?'

'Like what?'

'Afraid.'

Warren parted his lips, but Norbert nearly growled at the younger man, 'Shut up.'

'No.' Rory dragged a hand through his hair to keep from grasping the hilt of his sword. He turned to Warren. 'Belay that order. What has happened?'

When Warren glanced at Norbert, Rory raised his voice. 'I am the Lord of Rockskill. You answer to me.'

Warren answered, 'Lord Albert happened.'

'And his companions,' Norbert added.

'Mostly Lords Blackshore and Smithfield.'

Rory winced and raised his hand for them to stop. They didn't need to elaborate. He knew both men well enough to realise just what harm had befallen the villagers. No one would have been spared, no matter how young, or how old.

'Lord Albert does nothing to prevent the men's actions,' Norbert explained. 'And when we intervened, some of our men were cut down.'

Rory cursed. He wanted to assure these people and the guards of their safety going forward from this day, but until he knew the whereabouts of his men for certain, he wasn't about to make a vow he couldn't keep.

He did another quick survey of the village before advancing towards two elderly men sitting on a bench near the doorway of a cottage. Urging his horse closer, he asked, 'Are you able to travel to the Keep?'

Both men frowned. One asked, 'Who wants to know?'

'The new Lord of Rockskill.'

They slowly rose to their feet and doffed their head coverings. Wringing the worn cap between his gnarled fingers, the taller one said, 'You are Lady Gillian's new husband?'

Rory bit back a smile. Word travelled as quickly as a bolt of lightning. 'Yes. I wish your presence at the Keep tomorrow morning.'

'For what, my Lord?'

'The two of you most likely know more about this village and its needs and concerns than anyone else. I would like to address them.'

The men looked at each other, shrugged, then nodded.

Deliberately, Rory slowly trailed his stare to the woman and the girl still standing in the door of the cottage before turning his attention back to the men. 'All of the concerns. Do you understand?'

After a long glance at each other, the men nodded again.

He could only hope some of the people came to tell him what had befallen them. Short of catching Blackshore or

Smithfield in action, an eyewitness or victim would be the only way he could exact retribution for their deeds.

Certain the men understood, he led Norbert and Warren out of the village. There was someone else who needed to know the identity of the new Lord of Rockskill.

Rory halted at the inn just beyond the village, the one he'd stopped at between the two streams when first coming to Rockskill. 'I think something to drink is in order.'

He slid off his horse and tied the animal next to two horses he recognised by the markings on the saddle bags—four upright snarling wolves had been branded into the leather.

Norbert grimaced. 'Are you sure?'

Rory laughed. Norbert knew what had happened at the inn the day he'd arrived. 'I am fairly certain the innkeeper isn't going to make the same mistake twice.'

Without waiting for the guards to dismount, he entered the inn and pulled a dagger from his boot. Before anyone noticed his weapon, he stood behind a large man who sat facing away from the door, wrapped one hand around the back of the man's neck and pressed the edge of the dagger against his throat. 'This is how you serve your Lord?'

The man didn't so much as flinch. 'I would think my Lord would be far too busy with his new wife to know how I serve him.'

The guard seated next to him shrugged. 'We weren't even invited to the wedding ceremony.'

'It is a sad thing to have missed such a joyous event, considering how far we've travelled.'

'Not to mention the food and ale.'

Rory released his guard, slid the dagger back into his boot and approached the long bar. He couldn't hold back a smirk when the innkeeper saw him and dropped the full pitcher he had been holding.

'My Lord, I—'

'Did as you had been bid.' Rory leaned on the wooden bar top. 'Be warned, it will not happen again, to anyone, unless the order comes directly from me.'

Bushy white eyebrows disappeared under a fringe of hair just as white.

'Rest assured, as the new Lord of Rockskill, I do not require permission from my wife.'

The man nodded and poured a tankard of ale that he set on the bar. 'Your coin is of no use here, Lord Rockskill.'

Rory took the vessel, flipped a coin on to the bar and then waved Norbert and Warren to join him and his guards at the table. 'Where are the others?'

'Camped in a clearing just on the other side of the first stream we came to.'

Norbert choked on his drink.

His men were not on Rockskill land. The current conflict between Rockskill and the bordering lands made this dangerous. 'Is the camp marked?'

'Yes. Pennants are flying.'

'Mine?'

'We've been travelling under Lord Elrik's since it seemed safer.'

That much was true. Not many people would think to confront a group of soldiers flying Elrik's war banners with the four wolves standing, fangs bared, poised for battle. Still, they needed to get the men moved on to Rockskill land before anyone realised that all four of King David's wolves were not in attendance.

'Why are we here? King David's messenger said only to bring a force here to assist you.' The guard leaned over to study Rory's left hand. 'I see the rumours are true.'

'Yes, I am wed.' Rory thumbed the plain band. 'That's a

story for another time. Right now, I want the men moved to the Keep.'

Norbert tipped his head and frowned. 'Beg your pardon, my Lord, but how many men?'

'Twenty,' the smaller guard answered.

Rory rolled his eyes. 'Did you leave anyone on Roul Isle?'

'Lord Edan ordered us to take half. He will be arriving with the others by ship.'

Rory groaned. Just what he didn't want, or need, was the presence of any of his brothers. Not to mention the addition of even more men. Rockskill was a small Keep and didn't have the room to house the men who had already arrived, let alone double that many. But he wasn't dismissing his men until he had the situations at Rockskill under control.

A bigger concern was a ship—Edan's ship—sailing into an area with active smugglers. Losing Edan and half of Roul's troops was *not* something he wished to explain to Elrik.

'Move the men inside the wall and set up camp in the inner yard.'

His men shrugged. 'After the time in Normandy, we're used to making camp.'

True. They'd rarely resided inside a building during the last couple of years.

The larger man added, 'Lord Edan sent along fully equipped wagons, so we have plenty of food and drink to last until he arrives with the rest.' He leaned closer to whisper, 'And there is more than enough coin to pay for what we don't have with us.'

Edan had thought of everything. And knowing his brother, Rory was certain he'd also kept close account of what was loaded on to the wagons and the ship, along with exactly how much coin had been provided. By the time his tasks were completed here at Rockskill, and he returned to Roul Isle, he would likely owe Edan more time at the shipyard than he could imagine.

Except for making one final decision, he was done here. Rory finished his ale, set the tankard on the table, then looked at the larger man. 'Brent, follow this road and lead the men to Rockskill Keep. You will eventually run into Adam and Daniel. They can assure your entry into the Keep is unchallenged.' He'd had his men bringing up the rear on purpose. While he'd had no sign of Blackshore since that first night, neither had he heard news of the man and his men leaving Rockskill. He wanted his back protected and there were no better men suited to that task than Adam and Daniel.

Rory stood, turning his attention to the other man. 'William, you ride with me, Norbert and Warren.' The smaller man could more easily scramble over rocky terrain should the need arise.

After Brent left to gather the men, Rory pinned Norbert with a hard stare. 'I want to inspect the cliffs.'

The older man hesitated, grimacing, but finally nodded. 'As you wish.'

Gillian pulled the cloak tighter around her and tried not to shiver in the chilly dampness of the cave. While she could easily dismiss the cold teasing at her, the pain in her knee was harder to ignore.

She had fallen scrambling over the slick boulders and landed hard on her knees atop a pile of jagged rocks. Her nails were broken, fingertips scraped and bleeding from where she'd tried desperately to stop herself from falling. Other than that, she was uninjured.

Thankfully, her husband did not feel the need to enforce his marital rights. So, she didn't have to worry about him seeing her scrapes.

Jonathon, the leader of this group of thieves, approached. 'Lady Gillian, is there anything I can help you with?'

Anyone who didn't know Jonathon would find it hard to believe that this scarred man was only twenty-three—two years older than her. He was bitter and sometimes mean, but every now and then she caught a glimpse of the carefree boy he'd once been. More importantly, he was loyal and quick witted, which was why, after her father and first husband died, she had put Jonathon in charge of this detail.

'Yes.' She surveyed the contents of the cave and swallowed hard against the knotting of her stomach. The proof that the men had lured one of the King's ships to a fatal end was evident by the countless weapons and armour strewn about in piles on the floor. 'You can help me find a way to either get rid of, or hide, these weapons and armour quickly.'

At his frown of confusion, she explained. 'I am sure by now you have heard about my marriage.'

'Yes, of course.'

'And were you told it was to one of King David's wolves?'

The brief, slight widening of Jonathon's eyes attested to his surprise. He whistled softly. 'No, I wasn't told that. It could prove a bit dangerous having one of the King's men in residence.'

She nodded. 'It gets worse—he was also sent here to deal with the shipwrecks and smuggling.'

While that much was true, these men didn't need to know that their marriage hadn't been with the King's blessing.

'And I'm sure he already suspects that we...?'

She finished his question. 'Wrecked one of David's ships and killed his men? Yes, he does.' With a wave towards the piles on the floor of the cave, she added, 'So we need to rid ourselves of these items.'

'Do you know how much gold this haul can bring to us?'

'Quite a bit, I am sure. But only if you can find some-one willing to purchase the goods and I don't see how that's possible right now.' Once a buyer realised where these items came from, they would quickly back out of any deal made. It was too soon to offer up these weapons for sale and far too dangerous to keep them in storage.

Jonathon cursed. 'The quickest option would be to toss them into the sea.'

Since Gillian couldn't think of any other way to rid them-selves of this evidence, she agreed. 'I know the men will complain, but see that it gets done right away. My husband is out and about surveying the village today. It won't be long before he turns his attention in this direction.'

Jonathon picked up a sword and ran his fingertips along the edge of the blade as intently and lovingly as he might a woman's body. The admiration for the finely made weapon was obvious in his steady gaze and touch. With a sigh, he lowered the blade to his side. 'And what do you suggest we do if your husband comes upon us before these are gone?'

She glanced at the weapon, then back up at the man to warn him in a rush, 'For the love of God, Jonathon, do not kill him.'

He must have found her tone amusing, because he threw back his head and laughed boisterously in a manner that so reminded her of the days they'd both been carefree children. It had been such a long time since she'd heard that laugh that she couldn't help but smile. The familiar feeling made her wonder if perhaps he might have been the better choice as a husband. He was known and the men listened to him. She wouldn't have had to keep track of any lies.

After wiping the tears from his eyes, he chided her, 'Oh, come now, Gilly, you know full well you aren't ever going to be happy until you've taken a cook's son as your husband and that can't happen with this current husband still breathing.'

She swatted his shoulder and reminded him, 'That would never happen. We were like brother and sister.'

He rolled his eyes. 'Perhaps my memory fails me, because that's not quite how I remember it.'

'Your memory doesn't fail you. We both agreed.'

'Pity we didn't ignore our first instincts.' He paused to slowly trail his gaze from her toes to finally meet her stare.

Uncomfortable by his bold attention, Gillian stepped back. No, this was not the man to have made her a good husband. While it made her nervous, at least Rory's speculative gaze didn't make her blood run cold.

Jonathon must have recognised her sudden change of mood because he tossed the sword back atop the pile, spread his arms and then also took a step away. 'Lady Gillian, please, forgive me. I meant not to alarm you.'

His apology made her feel foolish for taking his bantering so seriously. She shook her head. 'No, it is I who should be sorry. I don't know what has made me so skittish of late.'

'Anyone in your position would be on edge.' He nodded towards the weapons and armour. 'We need to remove these before your husband finds them.'

'Yes.' Perhaps the fear of Rory discovering such proof was what made her so ill at ease. 'To answer your question. If my husband should happen upon this cave before it has been cleared, I suggest you and the men hide. Do not let him find any of you.'

'We can do that easily enough. I'll post a couple of the more agile lads as lookouts, they'll give us quick enough warning should anyone approach, to get the men into hiding.'

She nodded in agreement. There were plenty of tunnels leading from one cave to another in these rocky cliffs. Unfa-

miliar with the layout, Rory would spend useless time searching for men who could navigate these tunnels in the dark.

'You do realise that eventually he is going to find one of
the storage caves. What will you do then?'

Jonathon was right, she knew that. 'Before that happens, I
will have confessed to being responsible for the crimes committed and will likely lead him here myself. So you need to
make sure there is nothing from the royal ship to find.'

'Gilly, you can't do that.'

'I must. Don't you understand? The wolf is here not just
to stop the activities but to return the person responsible for
the sinking of the King's ship directly to King David. I can't
let anyone else risk their life for Rockskill.'

He stared down at her as if she'd sprouted another head.
'And you understand that I'm not going to let that happen.'

'Jonathon—'

'Jonathon! Sir!' The shouting cut off anything she was
about to say.

A breathless boy skidded to a halt before them. His reddened cheeks and heaving chest spoke of great haste. 'Someone approaches.'

Jonathon looked from the boy to her.

Gillian swallowed hard and clutched at her cloak. 'How
many men?'

'I counted four.'

Rory had left with only two men. 'Did you recognise any
of them?'

'Only Sir Warren. The others were behind him.'

An unladylike curse escaped. She needed to get out of
here and back to the Keep quickly.

Jonathon asked the lad, 'How close were they?'

'Just came out of the woodlands.'

'Good. Tell the men I said to hide and let the other boys know to keep out of sight.'

When the boy ran off, Jonathon reached out to pull the hood of her cloak up and tucked her braid inside. 'Come. Let's get you back to the Keep.'

She agreed, she needed to return before Rory saw her. 'I can go alone. You should see to the men.'

'I'll not argue this with you.' He tugged on her wrist. 'The men can see to themselves. Come.'

Left with no choice, she followed him out of the cave. Keeping low, they scrambled quickly around and over boulders until they reached the bottom of the cliffs. The trail from the woodlands was on the other side, so any riders approaching from that direction wouldn't see her and Jonathon.

Stepping on to the flatter ground, Gillian stumbled. Her knee seemed to be on fire and the effort of coming down from the caves had left it weak.

Jonathon caught her before she fell against the hard rocks. 'What did you do?'

She shrugged off his hold. 'I took a tumble on the way up and injured my knee. It will be fine.' Her next step proved her wrong, as her leg seemed to fold beneath her.

She cried out in pain and frustration. How was she going to make it back to the Keep if she couldn't walk?

'Gillian, let me help.' Without waiting for her approval, Jonathon drew her arm around his neck and slung his own arm across her back. 'Come, let me bear your weight.'

They had taken no more than maybe a dozen awkward steps when the fine hairs on the back of her neck stood on end. Someone was watching them.

'Stop.' She pulled her arm from around his neck and turned to look behind them. At first, she didn't see him, but when she checked closer, slowly scanning the area with sharper intent, she spotted him. Near the base of the cliff, on the side that curved towards the edge of the sea, stood a single mounted rider.

He wasn't close enough to identify by sight, but she knew who it was just from the way he seemed to stare directly at her.

His piercing focus set her heart racing. This odd sense of anticipation could only be caused by one man.

At her softly issued curse, Jonathon drew his attention to where she gazed and asked, 'Do you know who it is?'

'My husband.'

His curses were not spoken as softly as hers had been. 'You can't make a run for the Keep.'

'As I have done nothing wrong, I have no intention of trying to outrun him.'

'The cave?'

'He doesn't know where I have been. He can do nothing but guess. As long as neither I…' she paused to glance at Jonathon '…nor anyone else tells him otherwise, I was simply out for a walk.'

'A walk? And he won't question you being out unescorted?'

'On my own land?'

The rider started heading towards them.

Jonathon brushed his hair from his face. 'How do you plan on explaining my presence?'

'You saw me fall and offered to assist me back to the Keep.'

'I have always envied the way you could so easily construct a half-lie.'

'Half-truth,' she corrected him.

He rolled his eyes, before holding out his hand. 'I see no reason to stand here and wait for him.'

Gillian debated. He was going to be irate since she'd evaded the four guards he'd ordered to watch her. That and the fact that he could easily guess where she'd gone.

So, what would anger him more? Standing here waiting for him, or continuing her quest for the Keep?

What she truly wanted to do was run, but that wasn't an option. Even if her knee was whole, she wouldn't permit herself to give into that urge. Doing so would only confirm whatever suspicions were brewing in his mind.

She took Jonathon's hand and put her arm around his neck.

'You don't think this is going to fuel his anger?'

'What? Your help?'

'A man he doesn't know putting hands on his wife.'

'Ah. Fear not. I doubt it will concern him overmuch.' Wouldn't a man have to care about his wife for something so slight to bother him? That was one thing she never need fear—her husband caring about her.

Wasn't that what she'd wanted to begin with? A husband who would keep Albert at bay while essentially letting her go her own way?

Why then did that idea suddenly seem so unappealing?

She hit an uneven spot on the ground and stumbled against Jonathon. He tightened his hold. 'This would be easier if I just carried you.'

Her reply was cut off by the distinct pounding of horse's hooves rapidly drawing near.

Rory stopped his beast directly in front of them, blocking their progress. He stared down at her. After a few deadly quiet moments, asked, 'Broken?'

Suddenly uneasy, she shook her head. 'No.'

He slid from his horse.

Jonathon released her and took a step back. He bowed his head. 'My Lord.'

Rory did little more than nod in acknowledgement before he lifted her in his arms and helped her on to his saddle. He then went and spoke to Jonathon.

The men kept their voices low, so she couldn't hear what they said, but since neither one took an aggressive stance, she assumed the conversation was nothing more than a discussion about what had happened. She hoped Jonathon kept to the story she'd devised.

When they were done talking, Jonathon headed towards the Keep. Rory took the reins to the horse and started walking in the same direction. Her husband was eerily silent, leaving her wondering what he was thinking.

'Jonathon is the cook's son and we grew up together. He was a childhood playmate and now a friend.'

He ignored her explanation, but she could almost feel the tension thicken in the air around her. The building nervousness in her stomach prompted her to explain further. 'Like everyone else I have been stuck inside the Keep these last four days because of the rain. I only sought some fresh air and the chance to stretch my legs.' Even she could hear the rush of her words and paused to take a breath. 'I tripped over a rock and twisted my knee. Thankfully Jonathon came along and was willing to assist me in returning to the Keep.'

When nothing but silence met her, she hiked up her gown so she could throw a leg over the saddle. She would rather hobble back to the Keep on her own than endure his quiet rage.

Chapter Eleven

'If you get off that horse, I will tie you to the saddle.'

Gillian gasped at the clipped, steady tone of Rory's warning. Yes, he was angry—very angry. But she doubted he would truly do as he'd warned and she wasn't about to suffer any more of his surly presence.

She slid to the ground, making sure to land on her good leg before turning to head back to the Keep. Two steps were all she managed before she stumbled. A strong arm wrapped around her waist prevented her from landing on the hard ground.

He swung her up and around to face him, keeping his arm about her to pin her against his chest.

She pushed at his shoulders. 'You—'

The slight wing on one brow should have been enough warning. But she caught the subtle movement too late. In less than a heartbeat his mouth locked over hers, effectively cutting off her curse.

There was nothing gentle in his kiss. He was seeking only to force her to his will. The heat of rage burned in her chest. She hated this man she'd forced to become her husband.

He reached up to curl his fingers against the back of her head and tilted it before stroking his tongue across hers.

She might very well hate him, but the heat of rage turned

hotter, leaving her wanting more than just his kiss. Gillian freed one arm from between them to reach up and stroke her palm against his stubble-covered cheek. Yes, she hated him, despised what he did to her with just a kiss. But as their tongues tangled, she wanted nothing more than for him to tumble them to the ground and take her, right now, here in this open rock-strewn field.

He broke their kiss to stare down at her. When she turned to look away, he only tightened his hold on her head to keep her in place. 'Gillian, I am done with this. You are my wife. Mine. I am weary of this game you play. I am not simple-minded. You were coming back from the caves, not simply out for a walk.'

She glanced at the ground. A low rumbling, like a growl, drew her attention back to Rory. 'Tell me, Wife, must I now look at every man and wonder if he is a past lover, or just a childhood friend as you claim?'

Shock at his question raced clear to her toes. 'Now who is the one lying? You really don't expect me to believe you are jealous, do you?'

'Jealous? Is that what you want me to be?' He shook his head. 'A weak, insecure boy becomes jealous. I am neither weak, nor insecure.' He pulled her tighter against him. 'And I am not a boy.'

She couldn't disagree with what he'd said, but she forged ahead regardless of the danger she could be walking into. 'Perhaps, but you forgot one thing. You would have to care for me to ever become jealous of another.'

'You are my wife. I own you, body, and soul. Of course I care about you. I always care for and protect my possessions. But you make my responsibility harder than it needs to be.'

Gillian closed her eyes and silently cursed the unwanted moisture building behind her eyelids. Ah, yes, she had willingly walked into dangerous territory. This wasn't a love match. Why then did his words sting in such a piercing manner? Swallowing hard to ensure she could speak without her voice shaking, she said, 'Yes, I am your wife. Thank you for informing me in no uncertain terms that I am an item you own, worth no more or less, I hope, than your sword.'

'My sword is worth far more gold.'

Gillian gasped at the sudden pain caused by his nasty comment. She couldn't stop the tears, no matter how tightly she closed her eyes.

Rory caressed her cheek, made a grunting sound and then wiped at her tears with his thumb. 'However, my sword does not cry, or share a kiss. Nor does it keep me warm at night.' He paused, waiting for her to look at him. When she finally did, he said, 'The worth of some things cannot be measured in gold, Gillian. You are one of those things.'

He rolled his eyes at her sniffle-choked laugh. 'When you are done with these womanly tears, let me know so I can properly and soundly chastise you for taking such a foolish risk.'

She sniffed again and then nodded.

Rory lowered her to her feet, but kept a hand threaded through her hair. 'Gillian, I am done with this cat-and-mouse game. Before the sun sets on this day you will tell me everything. No more lies. No more of your half-truths. I want to know everything you know.'

He pulled her closer, saying, 'I will do whatever I must to get the information I need. Consider yourself warned.'

She closed her eyes against his unwavering stare. Not for one heartbeat did she believe his softly spoken, but deadly earnest threat was anything less than a warning that he would make good on his vow.

He released his hold on her head to tip her face up to his

with a fingertip beneath her chin. This kiss was gentle and afterwards he whispered against her lips, 'I have made many promises these past days. I will break none of them.'

Which promise was he referring to? Was it the promise to protect her and Rockskill? Or perhaps one not to take her unless she wanted him? Or maybe the promise not to hurt her? Or this last—the one to get the truth about everything going on at Rockskill?

Before she could guess at his actions, he swept her off her feet and back on to the saddle of his horse. Resting a hand on her thigh, he asked, 'Do I need to tie you there?'

She shook her head and he led the horse towards the Keep.

Their trip back to Rockskill was done in silence until they neared the wall. 'Which gate?'

Gillian knew that eventually he would find the postern gate, so she directed him there. He spared a glance for the single guard, but didn't stop until they rounded the Keep to the inner yard. The bailey was a flurry of activity. Men—armoured men—strangers, neither hers, nor her cousin's, were setting up tents.

'Who are these men?'

Rory ignored her question and wrapped his hands about her waist. Instead of lowering her to the ground, he held on to her, settling her against his chest, and carried her into the Keep.

Only about a dozen men were inside the hall, but most were known to her. Unfortunately, four of those were the ones he'd tasked with guarding her.

Rory stopped before them. Thomas glared at her, Richard turned his attention to the floor, while the other two Rockskill guards both had wide-eyed, open-mouthed expressions of shock as they looked from her to their Lord.

'My Lord, I...we—'

Thomas broke the silence first, but Rory cut him off. 'Not a word. Get a tub and plenty of hot water up to my chamber. I will deal with all of you later.'

Gillian winced. Oh, yes, he was angry—very, very angry. If the tense muscles of his arms and chest hadn't been enough to signal his mood, the deep, clipped tone of his voice gave evidence of anger.

She withdrew the hand that she'd cupped around his neck, wanting nothing more than to jump from his hold and hide.

He glared down at her, but still didn't say a word. Instead, he carried her up the stairs and into their chamber.

Catherine jumped up from where she'd been sitting by the window. Her mending fell to the floor as her gaze flew to the bed where a young maid had the covers in her hand as if she'd been about to climb beneath them.

'Lady Gillian, my Lord…' At an unusual loss for words, she sounded as flustered as she appeared.

'Out.' Rory's one-word order served to fluster the older woman more.

Catherine retrieved the sewing items from the floor, dropping some more than once before she secured them in the skirt of her gown. She waved at the maid who seemed frozen in place.

As the women were leaving the chamber, a couple of younger men arrived with a wooden tub that Rory had them place near the brazier. Catherine turned back to the room. 'I can assist—'

'Out!' If Rory's shouted order hadn't been enough to send the woman racing from the chamber, his dark scowl would have done the deed.

Once they were alone and the door had been closed, Gillian pushed against his shoulder. 'You can put me down now.'

He turned and dropped her on to the bed. Before she could

right herself, he loomed over her, his fisted hands on either side of her on the bed and asked, 'Where is it?'

She knew exactly what he meant, but intentionally chose to misunderstand. Even though there was no sensible reason to do, and could prove dangerous, something inside urged her to be contrary. Taking off her cloak, she responded, 'Where is what?'

Rory grabbed the cloak from her hand and threw it so it landed half on the bench and half on the floor. 'The door to your hidden passageway.'

Gillian frowned as if confused. 'What hidden passageway?'

'Enough!'

Rory shoved off the bed uncertain whether he was angrier that she'd evaded her guards to sneak off to the caves, or that she was now playing some childish game with him. He turned to study the chamber. After a quick glance in her direction, he stomped into the alcove. The tapestries that helped keep the chamber warm were also big enough to conceal a door. He tore all three of them from the walls and threw them in a pile on the floor.

A flicker of light glinted across a metal latch on a side wall. Rory flipped the latch and shook his head at the thin metal that wouldn't keep a child from breaking into the chamber. There were no visible hinges, so it was likely the panel slid open—something that would be fixed immediately. The last thing he wanted was for someone to surprise him in his bedchamber.

He pushed the narrow panel aside and then turned to stare at Gillian. 'Where does this lead?'

At first her tight lips made him wonder if she would tell him, but eventually, she shrugged and said, 'It leads out to a garden in the bailey.'

'Your neglected herb gardens?'

She nodded.

Rory was amazed at finding a door anyone could break through leading to a stairwell that led out to a nearly un-guarded postern gate. This would not do. He headed towards the chamber door, asking, 'How have you all not been killed in your sleep?'

Pulling open the door, he stepped into the opening, and shouted for Daniel. When the man arrived, Rory led him to the alcove. 'There will be woodworkers among the guards who have arrived from Roul. I want this fixed. Until the door at the bottom can be sealed off, get a hinged door on here and put at least three heavy locking bars across it on this side. Have them gather the materials and await word from me as to when they can begin working.'

Daniel studied the panel, sliding it back and forth, then whistled. 'Isn't Rockskill always at battle with their neigh-bouring lords?'

'That's my understanding. Hard to believe how witless the previous lords have been, isn't it?'

'Either witless or extremely arrogant.'

'Which makes me wonder how many more of these secret doors exist in the Keep.'

'Adam and I will find them.'

'Today. And I want them secured. Today.'

As Daniel was leaving, half a dozen lads arrived, carry-ing buckets of steaming water.

Catherine followed, carrying towels and soap. 'I can as-sist with your bath, my Lord.'

'The water is for my wife and we do not require your as-sistance.'

'But…' Her words trailed off as she looked to Gillian. 'Lady?'

Rory took the bathing supplies from her arms and set them on a table near the tub. 'You can leave now.'

Once everyone finally left the chamber, he closed the door and dropped the top locking bar across the heavy wood.

Only then did he take the time to study his wife. Between her ragged, patched gown and the filth on her hands and face, she looked more like a girl who had been up to mischief than she did the Lady of Rockskill. Her willingness to defy him so openly should have made him angry—and he was, to a point—but not as outraged as he would have thought. Oddly enough his anger was tempered by the idea of her being so headstrong and willing to get her hands dirty. He found that rather appealing. However, needlessly putting herself at risk wasn't appealing in the least.

Rory was well aware that shouting at her would get him nowhere. She only met his anger with a measure of her own. If he wanted his answers today, and he did, then he needed to change tactics. He took a breath to steady himself for the game he was about to play.

'Where is your leg injured?'

She looked away, refusing to answer him.

Her stubbornness suited him right now. He could be just as stubborn himself. Rory sat on the edge of the bed and grasped the calf of what he suspected was her injured leg. Removing the short, soft boot, he tossed it towards the bench near the door. If she didn't want to tell him where it hurt, he didn't consider it a hardship to discover the injury himself.

'What are you doing?' Gillian tried pulling her leg free,

While sliding down her stocking, he answered, 'Since you won't tell me where you hurt your leg, I'll find out for myself.'

'My knee. It's my knee.'

He held back a chuckle at her gasped rush of words. His attention was making her nervous and at this moment, he didn't care, since that was his intention. Being agitated was the least she deserved for sneaking off in such a manner after he'd ordered her to stay in the Keep.

Once the stocking joined the boot, he pushed up the hem of her gown, exposing her leg from the thigh down. The slightly swollen knee made him heave a sigh of relief—she might have twisted it, but at least it didn't appear to be broken.

Gillian pushed at the gown and batted at his hands. 'Stop it. I can see to it myself.'

He grasped her hand and turned it over. Dried blood and scrapes attested to how she'd injured her knee. 'You fell.'

'I know that.'

'Had you done as I'd instructed, you wouldn't be hurting now.'

'You mean as you'd ordered.'

Rory released her hand and snagged the other one. Broken nails and scrapes along the fingertips had been the only damage done. 'Call it what you will, either way you took it upon yourself to outwit your guards and leave the Keep.'

She pulled her hand free, clamped her lips closed and turned her head.

'You can ignore me all you want, Gillian. But the fact remains, you took unnecessary risk with your life and I'll not stand for such foolishness.'

She glared at him. 'It is *my* life.'

'You are *my* wife and until such time that changes your well-being and safety is my concern.'

'No, it isn't. Rockskill is your concern.'

'If I remember correctly, you required someone strong enough to keep *you and Rockskill* safe.' To intentionally feed her nervousness, he placed both hands around her ankle and started massaging the muscles of her leg, then asked, 'Has that suddenly changed overnight?'

He wasn't witless and knew full well that she had gone out to the caves to warn her men. Exactly as he would have done. But should danger arise, he could defend himself, where she could barely hold her own against a boy attacking her with a wooden sword on a practice field.

She didn't seem to understand how dangerous it was for her to hide the truth—even if it was done to protect those she cared about. She was putting her own life and future foolishly at risk. She was leaving him little choice but to coerce her into confessing what she knew and what part she played in the illegal activities.

If he had to kiss her senseless, so be it. He would go as far as he must to get what he needed.

By the time this day was over he would very likely despise himself as much as she claimed to hate him—if not more.

When she didn't respond, he prompted, 'Do you know exactly where your cousin Albert is at this moment?'

'No.'

'So, you thought it would be safe to head out to the caves on your own?' Taking his time working the muscles of her calf, he added, 'Without an escort or protection.'

'My own safety wasn't on my mind.'

Her unguarded admission was what he had been seeking. 'Ah. You were more worried about me finding your men in the midst of criminal acts than you were about Albert taking you unaware.'

At the widening of her eyes, Rory said, 'Come now, you can't for one heartbeat think I am so feeble of mind that I wouldn't know what you were doing out there?'

Gillian grabbed both of his wrists when he skimmed over her knee, stopping his progress up her thigh. 'You are doing this on purpose to distract me.'

His wife wasn't feeble of mind either. 'And it's worked well, hasn't it?'

'Perhaps, but I'll tell you nothing further.'

Oh, sweeting, one way or another, eventually, you'll tell me everything I want to know.

He kept that thought to himself and rose to offer her a hand. 'Come, before the water gets cold.'

She batted his hand away. 'You are not getting me into that tub.'

'You really should learn not to issue challenges like that.' He leaned over and drew her across his shoulder. 'They are far too hard to ignore.'

Gillian gasped for breath as she landed across his shoulder. What did this oaf think he was doing?

'Put me down.'

He walked towards the tub. 'I plan on doing so.'

'Stop!' She pounded a fist against his back. 'If you are trying to get me riled, you have succeeded. Now, stop!'

To her amazement, he did stop and slid her off his shoulder. But before she could scurry out of his reach, he spun her around and ordered, 'Raise your arms.'

Having no intention of letting him remove her clothing, she stepped away. Only to be brought up short when he grasped the neck of her gown and tore it down the back.

'I do not think another patch will be noticed.'

'Why, you…you—' She spun around gingerly, her knee already feeling weak and found herself tightly pressed against his chest.

'I think we covered this before. I am a beast, a monster, an animal and a whoreson of the devil if I am not mistaken.'

'Yes!' She wasn't about to disagree with the obvious.

'You do realise, Gillian, that few would fault me if I were to hand you the same treatment you gave me by chaining you to a wall in a cell below? Especially once they discovered it was the only way to keep you safe.'

The sudden huskiness of his voice caused her to look up at him. His heavily lidded gaze did not speak of the anger she'd expected to see. Instead, it spoke of seduction and sent visions to her mind that had nothing to do with punishment or torture. The flash of being chained to a wall naked while his large, calloused hands roamed over her body was brief, but it left her breathless, trembling and wanting.

What was wrong with her to have reacted so indecently to his question?

He relaxed his hold slightly. 'Anyone could guess at the thoughts tripping through your mind.'

He truly was a whoreson of the devil. How else could he have seduced her mind so easily?

Without further thought she shoved out of his hold. Unable to bear her weight at the sudden movement, her knee seemed to fold beneath her and she tumbled towards the floor.

Rory caught her mid-fall and placed her on a chair. He knelt to remove her other boot.

She cursed in frustration and batted at his hands. 'Leave me alone.'

'No. I already made that mistake once. I'll not do so again.'

His fingertips brushed along her leg as he slipped her stocking free. She closed her eyes at the slight touch that served to once again fire images no lady should entertain.

A soft chuckle and his warm hands resting on her thighs made her look at him. He was so close. Too close. Yet she found herself wanting to reach out and draw him even closer.

Light from the torches danced in his eyes, making them shimmer as he returned her gaze. This was not the stare of a wolf. It was too warm. Too inviting. Too enticing. She could drown in that gaze and be content to do so. When he looked at her as though she was the only person in the world that mattered, she knew that she would tell him anything, promise him everything. Before she did something foolish, she looked away. 'What are you doing to me?'

'Doing? I am doing nothing but getting you ready to soak in a warm tub. Whatever you are imaging is the working of your own mind.'

He brushed her cheek with his fingers, before coaxing her to face him. 'Gillian, you do the same to me. But I swear I mean only to get you into the bath. That is all.'

The heat of embarrassment warmed her cheeks. She glanced down at the floor. How did this man, a stranger, know her thoughts with such ease?

'Come. Stand up so we can remove this.' He freed the ties at the wrist of her chemise.

The last thing she wanted to do was to stand naked before him. But she knew that he wasn't going to stop until she was in that tub. And right now, soaking in the warm water sounded inviting.

'You swear, nothing?' At his nod, Gillian put her hands on his shoulders and stood.

Before she could become embarrassed any further, or change her mind, she found herself stripped of her undergown and lowered into the warm water. His dark, brooding stare meant she could guess at what he was thinking. The fact that he'd stepped away from the tub proved he was going to be true to his word.

Gillian rested her head against the edge of the tub and sighed. The stiffness and aches eased in the warmth of the water.

From across the room, she heard the clinking of mail as Rory removed his armour and then the thud as it landed on the floor.

'Why did you feel such a need to warn your men?'

Every muscle in her body tensed. She should have known he was going to get back to his questioning sooner rather than later.

Trying to feign innocence, she asked, 'Warn them of what?'

'That the new Lord of Rockskill was out and about. Or perhaps that he was one of the King's men sent to stop the smuggling.'

His voice rose with each word. Not because he'd spoken louder, but because he'd moved closer to the tub and now stood alongside, staring down at her with that focused gaze that made her limbs weak and mind even weaker.

Gillian drew in a breath and gripped the edge of the tub with both hands. If she kept up the pretence of not knowing what he was talking about, he would once again resort to making her nervous enough to spill everything. She'd already learned how easy it would be for him to accomplish that feat.

She would tell him all—eventually. Stopping Albert and the happenings here at Rockskill was of the utmost importance and that would require Rory's help, but not until the goods from the King's ship were disposed of. For now, what if she gave him nothing more than a short, direct answer? Would that satisfy him?

'Both. I warned them of both.' The huskiness of her voice surprised her. She swallowed, before asking, 'Wouldn't you have done the same?'

He nodded. Then moved behind her and tapped the back of her head. 'Lean forward.'

The water behind her swished. And the rising scent of rosemary and lavender filled the air. He wasn't going to bathe her, was he?

The slick warmth of a calloused hand sliding down her back answered her question. Yes. He was.

Rory dragged his knuckles slowly down the length of her spine, rubbing out any kink and every tight spot. Gillian arched her back, then relaxed.

By the time he started on her shoulders and neck she feared he would have her so limp, she would melt into the bath.

'I would.'

Confused by the sudden break in the silence of the chamber, she could only ask, 'Would what?'

'Warn my men if perceived danger were near.'

'Oh.' Her mind was currently as limp as her body and she wondered if that had been his intention.

'But…' She wanted to curse at her inability to think clearly. Sitting up slightly on the small bathing stool, she tried to focus. 'Were you not sent here by King David?'

'Yes.'

'And did he not task you with…' instinct advised her to be careful, to choose her words wisely '…with certain responsibilities?'

His deep chuckle warned her that he knew what she was doing. 'Yes. I was sent here to put a stop to the illegal activities. But I wed you knowing I was aligning myself with whatever was taking place here at Rockskill.'

Chapter Twelve

Rory slipped his hands over the front of her shoulders as he kneaded along her collarbone.

For a heartbeat she wondered if he would slide his fingers up to choke her, or down to stroke her breasts.

Instead, he slid his hands across the top of her shoulders to her arms. Against her ear he whispered, 'Your body gives away your thoughts. You tensed briefly, wondering if I would take the opportunity to strangle you. Then a slight hitch in your breath told me you feared I might caress your breasts.'

This time she did curse.

He moved to the side of the tub and grasped one of her hands between his. 'Gillian, I am very good at what I do for King David. There is no devil's magic at work here.' As he massaged each finger, then worked his way up her arm, he explained. 'Very, very few people can control their body well enough to hide what they are thinking. They will tense when afraid, or when lying. The dark centre of their eyes will enlarge when in the clutches of desire, when lying or when trying to hide something. There are subtle changes in their breathing, tone of voice, manner of talking and movements that give away much. You are no different.'

'No?'

'No.'

His voice had deepened, sending a shiver down her.

'Right now, were I to go back on my word and decide to seduce you, you would protest little, if at all.'

She hated that he was right. 'What makes you so certain?'

He released her hand and retrieved her other one to repeat his motion with that arm. 'When I speak softly, slowly and deeply, your eyes darken. You shiver.' He gave her a lopsided half-smile. 'Yes, just like that.'

She shook her head. That much was true. He could recite a prayer in that tone of voice and her mind would fly to thoughts completely unholy.

'Your breathing, while not heavy, is uneven. Much like the tiny pulse against your neck.'

Again, he was right. Her heart felt as if it were skipping inside her chest.

'You are naked, so it is obvious, but even beneath layers of clothing I would see that your breasts would welcome my touch, be it from my hands or mouth.'

She didn't need to glance down to know that her nipples were straining towards him. She could feel the tightening of the flesh.

'The fullness of your lower lip, the slight parting means your mouth wants to taste my kiss.'

Gillian ran her tongue over her suddenly dry lip. Yes, she did want him to kiss her. Immediately. And thoroughly.

'Were I to slide my hand between your legs, I would likely find heat.'

She pressed her legs together tightly with a groan. But it did little to stop the building desire pulsing to life. He had seduced her with nothing more than words. Hoarsely, she whispered, 'Stop.'

'There is nothing wrong with desire. Is it not a good thing?'

There was plenty wrong with desire. Had she not learned

that during her first marriage? There was more wrong with it when this man could sense it in her. 'Not when you can read me so easily.'

'Ah, but with a little patience you could do the same, if you wanted.'

He released her arm and grabbed a towel. 'Out. I want to bathe, too.'

'The water is getting cold.'

Rory chuckled. 'Right now, that would prove welcome.'

She looked at him, her gaze trailing from his half-lidded eyes, down his chest, past his waist and pausing on a gasp. If the tent against the front of his braies was any indication, she wasn't the only one he had seduced.

He held the towel out and repeated, 'Come.'

Gillian hesitated. She wasn't afraid that he would decide to break his word if she stood up. She was more afraid that she would throw herself against him and beg him to do so. He had sworn not to force himself on her until she was willing. At this moment, she was more than just willing.

Finally, certain she would do nothing so foolish, she rose. He immediately wrapped the towel around her and lifted her from the tub.

'Can you stand?'

Her knee no longer throbbed. 'Yes.'

He set her on her feet. She grasped the edge of the tub with one hand and the towel with the other, then tested her leg. She nodded to the cooling water. 'Go. I am fine.'

Gillian used the oversized bath sheet to dry herself off, all the while keeping an eye on him. Just as she had, he leaned his head back to rest against the tub and closed his eyes.

She wrapped the sheet about her, tucking in the ends to hold it in place as best she could, then picked up the soap, debating. When he'd been chained in a cell below, she had reached out to touch him, but confusion had stopped her from doing so. Today, she wanted to slide her hands over the hardness of his chest. She wanted to feel the heat of his flesh covering the muscles beneath.

More than that, she wanted to know if this want, this longing he'd reawakened in her, could be fulfilled with anything more than mind-numbing frustration that would leave her angry and filled with self-loathing for her own weakness.

Where Jonathon's attempts had frightened her and being bedded by her husband Richard had repulsed her, something about Rory drew her closer.

Her late husband had laughed and called her wanton the one time she'd mentioned feeling some kind of need. Any wanting from her was indecent and befitted only the basest whore. She'd been forced to share his bed in the manner he'd required—still and emotionless, as if it were nothing more than another chore to be performed.

But that had flown out the window since she'd seen Rory chained up in the cell. She knew that this desire, this longing, wasn't going to disappear on its own. The only way she could think of finally putting it to rest was to discover if it could be filled, or if she was indeed seeking something not meant for her.

Gillian reached down to swish the soap in the water.

Rory grabbed her wrist and opened his eyes. 'What are you doing?'

'I was going to help you bathe.' Her voice came out in a breathless rush that made her swallow in a useless attempt to calm herself.

Still holding her wrist, he stared at her a moment. 'I made you a vow. Your touch will make it difficult to keep.'

Knowing this was foolish, but never more certain of anything in her life, she held his stare. 'I release you from that vow.'

He pulled her closer as he sat up to slide a hand behind her neck and whisper against her lips, 'Gillian, if you have changed your mind, you need to say so.'

Instead of answering him, she nodded, then trailed the tip of her tongue along his lower lip and found herself caught fast in his kiss.

He released her wrist, pulled the sheet free and let it fall to the floor, then wrapped his arms about her and pulled her into the tub to straddle his lap. The water was decidedly cooler, but she leaned against him and the warmth of his arms, along with the heat from his chest, chased away any chill. The trembling of her limbs wasn't from the temperature of the water, but from a sudden bout of nerves. She wasn't afraid. It was more unknown anticipation than fear.

Rory broke their kiss to lean back against the tub. He retrieved the soap she'd dropped and placed it in her hands. 'You were going to help me bathe?'

Grateful for something to focus on, she spun the soap in her hands. 'Yes, that's what I had planned.' Nothing could have chased the tremor from her words, so she ignored it and set her mind on running her soap-slicked hands over his shoulders.

He mimicked her motions, lathering his hands with the soap before sliding them along her shoulders.

When she moved to his arms, he did the same to her. Gillian narrowed her eyes as she realised he was seeking to lessen her nervousness. Emboldened by his willingness to follow her lead, she stroked his neck, marvelling at the way his shiver mirrored her own. Was he simply mimicking her reaction to his light touch beneath her ear, or did he truly feel the same lingering spark of icy fire?

She closed her eyes and teased her fingertips along his collarbone. To her dismay, his hands didn't leave her neck—

until she opened her eyes. Only then did he brush his touch over her collarbone.

Embarrassed to have him watch her so closely, she forced herself to hold his gaze before she drew one hand down the centre of his chest.

His fingers shook slightly as he skimmed them between her breasts. Was his anticipation as great as her own? She took in a long, slow breath and flattened her hands against the muscles of his chest.

When he cupped her breasts, she closed her eyes. Thankfully, this time, he didn't stop his movements. His touch was warm and her already peaked nipples seemed to strain even more.

Gillian lightly circled one of his flat nipples with a fingertip. Surprise made her open her eyes. The small nub had hardened beneath her attention.

She gasped when he repeated that attention on hers.

His soft chuckle drew her gaze back to his half-lidded shimmering one. 'Kiss me, Gillian.'

She leaned towards him to follow his request. While his husky tone had been soft, there was nothing soft about his kiss. He wrapped one arm around her, pulling her tight against him before sliding it up her back and cupping her head with his hand.

He swept her away with the force of his onslaught, leaving her dizzy with desire and moaning with need. She grasped his shoulders, determined to hang on, not wanting him to stop.

She barely noticed his other hand skimming along her side, stroking fire against her hip, making her legs tremble as his teasing touch trailed the length of her thigh and came to rest at her core.

Gillian's breath caught, his kiss forgotten as she waited

and wondered. He pulled his lips from hers just far enough to ask, 'You need to tell me, do I stop?'

His question, asked in such a ragged, hoarse tone, beckoned her to respond honestly. She leaned her head forward, pressing her lips once again to his. 'Please, no.'

'Are you certain? The decision is yours.' He brushed a kiss across her forehead. 'Yours alone.'

She cupped his face between her hands. 'I am positive.'

Where his kiss was hard and demanding, his touch between her legs was gentle and coaxing. She couldn't have stopped the shivers rippling through her body had she tried.

Her pulse raced. She slid her hands down his cheeks and neck to curl her fingers into his shoulders. If she didn't know she was firmly planted against him, she would have thought she'd fallen over the side of a cliff. Everything seemed to swirl around her as all feelings centred beneath his touch.

A loud, insistent pounding on the chamber door was accompanied by a shouted, 'Lord Roul!'

Rory tore his mouth from hers, a curse already leaving his lips. 'What!'

But he didn't stop his teasing touch. A whine built in her throat. He pulled her head closer, pressing her mouth against his neck.

'You are needed in the hall!'

Her body pulsed, quickly, repeatedly and she gasped in shock. To stop her cry from filling the air, Gillian clamped her teeth on his neck. She felt him flinch, but couldn't stop herself. The only thing she could focus on was the deliciously wonderful shattering of the lies Robert had told her.

'I will be down.'

He wrapped his hand in her hair and pulled her head away from his neck. 'Hold on.'

Hold on? To what? Why? She couldn't force her mind free of the dizzying spin that had captured her.

He wrapped his arms around her and rose. She wound her arms around his neck, her legs around his waist as he stepped out of the tub and dropped both of them on to the bed.

Her breath escaped in a loud whoosh as he landed on top of her. She started to slide her legs free. 'You need to go.'

'Like hell.'

'No, they need you—'

He reached between them and in one fluid move slid his cock into her, filling her, cutting off anything she'd been about to say.

Against her ear, he asked, 'Who needs what?'

'Me.' She tightened her legs around him. 'I need you.'

She laughed at his responding growl.

It was easy to follow his lead. Somehow, they seemed made for each other, as if they'd been sharing a bed for years, instead of just this day. They quickly learned where to touch, how to move, when to speed up, or slowly lengthen a thrust.

He could move so slowly, with such steady intention, that she feared her eyes would roll back in her head permanently. And she discovered a spot on his lower back that when she drew her nails lightly against it made him groan and shudder.

Soon, too soon, her body responded, but this time, instead of a quick pulse, it was more of a pounding need. She moaned and bucked against him. He grasped her hands, threading his fingers through hers before he rose up on his forearms to stare down at her.

'Shh, Gillian. Let me.'

Not knowing what else to do, or how to satisfy the want that seemed just out of her reach, she ceased striving for release and tightened her fingers around his.

He steadily sent desire to a fevered pitch and swiftly took

them both tumbling over the edge. Gillian cried out as she felt herself falling and he caught the cry with a fierce kiss, wrapping her safely in his arms until they both fell limp. Their satisfied sighs mingled in the quiet of the chamber.

Rory rolled off her, on to his side, bringing her along with him. 'I need to go.'

Since he made no attempt to move, she only nodded and agreed, 'You do.'

He kissed her forehead. 'I should get up.'

'Yes, you should.' She snuggled tighter against the warmth of his body.

His mouth was on her neck, his lips teasing at the soft spot beneath her ear, making her shiver. 'I need to go.'

Against his chest, she whispered, 'I know.' Then slipped a foot between his ankles.

'You need to let me go.'

Gillian laughed. 'I am not stopping you.'

One loud pound on the door was followed by a shout, 'Rory!'

Unlike the first one, this voice she recognised as Daniel's.

Rory groaned against her neck, kissed the end of her nose, untangled himself from her and sat on the edge of the bed. 'What?'

His man tried to push the door open, but thankfully the locking bar prevented him from entering.

With a curse, Rory flipped the edge of the bedcovers over her and grabbed his braies as he headed to remove the wooden bar.

Daniel marched into the chamber and came to a dead stop as he stared from Rory to her and back to Rory. He shook his head, snorted, then shrugged. 'Your prisoner is demanding an audience. Rockskill's men are growing uneasy and grumbling loudly.'

Holding the covers to her, Gillian sat upright. 'What have you done?'

Rory hastily pulled on his clothes, then pointed at her once he had his boots on. 'Stay in that bed. We aren't yet finished.'

As he walked out the door, he paused to look back at her and warn, 'Don't try to escape. It'll only cause more trouble for those below.'

Angry voices and an occasional shout echoed up the stairwell. Rory clenched and unclenched his hands, trying to prepare for whatever mayhem awaited below. He'd expected Rockskill's men to take umbrage over holding one of their men captive sooner or later.

However, right now was *not* a good time. He was far too relaxed and mellow to deal with it. Hell, he'd rather be wrapped up in the bedcovers and the soft woman above than tromping down the stairs to face down a group of angry men.

He checked the buckle of his sword belt and gripped the hilt of his weapon before stepping down into the hall.

One glance at the irate faces and defensive stances let him know he needed to gain control immediately. He pulled his sword free, widened his stance and yelled, 'Cease!'

The din of noise in the hall fell to hushed whispers, replaced by the sound of shuffling feet as the men turned to glare at him.

Rory motioned towards Daniel and instructed Adam, 'Get Roul on the perimeter.'

The men from Roul fell back to surround the group. Then they closed ranks, pushing Rockskill's men tighter together, giving them no room to fight.

He motioned Gillian's man Thomas to him. 'Go guard your Lady. Nobody enters the chamber except for me. And she doesn't leave it either. Understood?' Thomas nodded, then headed up the stairs.

Stomping over to the raised dais, Rory stepped up on to a stool, so he stood above the gathering.

'You know who I am.'

Half-whispers of wolf, rabid dog, reached his ears. Used to the comments, he ignored them. 'You also know I am the Lord here. My rule is law.'

It was surprisingly easy to stare them down. One steady sweep of the room had most of them looking at the floor. Daniel and Adam would note those who didn't and keep a closer watch on them.

'Rockskill is guilty of smuggling. I was sent by *our* King to put an end to the activity.' He once again scanned the gathering. Now the shuffling started back up. Nervousness or guilt? Either was a good thing—maybe one or more of them could be convinced to provide the information he needed. 'I want the person, or persons, responsible for the deaths of King David's men.'

From the back someone shouted, 'It wasn't Jonathon.'

Rory wasn't so sure about that and the suddenness of that declaration made him less sure. 'And he will have the opportunity to explain his guilt or innocence soon.'

When the grumbling stopped, he told them, 'You have a choice to make. Either you will all pay for the deeds done here, or you will hand over those who are responsible.'

Someone in the front asked, 'What about Gillian? Is she your prisoner, too?'

'Lady Gillian is my wife. As such she is afforded my full protection.'

The rumbling of dissent rippled through the men. Either she was more responsible than he'd imagined, or some of these men hadn't heard about their marriage. 'So, the outcome of my task for the King is up to you. Make your decision quickly. I'll not wait long for your response.'

He jumped off the stool, stepped off the dais and beckoned Daniel over. 'I need to speak to my wife before interrogating our prisoner.'

Daniel snickered. 'You didn't have time for that earlier?'

Rory glanced at the men departing the hall as he growled at Daniel in reply, 'Don't.'

A meaty fist smacked him on the shoulder. 'I've been married, Rory. Did we not warn you?'

Yes, they had. However, he had never planned on actually seducing his in-name-only wife quite so thoroughly. And just as he had feared, he hadn't come out of the encounter as unaffected as he'd hoped.

He glanced at the stairs, impatient to be back in their bedchamber, alone, just the two of them.

Daniel laughed. 'Go. I'll see to it that the prisoner knows to expect you…eventually.'

Rory took the stairs two at a time, then paused outside their chamber door. He dismissed Thomas. 'Make certain nobody comes up those stairs. Nobody. Unless an armed enemy is at our gate, I do not wish to be interrupted.'

The older man's eyes widened, but he nodded. When he finally heard Thomas's feet on the stairs, he placed his hand flat on the door, wondering what he would discover inside.

Chapter Thirteen

Gillian sat on the edge of the bed facing the door, waiting for Rory to enter. She'd heard him speaking to her current nursemaid Thomas, so she knew they were both in the corridor. A moment later she heard the heavy footsteps of a single man walking away and assumed that was Thomas.

Finally, tired of waiting for Rory to decide if he would enter the chamber, she rose and donned a sleeveless surcoat, tying a belt around it as she crossed the chamber to pull open the door. 'Are you coming in?'

'I haven't decided.' He shrugged. 'I was thinking about standing out here all night.'

When she moved to close the door, he grasped the edge and stopped her. 'Of course, I had planned on joining you.'

Once inside, she spun around. 'What have you done?'

'About? With?'

'Oh, now you seek to play a witless fool. What have you done with Jonathon?'

'Ah.' He appeared to ignore her as he sat on the bench to remove his boots, then unbuckled his sword belt. He stood up to approach her. But instead of stopping in front of her, he kept walking, pushing her back towards the bed as he moved.

When the back of her legs hit the bed, he stopped and deftly undid the fabric belt she'd tied around the surcoat.

He pushed the garment off her shoulders, letting it rustle to the floor, then he simply fell forward, pinning her beneath him on the bed.

Gillian brushed his hair from his face. 'What are you doing?'

'I was hoping to keep my wife still and quiet, so we could talk.'

'Talk? As in an exchange of words, or interrogate?'

He kissed the end of her nose. 'Oh, we'll have an exchange… of that I am certain. Whether it be of words or not hasn't yet been determined.'

'So, interrogate. Rory, there is nothing I can tell you.'

'Gillian, a man's life hangs in the balance at this moment. A man you claim to be a friend. So, listen to me carefully. I vowed to keep you safe. But I cannot do so if I do not know what danger lurks around you. Whatever evil surrounds you, surrounds me, also. Help me to help you. No matter how it came about, I am your husband, not your enemy. Even if it is discovered you ordered the ships be lured to their destruction, I will protect you. On my honour, I will keep you safe, but I need to know so I can plan the best approach to do so.'

She so wanted to believe him. But a part of her warned that he wasn't to be trusted, not yet—not fully. Would a trustworthy man have put her friend in chains? Would that same man have seduced her so thoroughly just moments ago, after swearing he would never do so?

'Why?' Gillian pushed at his shoulder. 'You will be gone from here as soon as all is in order, so why do you even care?'

He grasped her face between his palms. 'What we did here earlier might have consequences that change those plans.'

She shook her head. 'No. I was wed for over two years before. As you know, there were no consequences. I am barren, so you have no fears that you will be forced to stay here at Rockskill because of any children.'

'And you know you are barren, because an old man couldn't get you with child?' He shifted on top of her to pin her legs between his. 'I am not an old man.'

Thankful for the turn in the conversation, she arched up against him. 'No, you are not an old man, are you?' Fluttering her eyelashes, she asked, 'What would a younger man be doing right now with a woman trapped beneath him?'

He chuckled. 'You'll have to try harder than that to distract me. Tell me what I need to know.'

'Where is Jonathon?'

'You are naked beneath your husband asking about another man? Strange tactic to avoid the topic at hand.'

'Where is he, Rory? What have you done?'

'He is safe in a cell below. I managed to survive, so I'm certain he will also. At least until I go below, then I can promise nothing.'

She squirmed enough to slide out from beneath him and sit on the edge of the bed. Staring at the floor, she asked, 'What are you planning?'

He sat beside her and draped an arm across her shoulders. 'If you refuse to tell me what I must know, I will have no choice but to get the information in any manner I can.'

'Any manner?'

'Yes, Gillian. Any manner it takes be it simple words, my fists, a dagger, sword, lash or hot poker. I will not sleep again without having the information I want.'

He stated his intentions with such a lack of emotion that Gillian had to swallow hard to keep her stomach in check. She had little doubt that he would do anything and everything imaginable to force Jonathon to talk.

Unfortunately, she'd known Jonathon all her life and knew

the fool would hold his tongue at the cost of his life before spilling any information.

She hung her head. What was she to do? If she talked, her childhood friend might forfeit his life alongside her for his part in all of this. But if she didn't talk it was also likely he would die during Rory's interrogation.

And if she didn't talk, her husband would have little reason to trust her at all. Not that he did now, but at least at this moment, they seemed to have some semblance of a relationship. To her surprise, that was something she truly didn't want to lose.

However, Rory would be leaving. Jonathon would still be here. While she wanted nothing physical between her and Jonathon, he was her friend. He had often protected her, championed her against Robert and Albert.

Yes, he was involved with the smuggling, but so were many others at Rockskill. They did so because they were ordered. What choice did they have?

Even though she had a sinking worry deep in her stomach that Jonathon had taken it upon himself to give the orders to take the King's ship, she would still do everything in her power to protect him and the others. If it truly had been him, she knew he'd done so only because she relied on the coin from the goods gained. How else was she to feed those at Rockskill? How else could she purchase, or barter for, the materials needed when the Keep or the cottages needed repairs, or for medicines when any of her people got sick?

'Me.' Gillian closed her eyes and took a breath. 'I am responsible. The men of Rockskill act only on my orders.'

The silence in the chamber was frightening. She wondered if this is what it felt like the moment before one died—complete and utter silence. A quiet so stark that her heartbeat roared in her ears.

Rory rubbed his hand across his brow, but said nothing. Instead, he rose, stared at her a moment, before putting his boots back on and grabbing his sword belt from a hook on the wall.

'Where are you going?'

The glare he turned on her took her breath away. 'To find someone who doesn't think I'm a complete lackwit. Someone who I can force to give me the truth. Because, Wife, what just spewed from your lips isn't even close.'

'Jonathon will tell you the same.' At least she hoped he would stick to her plan.

Rory buckled on his belt and then gripped the pommel of his sword. 'Tell me, Gillian, since you know him so well, how many body parts will he be willing to lose to back up your lies? An ear? A hand? Will it take one, or both arms? Or perhaps just his cock will suffice. Do you think your friend will then be willing to tell me what you won't?'

She knew he wasn't speaking out of turn just to frighten her—the King's wolf would do any or all those things to get the information he wanted. She flew off the bed. Ignoring the searing pain in her knee, she dropped to the floor at his feet. Wrapping her arms around his legs, she pleaded, 'Rory, please, no.'

Gillian shuddered as the end of the leather-wrapped wooden sheath came to rest beneath her chin, tipping her head up so that she was forced to look at him. 'Would you care to try this again?'

She nodded, then whispered, 'Yes.'

'Who. Gives. The. Orders?' he asked in that slow, steady tone of anger.

When she paused a heartbeat too long, he lifted her chin higher. 'Answer me.'

'Albert.'

'Who is his second-in-command?'

His hard glittering stare never wavered. If she lied to him again, he would know. Gillian swallowed, then softly said, 'Jonathon.'

'Damn you, Gillian. And you seek to protect him?'

She closed her eyes, unable to hold his gaze any longer. 'He is my friend. My only friend.'

'Friend.' Rory snorted. 'Is this the same friend who split your lip on our wedding day?'

'Yes.'

'For that alone I could kill him.' He reached down and grasped her under the arms. 'Get up.'

She leaned against his chest. 'Rory—'

He stepped away, cutting off anything she would say, and ordered, 'Get back in that bed.'

'What are you going to do?'

His sigh was loud, and long. 'As much as I would like to throttle you right at this moment, you wouldn't provide much sport. So, we're going to talk instead.'

She dropped down on to the edge of the bed. 'Oh.'

He once again removed his boots and sword belt, then joined her. 'How did all of this start?'

Rory caught the first tear with a fingertip. 'Gillian, don't.' He pulled her closer to his side. 'It can't possibly be as bad as you seem to fear. Just start at the beginning. Place your fears on my shoulders. I am more than willing and able to bear them with or even for you. Who started this smuggling campaign?'

She shook her head. 'I cannot. Not when you are watching me so closely.'

He turned so his back was against the head of the bed, stretched out his legs, then pulled her to him, resting her head on his chest. Rory jerked the bedcovers over them and wrapped his arms around her. 'You are safe. It is just you and me, nobody else is here.'

Rory relaxed as she took a shuddering breath. He knew she was finally going to surrender. Earlier he had told her he wasn't jealous of Jonathon. And he wasn't, not then and not in the way she had meant. But he'd be lying if he said it didn't chafe that she was now willing to tell him things because of her concern for Jonathon when she hadn't been willing before. His brothers would get a good laugh if they knew of the feelings buffeting him at this moment.

She twisted the edge of the cover in her fingers. 'What do you want to know?'

'Everything. Start at the beginning.'

Tipping his head back to rest against the solid wood headboard, he silently waited.

'A ship crashed on the rocks. It sank, taking all the souls with it. My father and Albert scuttled the wreckage finding usable goods and gold. Albert talked my father into purposely drawing ships to their demise, convincing him it would bring Rockskill wealth. And it did. But eventually it wasn't enough, so Albert again convinced my father that he needed to start taking land from the neighbouring lords to gain extra coastline which would provide more ships to lure on to the rocks.'

He remained quiet as she continued to tell him of the wrecks, the battles with the neighbouring lords over property and what had happened when she tried alerting King David to the things happening here.

Rory couldn't help but feel sorry for the young woman who was helpless to do anything to right the things at Rockskill that had gone horribly wrong. He closed his eyes when she told him about being forced to wed and endure a husband nearly as old as her own father. And then upon his death to endure the cruelty of her cousin.

He'd been correct with his first assumption—the men in Gillian's life had not been kind.

While he felt sorry for her, he noticed that she didn't. His wife hadn't shed one tear during the telling of what was essentially her miserable life.

She had tensed when speaking of her father. Trembled slightly over speaking of her first husband and shook as she'd told him about Albert.

When she paused, he asked, 'When your father died, did your husband take over?'

'Yes. Robert and Albert made quite the pair. I don't think there is a single landowner in the area who doesn't despise Rockskill.'

'We can amend that, later. So, the two of them kept up the operation?'

She nodded and told him of the increase in shipwrecks and lives lost. Gillian sighed and explained how her older husband had died from a wound received when a survivor refused to simply drown.

'Which left you to your cousin's tender care.'

She snorted. 'Yes.'

'Did you ever get along with him?'

'No. Never. He was nasty even as a child and mean. From the moment he moved into Rockskill it was obvious he was after the Keep and any gold he could get his hands on. He constantly badgered my father, then my husband about how stupid it was to leave any of this to a mere female. He still doesn't know that this Keep belonged to my mother's family and was always to come to me. I have the King's writ hidden where Albert will never find it.'

He toyed with a lock of her hair, still besotted by the way it would spring back into a perfect curl when he stretched it out, then quickly released it.

'So, when did your cousin decide you needed a monster for a suitor?'

'He moved them in before Robert's body was barely cold. When I complained and threatened to go to King David, he dragged me to Hell's door and hung me out the opening. It was enough to convince me not to complain any more.'

Rory shook his head at the cruelty of the man and said, 'Albert is the one who issues the orders pertaining to the ships.'

She nodded. 'Yes. It is solely his decision.'

'What is done with the goods taken from the ships?'

He felt her tense against him and knew he wouldn't like her answer, but he remained silent, waiting for her to speak.

'They are kept in the caves until I take inventory and decide when the time is right to distribute them for sale.'

He'd known there was a possibility that she was directly involved. It would take some expert manoeuvring on his part to keep her safe. 'Are there listings of the inventory?'

'Yes, in my chest. I kept them all, except for one.'

'Which one?'

'The royal ship. I haven't had the chance to go through the items with Jonathon yet.'

Yet? Did she truly believe he was going to permit her to carry on after this? Rory cleared his throat. 'Who sets the prices for the items and collects the gold?'

'Jonathon and I set the price and decide how best to dispose of them, then Jonathon takes care of the exchange. Albert collects the gold and pays the men.'

'What do you gain out of this…enterprise?'

'Nothing for myself, but just enough to keep Rockskill's people fed.'

'Did you know they attacked one of David's ships?'

'I heard rumours, but I didn't know for certain until after we were wed.'

'Ah, when I told you why I was here to begin with.'

She nodded.

'Where are the goods from the ship? The weapons, armour and the chests of gold that were supposed to be heading to David's niece?'

Weapons, armour and gold that Rory knew were desperately needed to help Lord Geoffrey retain and enforce his dominance in Normandy.

She groaned. 'I gave orders to hide it all, to dump it into the sea if necessary. But I know Jonathon didn't pass on those orders, so I can only assume the goods are still in the cave.'

'Looks as though tomorrow you and I are headed to find out.' Rory heaved a heavy sigh. 'How many men are guarding the caves and who are they?'

'Some are villagers, some are Albert's men, and some are Rockskill's guards—maybe fifteen to twenty in total. There are also about five boys on lookout duty.'

'That explains the absence of men in the village.'

She again nodded.

'What about Thomas, Richard and the others?'

'No. They have nothing to do with the ships.'

Her answer was a bit too specific. 'What do they do while the others are occupied with the ships?'

'They guard Rockskill's gates and land.'

Rory hiked an eyebrow. 'To ensure nobody interrupts the tasks at hand?'

'Yes.'

'Then all the guards are well aware of the happenings here.'

She nodded.

'And they did nothing.'

Gillian asked, 'What could they have done?'

'Are there no men at Rockskill who possess any measure of honour?'

She sat up to stare at him. '*You* speak to me about honour?'

Rory knew she referred to their lovemaking earlier. 'I gave you more than one chance to change your mind. *You* chose not to do so.'

'Oh, yes, you gave me the choice after you knew full well I wasn't capable of telling you to stop.'

He laughed. 'So, it's *my* fault you are unable to control your desires?'

'Yes, it is.'

'I didn't realise you were suddenly that weak of will. When did this change come about?'

A flush crept up her neck and face. She looked away. 'The first time you kissed me.'

He rolled his eyes. Yes, that was the effect he had on all the women of his acquaintance…in his unimagined dreams maybe. Guilt plagued him. He was tormenting her solely because he knew he could—she was far too inexperienced to bedevil in this manner. He turned the conversation back to where it belonged. 'We are in need of men to guard the walls and men to help plant the fields. It is time they gave up their cave duties.'

She remained silent.

'Is there anything else I need to know?'

'Not that I can think of.'

'What about your relationship with Jonathon?'

She turned to gaze at him. 'Honestly, Rory, there is nothing of a physical nature between us. He is just a friend. Someone I trust with my life.'

He truly didn't want to know, but had to ask, 'Then why did you not marry him? You only wanted someone to protect you and Rockskill. Why not someone you knew and trusted instead of a stranger?'

'He is not a warrior. Nor does he have the wealth required to maintain Rockskill. Besides, nobody here would believe the two us were truly wed. Least of all my cousin.' She reached up to stroke his cheek. 'You have nothing to fear from Jonathon. Nothing.'

He grasped her hand and kissed her palm. 'I do not fear anything from him. I fear you defending him overmuch if anything goes wrong.'

'Goes wrong?' She tried to pull her hand away, but he held it fast. 'What are you saying?'

'Gillian, I will protect you with my life until the day I die. I will do everything I can for our men, but I will not trade my life, nor yours, for them.'

'But…'

'But nothing. I wed *you*. My life is entwined with yours, not theirs. If King David decrees they all perish, so be it. I will ask for leniency, but I cannot do more. I already suspect that your cousin will pay for his crimes with his life, as will any others who gave the orders. But I do not know what will happen to the others. They have killed innocent men and royal guards—there is bound to be some penalty. I can only ask that penalty be in coin, money that I will pay for them, but I cannot promise you anything on that score. Do you understand?'

Her lower lip quivered. He let out a heavy sigh. 'Stop. Tears will change nothing. Just stop.'

She tightened her lips for a moment, then answered in a steady voice, 'Yes, I understand. I do not like it, but I understand.'

'Good.'

Tired of this conversation, he pushed her down on to the bed, soundly kissed her, then raised his head far enough to say, 'You should get some sleep.'

She threaded her fingers through his hair and tried to

bring his lips back to hers. But Rory sat up. 'Sleep, Gillian. We have a long day tomorrow that is going to start early.'

'Doing?'

'First I need to speak to your Jonathon.'

'You won't harm him?'

'No need, now that you have finally told me what I needed to know. I just want to discover what's been done with the King's supplies and see if he will join us in our jaunt to the caves.'

'I'm sure he will. But that won't take all day, there's no need to set out early.'

'Ah, but the villagers are coming tomorrow to tell me what's been happening to make them act like frightened rabbits. Especially the children.'

'I can answer that. Albert and his companions happened,'

'I want to hear it first hand, from the people it happened to.'

She rolled her eyes, but nodded in agreement. Before he could rise from the bed, she grabbed his wrist. 'Rory, stay. I don't want to be alone tonight. Please, stay.'

The last thing he wanted to do was to spend the night next to her. What if... With a sigh, he rose to take off his clothes, then slid under the covers. 'You are such a shrew. Come, join me.'

Snuggling against him, she rested her head under his chin. 'You wouldn't be happy married to a meek, mild log, so stop complaining.'

He kissed the top of her head and wrapped her in a tight embrace, asking, 'Who's complaining?'

Chapter Fourteen

Gillian opened her eyes and rolled over, asking, 'How early did you—?'

The empty space beside her in the bed stopped her question abruptly. She sat up and did a quick survey of the chamber for any sign of her husband.

Where was he now? How long had he been gone?

She glanced towards the narrow windows. Daylight had not yet begun to break, so it was far too early for him to be up and about, unless... She tossed off the covers, slipped into her surcoat and went out into the corridor to grab a lit torch. After securing it in a wall sconce, she rooted through her clothes chest. Had Rory changed his mind and decided to interrogate Jonathon?

What else could he possibly hope to learn? Going against her initial instinct, she'd told him almost everything. So, now that she'd ignored her gut feeling, King David's wolf knew enough to ensure her death or a lifetime of imprisonment. He'd sworn to protect her and even though she wasn't certain she could believe him, it was no longer in her hands.

It wasn't just her life she fretted over, but the lives of men who had only obeyed orders. What if Jonathon admitted how deeply he was involved? Not only would she lose her friend, but she would lose her husband instantly instead of later when his tasks were completed.

No. There had to be something she could do to prevent that.

Gillian straightened out the skirt of her chemise and paused. Mere hours ago, she had given Rory everything. Had told him all about the smuggling activities, what had happened to King David's ship and men, had truly taken him as her husband in more than just name and somewhere along the line she had surrendered a piece of herself to him.

She wasn't foolish enough to think she'd given him a piece of her heart—that could never be allowed to happen, not when she knew he would be leaving Rockskill for good. But she'd told him things she'd never given voice, to anyone. For a matter of moments…she'd trusted him. She'd willingly made herself vulnerable on the slim hope that perhaps she could have a taste of being wanted, even if it was for just a short time.

Now, she couldn't help but wonder if he would betray that trust.

How well did she truly know this man?

Dragging on her gown, she shook her head, trying to clear it of the myriad of thoughts threatening to drive her mad with worry. No. Right now she needed to focus on making certain Jonathon remained safe and kept his mouth shut.

Gillian took her stockings, garters and boots over to the large, cushioned chair and sat down. Before she could slip on her boots, the door to the bedchamber creaked open slowly.

Rory peered around the door, looking first to the bed, then towards her before entering the chamber carrying a leather bag, sword and boots.

'Do not dare tell me I am dreaming.' Gillian glared at him. 'Where do you sleep at night, since it obviously isn't with me?'

She took a breath, then continued, 'Weren't you the one who said we would be sharing a bed so that nobody would think to question our marriage?' Before he could answer, she asked, 'Are you sleeping in somebody else's bed?'

He hung up his sword, then dropped his boots and the leather bag. 'And a fine good morning to you, too.'

'Do not.'

Casually crossing the chamber, he asked, 'Do not, what?'

'Do not come in here acting all innocent as if nothing is amiss and then try to pass it off as my imagination.'

He sat down on the edge of the bed. 'What has you so fired up this early in the day?'

She frowned. He was trying to distract her by turning the conversation to her actions. No. Not this time. 'Are you?' She swallowed, then keeping her voice as calm and even as possible, asked, 'Are you sharing someone else's bed?'

His lopsided smile made her grit her teeth. Damn him to hell. She would not fall prey to his oh, so, mind-robbing smile.

'Well, are you?'

'No, Gillian, I am not sharing a bed with anyone but you.'

His slowly spoken answer told her he wasn't lying, but it still didn't answer her question. 'Then where are you sleeping? Because I know it isn't here. Do I disgust you so much that even after asking you to stay the night with me, you found it less objectionable to sleep elsewhere, leaving me alone after…after…we…?' She let her question trail off.

Rory sighed. This was not how he had wanted to start the day. Normally she didn't rise until the sun did. What was so different about this day?

'Why are you up so early?'

Her eyes widened and she nearly shouted, 'Answer me.'

He had already guessed that given the opportunity this

wife of his could easily turn into a raging termagant. His mistake had been not knowing what would tip her over that edge. Obviously sharing a bed was that tipping point.

Not wanting to spend the entire day in this manner, he needed to calm her down.

She sprang to her feet, her hands fisted at her side. 'Damn you, Rory.'

Ah, yes, she was in a fine mettle. He rose, slowly, deliberately stretching every muscle in his body as he stood, wanting to intentionally intimidate her.

She looked up at him and swung an open palm towards his face.

He grabbed her wrist before she made contact, warning, 'That is not the best idea you have ever had. I have never laid a hand on you. I expect the same in return.'

She stomped her foot. 'Yes. I know you are bigger and stronger than I am. Do you need to prove that?'

Rory lightly grasped her other wrist and brought her hands between them. 'Since we are both aware of my size and strength, abusing you would prove nothing.' He lifted her hands and kissed her knuckles. 'I had things to prepare for today. I spoke to Thomas and Daniel about guards, weapons and wagons. Then informed Jonathon of what was going to happen. Since the villagers are coming later this morning, I made the cook aware so she could prepare something for them to eat and drink upon their arrival. I know that you rise with the sun, so I tried to return before then.' He paused to take a breath and gather his thoughts. He realised that even though he thought her complaint minor, she didn't. And he had been the one to cause her this distress. 'Forgive me for not returning on time. I am sorry my absence put you in this state.'

She sighed and shook her head. 'You are just trying to be nice so that I calm down.'

Since she wasn't entirely wrong, he simply nodded.

'Well, stop it.'

And just like that her rage seemed to vanish. He released her wrists and drew her against his chest. 'Gillian, trust me when I say I wanted nothing more than to hold you all through the night, to kiss you senseless once again and to wake up with you in my arms. But I could not, there was too much to do before the sun rose.'

'What if I had needed you in the night?'

'Then you could have just shouted for me.'

She eased away. 'We have much to accomplish this day. I need to finish dressing.'

Rory hung on to one of her hands, preventing her from walking away. 'Are we at peace with each other now?'

She shrugged. 'As much as we can be, I guess.'

That wasn't going to be enough. They had to show a united front not just at the caves, but also before the villagers. He despised grovelling, but he saw no other choice. 'Gillian, please, tell me what I must do to make this right between us. We need to be husband and wife, united, in agreement on all things today.'

She looked up at him. 'I don't know.'

He could see the shimmer in her eyes and wanted nothing more than to take away her worry. Rory tugged her towards him. 'Come here.'

Gillian buried her face against his chest, whispering, 'I am not certain I can do this.'

'Do what, Gillian?' He knew what she meant, but wanted her to give voice to her fear, hopefully lessening it in the act. 'You are braver than half the men I know. What is it the woman who captured a wolf thinks she can't do?'

'How am I to face the men and tell them it's over? Everything. The smuggling, the booty they need for their families and possibly their freedom…' her voice broke, but she continued '…if not their lives?'

'Shh.' He brushed a hand down her hair. 'You need tell them nothing. That is my place. King David only wants the ones in charge, not the men under them. What happens to those men is up to me. I have no intention of killing any of our men unless they stupidly do something that begs for death. We need them. Rockskill needs them. I need them loyal to me and hope a touch of leniency will help gain some of their loyalty.'

When she remained silent, he added, 'Gillian, nobody need die this day. I swear to you that I will treat them fairly. But I need you to show them that you trust me, that you agree with me. That, too, will go far in convincing the men to give me their allegiance. I would rather gain their allegiance, than demand their fear. Can you stand by me, even if it is for just this day?'

He felt her nod against his chest.

Rory dropped a kiss on the top of her head. 'You aren't alone in this. I will be right by your side.'

'Until you are no longer here.'

He closed his eyes and sighed. As enjoyable as yesterday had ended, it had been a mistake. One he'd sworn not to make. But he couldn't undo anything. However, he needed her unwavering loyalty and trust to be apparent to all. 'Gillian, for just this one day can you not think about what tomorrow might or might not bring? Can you simply think only of what is happening between the rising and setting of this one sun?'

'I can try.'

'I need you to do more than try. We are partners, comradesin-arms who have each other's backs. It is imperative I...*we* put an end to the smuggling. Rockskill's men need to understand it is over. Finished. There can be no doubt in their mind of this. None. While I hope nobody perishes today, if even one more ship is lured to the rocks all involved will die by my sword. No questions asked. My orders along with *our* will must be obeyed.'

'You are asking me to assist you in completing your tasks for King David?'

'No. I do not require your help with my tasks. My brother Edan is on his way here. If his ship is sunk by Rockskill's smugglers, I can promise you without a single doubt that Elrik and Gregor will tear this Keep apart stone by stone. I could not stop them. No one will be spared in their united frenzy. And they won't be alone in their quest for the destruction of Rockskill. Edan is not just another one of David's wolves, he is also a royal shipbuilder. The King will have men here quicker than you can imagine.'

'Why is your brother coming here?'

Rory chortled, then shrugged. 'Probably to assure himself that his little brother doesn't need any assistance. Did you notice the activity in the bailey yesterday?'

'Yes. I was going to ask about it but was...distracted.'

'All those men, the tents, horses, wagons, supplies, weapons, they are my troops from Roul, here by the King's orders. They didn't leave Roul without Edan's help. He isn't going to lend assistance without discovering the why of it first hand.'

'That'll be a surprise for Albert when he arrives.'

'Your cousin is the least of my concerns. Today is what matters. Can you, will you, stand at my side?'

She tipped her head back to look up at him. 'Today. From when the sun rises until it sets, I will do nothing to make you, or anyone at Rockskill, doubt that my allegiance rests solely with Roul.'

'It would be better if your allegiance and mine rested with Rockskill and its future safety.'

She nodded.

Rory glanced at the light streaming into the chamber and nodded towards the window. 'It is time.'

Gillian stepped away to tug on her boots. 'Then we best get busy. It might take a few moments of conversation to fully convince Jonathon of this plan. It usually takes him a talk or two to accept any idea that is not his.'

She had been correct in one aspect. It had taken more than a few moments to convince Jonathon of the wisdom of assisting them in this task. The man had done more than just baulk at the idea; he'd argued vehemently against it. He had some odd idea that it would be better to wait until Albert returned before doing anything to upset the current situation at Rockskill. There was something about his argument that didn't settle well with Rory and he doubted another conversation would alleviate that nagging doubt.

Was it possible that Gillian's friend did more than simply take orders from Albert? If so, if Jonathon and Albert were partners in crime, did she know? If not, then his wife had placed her trust in a man who could be a danger to her. But he wasn't about to tell her about his misgivings. He would drop hints later and hope she listened.

'I hope he is convinced, because he is waiting below in the hall with our men. Thirty men from Rockskill's and Roul's guard have been summoned along with wagons to collect any goods found in the caves.'

She blinked. 'Did you sleep at all last night?'

Rory shrugged. He'd learned long ago that some things were more important than sleep. 'I had enough sleep.'

When she rose, he retrieved her hooded mantle from the wall peg and swung it about her shoulders. 'The morning air is a bit chilly.'

As he tucked her hair beneath the hood, she reached up and placed her palm against his cheek. 'There will not be much time today for you to be anything other than the Lord of Rockskill and possibly King David's wolf. Before you put on your intimidating scowl, kiss me, Husband. I wish to have a taste of Rory before he gets stowed away.'

He lowered his lips to hers, whispering, 'Such a demanding wench', then silenced her soft laugh with the kiss she requested.

Still unsteady from his kiss, Gillian headed towards the door. Before she left the chamber, he asked, 'Could you ask Daniel or Adam to send up my squire?'

She turned away from the door. 'I can help you don your armour.'

'Not today.' He shook his head and chuckled. 'If you help me shed these clothes to dress for battle, we will never leave this chamber.' He glanced towards the bed. 'Not with that so nearby and handy.'

Her cheeks burned as she left the chamber to head below.

Gillian couldn't remember a time she'd ridden a horse to the caves. The walk wasn't all that far. She glanced over her shoulder at the long line of armed men, older boys acting as squires, and the wagons trailing behind them and shook her head. If Rockskill's men decided they didn't agree with having their livelihood taken away, there wasn't much they could do about it—not with the size of the force Rory had gathered. Any fight would be over before it truly started.

She glanced at Jonathon before turning her gaze to the spot between her horse's ears. Something wasn't right with him today. When she had arrived in the hall, he had avoided her and walked away without comment when she greeted him. In all the time they'd known each other, he had never done that before. Thomas must have found it odd, too, because he'd scowled at Jonathon's retreating back, but he hadn't said a word.

Had other words, besides about what would take place at the caves, taken place between Rory and Jonathon? Had Thomas been involved in that conversation? He must have been, because otherwise they had no reason to be at odds with each other. It made no sense to her. She could only hope that everything went as planned today. She shivered—what would she do if her friend and husband came to blows?

A cold chill crept up her neck—she sensed him watching her, studying her. She turned her head and met Rory's stare. He reached out to place his palm against her cheek. When she leaned her head into his touch, he relaxed just long enough to give her that lopsided half-smile before turning away to speak to Daniel.

She briefly closed her eyes. No matter what happened she would stand by her husband. Not just this day, but her future rested with him. Considering how she'd forced him into this marriage, he'd been more than honourable and whether he wished to believe it or not, he'd been kind, even when he had little reason to treat her with any kindness. She didn't believe she could have chosen a better man.

Gillian swallowed a groan. Dear Lord, she *had* given him a piece of her heart.

In a few short months he would be gone. What was she going to do to ensure her heart was intact when he left?

Stop. Today she could not let worry distract her. Just get through the day from when the sun rose until it set. Don't fret about tomorrow. Just focus on today. If she had to, she would repeat that until she believed that this day was all that mattered.

When they reached the base of the hill, Rory raised his arm, signalling a halt to those in the formation. He looked towards Jonathon. 'Where?'

When no answer was supplied, Gillian pointed towards the left of the hill. 'There. The entrance is larger and easier to reach so the men will not have to enter single file.'

As they continued, she turned towards Jonathon and asked, 'What is wrong with you?'

'Me?' He glared at her. 'Nothing is wrong with me, but I could ask the same of you.'

His tone—curt and accusing—stung. It gave her a twinge of guilt. She'd told her husband—the man Jonathon obviously considered his enemy—the truth of what had been happening here at Rockskill. Apparently, just as she had suspected, he never would have done the same and thought less of her for doing so.

'He is my husband, Jonathon.'

'You do not need to remind me of that. It has been made perfectly clear.'

Yes, the two of them had discussed more than just this jaunt to the cave. 'I thought I was protecting you.'

'You thought wrong. I never needed, nor wanted, your protection. And now you have put all of us at risk.'

Did he know something she didn't? Had Rory lied to her when he said no one need die this day? No. He had been very direct. He'd made certain to speak clearly, slowly, in that way he had when he wanted there to be no misunderstanding.

Regardless, something was...off...wrong. Yes, of course

Jonathon was angry. He was about to lose a sorely needed way of gaining coin. He would also lose his opportunity to be in a position of leadership. Her gut told her it was more than that—however, she couldn't quite figure it out.

To ease his concerns, she said, 'Jonathon, nobody is at risk. If the men do as they are bid, all will be well.'

He laughed bitterly. 'So you say. You cannot know what this man of David's will do when he discovers what's being stored in the caves. I am supposed to believe the word of a wolf—a known murderer of men who cross the King?'

'I would hope you could believe my word.'

'Your word? You are nothing more than a woman. One who gave herself willingly to the enemy. Tell me, Gillian, do you plot his death, or do you simper and sigh as you lay beneath him while he takes advantage of such an easily cowed whore?'

Gillian jerked back in shock. 'How dare you!'

Before she could take hold of her temper, a horse moved between them. Rory reached over and grabbed the reins from her hands. 'Come.'

He quickly led them ahead, far enough away from the others that nobody else would hear them. 'Anything we need to discuss?'

She tore the reins from his hands. 'No.'

'Easy.' He placed a hand on her shoulder. 'He is angry, Gillian. Do not take his words to heart.'

'His anger gives him no cause to speak to me in that manner. He called me—' She clamped her lips together.

'Whore. He called you an easily cowed whore.'

'You heard.'

He nodded.

'And you are going to do nothing about it?'

'This is your friend, remember? It is between the two of you. I am certain you can deal with this without me coming to your rescue. If I am wrong, you need tell me so. Because at this moment, I have no qualms about feeding him his teeth for calling my wife a whore. In fact, it might relieve some of the tension I'm suddenly experiencing.'

'Tension?'

'Yes, because I also heard the doubt in your voice when you told him nobody would be at risk.'

'It isn't you I doubt. Something is wrong. Off. Nothing I can put my finger on, but my gut is sending warning shouts to my head. I am uneasy about this.'

'Good. At least you recognise the unease. Never doubt those signals. Keep your eyes and ears open. Rest assured that Adam and Thomas will be at your back, at all times. Daniel and Richard will be at mine. Nothing is going to happen that our men can't control.'

She sighed. 'You wouldn't have put those arrangements in place if you didn't feel it, too.'

'I had no intention of doing this unprepared. Gillian, if for any reason we get separated, promise me you will do whatever Adam or Thomas tell you to do.' He paused, then added, 'Without arguing.'

The flutter of wings loosened in her stomach. She swallowed, fighting to keep the building fear at bay. 'What are you expecting?'

'Blackshore and Cranwell are both confined in cells. The men could not find Smithfield. While I do not expect to find him at the caves, there is no way for me to be certain. Your safety is my primary concern.'

'And you wait to warn me of that now?'

He slid his hand to cup the side of her neck and stroked his thumb beneath her ear. 'Had I done so earlier, you would have worried this entire time.'

'Don't seek to distract me.' She leaned away from his touch. 'You could have at least let me arm myself.'

He reached down, pulled a dagger from his boot and handed it to her.

Having reached the path that would lead up to the mouth of the cave, he brought his horse to a stop and assisted her from her saddle. Instead of releasing her, Rory tipped her head up for a brief kiss. 'If things become so dire that you need to make use of that weapon, do not forget your training.'

'Go for the kill.'

'Hard and fast.' He kissed her again. 'Do not risk sparring with anyone. You do not have the stamina to do so.'

Multiple sessions on the practice field had made her well aware of that fact. 'I won't.'

They heard the others approaching and drew apart. Even though the air was chilly, Gillian removed her heavy cloak and secured it to her saddle. The long fabric would prove a hindrance if anything did happen and she needed to move quickly.

Once the men dismounted, he took her hand. 'Ready?'

She slid Rory's dagger behind her, beneath her belt. 'As ready as I can be, yes.'

She led the way up the path, relieved her knee gave her no complaint, with Rory behind her. Daniel and Richard followed. Behind them Jonathon, with Thomas and Adam at his back. The others fell in line bringing up the rear.

When they reached the mouth Rory ushered Jonathon ahead.

He turned to glare at Gillian before shouting, 'To the ready!'

Chapter Fifteen

With a shout of shock and dismay, Gillian shoved past Rory to follow behind the retreating Jonathon, yelling, 'Rockskill hold. Hold!'

Did Jonathon truly believe she would stand idly by while her husband and their men were ambushed? Thankfully there were lit torches lining the walls of the tunnel, so she could see Jonathon's back. Without slowing, she reached behind her to retrieve the dagger. 'Hold!'

The scraping of weapons being drawn behind her and the pounding of booted feet let her know Rory and the men understood what was happening. Jonathon's shout had warned the smugglers that they were in danger and needed to prepare to meet the enemy.

She knew they would gather at the main cavern. That's where the weapons were stored. Waving the others ahead, she yelled, 'This way.'

The tunnel was wide enough that Thomas was at her right side, Adam was at her back.

Thomas was talking to her, but she couldn't hear him over the loud pounding in her ears. He was probably trying to stop her mad dash and that wasn't going to happen. She knew the way to the main cavern and she was not going to let her husband—a stranger to most of the waiting men—

be the first person to enter that cavern. The men would be unlikely to kill her—she didn't think they'd afford Rory the same regard.

As she turned to take the tunnel to the left, a hand grabbed her arm. Without thought, she grasped the hilt of the dagger and thrust with all her might.

A familiar curse and a thud made her shiver. She'd stabbed Smithfield's shoulder and gasped as a sword sliced the air, barely missing her chest. Thomas shouted for Rory as he wrapped an arm about her waist, pulled her from her feet and swung her to his other side, causing her to stumble and fall.

Without even a whisper of warning Rory lunged towards Smithfield. Her husband's weapon did more than just slice through the air. She looked away as Smithfield's lifeless body hit the floor with a heavy thud. Smithfield's death had been quick and certain.

Rory pulled his weapon free, then turned to pull her roughly to her feet, demanding, 'What is wrong with you? Are you seeking death?'

Daniel stepped behind his Lord and vigorously shook his head at her. Gillian took the obvious hint and remained silent. Her husband was more than just angry. From the tight, bruising hold on her arm, the hard glint in his stare and a tic in the side of his cheek, she'd done more than rile him.

Rory sucked in a deep breath and pushed her behind him. He jerked a thumb at Thomas and Adam, silently ordering them behind her while Daniel and Richard moved in to follow Rory.

He led them further along the tunnel at a fast pace. 'When this tunnel ends, it will abruptly open up into a large cave,' Gillian informed them, adding, 'The men will be gathered there and armed.'

She wasn't telling him something that he hadn't already

guessed. Of course, the men would be armed and waiting. Jonathon had made certain of that. He only grunted in acknowledgement.

Right now, he was too angry and shocked to do much more than put one foot in front of the other. Not even in his youth, when experiencing his first battle, seeing, hearing and tasting death for the first time, had he been this frightened. What the hell had she been thinking to have bolted ahead in that manner? She could have been killed.

Rory now understood why Elrik refused to permit his wife anywhere near a field of battle. Apparently choosing a headstrong woman to wife had its drawbacks—clearly, they reacted emotionally instead of rationally. The mere idea of following orders was beyond their comprehension. Worse, their misguided reaction was terrifying to behold. He swore his heart had come to a complete stop when she had raced down the tunnel alone.

If he knew nothing else, he was dead certain Gillian would never again be at his side when any battle, large or small, might be a possibility.

Never.

He didn't care if he had to confine her in a cell to keep her safe. He was not going to lose her at the point of someone's sword.

Rory sucked in a breath. Dear Lord, now was not the time to realise he cared for this wife of his. Cared overmuch. Oh, yes, of a certainty yesterday had been a huge mistake on his part.

He shook his head, trying to clear the thoughts running rampant. He needed to focus on the task at hand. These riotous feelings would have to wait until later when he had the leisure to sort through them.

'We are close.'

Her voice had come from right behind him. Rory stopped so abruptly that she ran into his back. He raised his arm, bringing the formation to a halt. Slowly, he turned to glare down at her. 'What are you doing?'

'I only wanted to tell you that we're close to the cave.'

'Do you think I can't tell that by the change in the airflow? Or perhaps the scraping sound of booted feet shuffling about on rock ahead didn't give that away?' He extended the hilt of his sword to her. 'Perhaps you need to explain to me how to go about this.'

When she took a step back and shook her head, he ordered, 'Get back with Thomas and Adam. Now. Do not come forward again unless I bid you to do so. Or I swear, Gillian, I will haul you bodily down the hill, tie you to a horse outside and send you back to the Keep.'

'I'm sorry, my Lord.' Thomas stepped forward, grasped her wrist and tugged her away. 'My Lady, please, stay with me.'

She didn't look the least bit happy. He didn't care. The woman had no idea what being unhappy truly was at this moment. Nor did she seem to realise the danger in angering him further. If her intent was to unman him in front of the men, she was coming exceedingly close. He was nearly ready to rage at her and swallowed hard to keep his temper in check.

He relaxed his tight hold on his weapon and turned back.

Daniel's fist bumped his shoulder. 'They are an aggravating lot, my Lord.'

Rory couldn't help but snicker at his man's attempt to distract him. 'That they are.'

When the tunnel widened, he stopped. Daniel and Richard took their places on either side of him. The rest of the men came to a halt. After making certain Thomas still had a hold on a frowning Gillian, Rory shouted, 'Your Lady is with me. If one hair on her head is misplaced, all of you will die.'

He waited a moment, then ordered, 'Drop your weapons and come forward.'

The sound of shuffling feet and mumbles as they talked among themselves met his command. He shook his head. Was everyone at Rockskill daft today? 'I am Rory of Roul, the King's wolf, and the Lord of Rockskill by marriage to your Lady.' He paused. 'I am your Lord and I will solely decide whether you live another day or die on this one.'

He hoped it didn't come to that. There were men currently in his company that had likely never taken a life. He didn't want their first time to be against men they'd grown up with, men they shared meals with—a slight hesitation on their part could prove fatal. To his relief the sound of first one weapon, then another and another clattered as they hit the cave floor. Slowly, one by one, the men stepped out to the opening of the cave. All but Jonathon.

At Richard's nod, Rory assumed most, if not all, of the men were present. They did not appear pleased to have been called out, but they stood there unarmed, looking down at their feet.

Rory stepped to the side and beckoned Gillian to join him. She came forward, her face expressionless. Thankful that her glare of displeasure was gone, he took her hand. She curled her fingers around his and squeezed lightly.

'Your Lady and I demand the activities here end. Now.'

A few of the men lifted their shocked gaze to Gillian. She moved closer so her shoulder rested against his arm and nodded in agreement.

'We know what you will lose and we guarantee that you, your homes and your families will be cared for.'

An older man asked, 'And what will be expected for this care?'

It was a legitimate question as nothing came without a price.

'Fields need tending, fish need to be caught and sold or bartered, walls need to be guarded and rebuilt. And, from what I have seen, cottages need to be repaired.'

Gillian asked the men, 'Is that not a fair exchange?'

The men shuffled about, but they all seemed in agreement.

Rory added, 'And I want the names of those who gave you your orders.'

It took a few moments but finally a younger man shrugged, grimaced, and then shouted, 'Lord Albert.'

Another said, 'And his companions.'

A boy—barely old enough to be away from his nursemaid— whispered, 'Jonathon.'

The man standing next to the child batted his backside, grabbed him, then pushed the boy towards the rear of those gathered. 'Ignore him. The boy speaks out of turn.'

Rory wanted to sigh in relief. At least his wife hadn't lied to him when she'd admitted that Jonathon acted as Albert's second-in-command. Although he still wondered if it was more than that.

Dragging his attention back, he motioned the guards forward with a wave as he told the men, 'The King's goods must be returned. You can all help load the items into the wagons waiting below. See that every single item is brought to the Keep, then report to the hall.'

He ordered the guards, 'Gather the weapons first.'

While they were doing as they were bid, he informed the others, 'If one more ship meets its end, anyone involved will forfeit their life, their home and their family.'

'You would kill our children?'

He swallowed a cry of denial, before saying, 'Not outright. But they will no longer be welcome at Rockskill, making their future bleak. Keep that in mind should you think to scuttle another ship. I will deal with you honourably and fairly, but you must do the same in return. Am I understood?'

To a man they answered, 'Yes, my Lord.'

Once all the weapons had been removed, he waved the men back inside. 'Get busy, you have work to do.'

Turning to address Daniel and Thomas, he said, 'Richard and Adam are with me. You two stay and oversee all is loaded into the wagons and that these men follow along to the Keep. Have a couple of Roul's guards deliver Smithfield's body to his camp. I understand they, along with Albert's men, are camped in the field behind the stables, outside the wall.'

'In any particular manner?'

Rory snorted at Thomas's question. 'We are not going to prepare him for burial, if that's what you are asking. Sling him over the back of a horse and dump him in the middle of his camp.

'Daniel, I want a message delivered. Smithfield's and Albert's men have until sunrise tomorrow to get off Rockskill land. If they are still here in the morning, they will be dispatched by Roul's guards.'

His man's smile stretched nearly across his face. 'I will deliver the message myself.'

'Take enough of our men with you to quell any objection.' Rory tugged on Gillian's hand. 'Come, we are done here and need to prepare for the villagers' arrival.'

To his relief she followed along silently.

When they reached the bottom of the hill, Richard and Adam mounted their horses and moved away. Rory untied Gillian's mantle from her saddle and swung it around her shoulders. He pinned it closed and pulled up the hood. 'You have nothing to say to me? Nothing at all?'

She bit her lower lip and kept her gaze on the rock-strewn ground. 'I am sorry.'

'Of course you are. You always are. That is your normal method of doing things. You do what you want, no matter what anyone else thinks, wants or needs, and then if you are unlucky enough to be caught, you are suddenly sorry. Your apology means nothing.'

He lifted her chin with the side of his hand. 'Let's try something new. What if you just explain yourself? Had you not raced after your *friend*, you wouldn't have been in danger. Smithfield would still be alive to face the King's justice.' He grasped her hands and lifted them palms up. 'And you wouldn't have these cuts and scrapes from hitting the rock floor when Thomas flung you out of harm's way. You put many people at risk. Was it worth it, Gillian? Is your friendship with this man so important that you risk the lives of our men and your own?'

Rory paused to study the area before turning back to her. 'Speaking of your friend, where is he? Apparently, his word means nothing.'

'I don't know.'

'You cannot possibly think I believe that, do you?'

'Rory, I...'

'No. Unless you are going to tell me where that traitor would go to hide, I don't want to hear a word, none of your excuses matter. Some of those men with us today have never seen battle. Had Jonathon's scheme worked, they could be dead. I would hold you responsible. You, Gillian. You would be the one explaining to their families the utter senselessness of their death. You would be the one arranging their burial. You would be the one shouldering the guilt and rightly so.'

He was being hard on her; he knew that, even if none of what he'd just said was true. Never would he have placed any of that responsibility on her. He was the one in command—all the responsibility for the outcome, good or bad, rested on him and him alone. But he wanted her to realise that her actions, or inactions, had consequences. Sometimes those consequences could be horribly unbearable.

'Do not. Just stop.' Rory tore off his gloves and swiped a finger at her first tear. 'Your tears are meaningless. They will not make me feel sorry for you. Pity is the last feeling I have for you right now. I am angrier now than I have ever been. If you were a man, I would beat you senseless and then turn you out.'

He jerked her hard against his chest and wrapped his arms around her, grateful that nothing had gone seriously wrong and that she was still here to berate. 'But you are not a man, you are my wife. You frightened ten years off my life. You will not ever do that again. Ever. Do you hear me?'

She nodded against his chest. 'Rory, I am sorry. I thought—'

His low growl stopped her from talking. 'I know what you thought. You have mistakenly been protecting a friend you thought was loyal to you. He isn't, Gillian. He isn't loyal to you in the least. And you surged ahead in the tunnel because you thought since you knew the way it was up to you to lead. It wasn't. It is never up to you to lead the way into danger. Never.'

He felt her silent sobs against him. Rory rested his chin atop her head and rocked from side to side. 'Where is he, Gillian?'

She drew in a shaking breath. 'At his mother's old rotting hut behind the village. But he likely won't be there for long.'

'He will gather supplies and leave, won't he?'

'Yes.'

Then he needed to ensure that didn't happen and quickly.

'Rory, I am sorry. Truly I am.'

'What you need to be sorry for is making me appear weak before the men. I am in command. I am their leader. They look to me for their cues. But if it appears I cannot control a mere woman, how am I to be trusted to control any situation?'

'I didn't think—'

'I know. You just reacted. That's what gets men killed in battle—reacting without forethought. That is one reason I train the men so hard. They need to know their next move instinctively without having to think. The thinking is my responsibility. Mine alone. You had no experience to draw upon. You could have got us all killed.' He drew away. 'We need to return to the Keep.' After placing a kiss on each of her palms, he drew his gloves over her hands. 'A little big, but it'll help lessen the sting of the reins against the raw flesh.'

'Thank you.'

'For what?'

She gazed up at him. 'For not beating me senseless and turning me out.'

He rolled his eyes and patted her cheek. 'The day is still young.'

Her laughter fell light against his ears. He doubted he would ever tire of hearing her laugh. Even though he was still angry at her, it felt as if someone had lifted a boulder off his shoulders. 'Come.' He helped her on to the saddle before mounting his own horse and then urged their beasts to catch up with Adam and Richard.

Seated at one of the tables set up in the hall, Rory stretched out his legs and took a long swallow from his goblet as he nodded at something the man next to him said.

The villagers had already entered the Keep when they'd returned from the caves. He and Gillian had listened to what the people had to say with interest. It mattered how the villagers were treated. Their lives and well-being mattered. It was important that they knew that.

What he had heard turned his stomach, but it wasn't anything he hadn't expected. It was truly a shame he didn't have the authority to kill Albert the instant the man set foot inside Rockskill. He would do so—gladly.

Gillian seemed to know her people well. She was standing near the door, talking and laughing with a group of older women. Rory excused himself and headed towards her.

A stooped-over, grey-haired woman, standing with her back towards him, reached out and touched Gillian's arm. 'My Lady, I must say being in love adds a nice glow to your cheeks and a lovely sparkle to your eyes. You remind me of your mother when your father first brought her here.'

Rory slowed his steps.

What had he done?

Gillian laughed softly and patted the woman's hand. 'Berta, I thank you, but I am sure it is just the sun that lends colour to my cheeks.'

He closed his eyes for a moment, hoping that was true.

'No, no, Lady Gillian, even if you have yet to admit the truth, it is obvious to the rest of us. You dearly love this husband of yours and we are all awaiting a precious little bundle to bring you even more joy.'

Rory blinked. As if sensing his nearness, Gillian lifted her head and met his stare.

He quickly veered around the group of women and headed out the door, silently cursing his stupidity. Somehow, he needed to find a way to fix this—before Elrik made him pay for his treason. And before he brought her nothing but misery. She didn't deserve that. This was his fault.

Chapter Sixteen

In the semi-darkness of their chamber, Gillian looked at the man sitting silently in the chair near the windows. It had been twenty-one days…three full weeks since he had done anything other than provide one-word answers to any question she asked—and then only if it was about Rockskill. He hadn't talked to her, hardly looked at her, hadn't touched her, kissed her and most definitely hadn't shared the bed with her.

But every evening he'd joined her as they'd mounted the stairs to retire. He'd positioned himself in the chair and stared out the window opening, waiting for her to undress, climb beneath the covers and fall asleep before he left the chamber. Then, in the morning, he'd return before she rose, taking up the same position in the chair.

She'd already tried arguing with him. He wouldn't argue. Repeatedly she had tried shouting at him. He remained silent no matter what horrible things she said—and some of her words had been unforgivably terrible and nasty. Last night she'd been desperate enough to try seducing him. He'd acknowledged her attempt with nothing more than a raised brow, which told her plainly that he thought she'd lost her wits, then he ignored her completely, leaving her feeling foolish and unwanted.

She sat up in the bed and stared at him, pleading, 'Rory, I need you.'

To her shock, he rose, but instead of coming towards the bed, he walked across the chamber, then straight out of the door without a word.

She waited until the door closed before beating her fists on the bed in frustration. Why was he acting in this manner?

When the villagers had come to the Keep, he had been fine. He'd listened to their complaints and discussed ways to better their circumstances—ways she'd not thought of herself.

Afterwards the two of them had gone their separate ways to speak with the villagers. Yes, he'd walked right past her when she'd been talking with the older women and while he'd looked…confused…he hadn't appeared angry. The next morning, he had seen to it that the changes promised to the villagers started immediately. He had gathered some of his guards, men with carpentry experience, to start repairing the worst of the cottages—some had already been completed.

Rory had done more than order the work, he had taken up tools himself to help. He had given some of Rockskill's guards the duty of protecting the village, ensuring no harm came to any who lived there.

While Cranwell and Blackshore remained confined to cells until they could be escorted to King David's court, and their men had been forced off Rockskill land, Jonathon had not been found. Rory had only asked once where to find him since he wasn't at his mother's old hut. She'd honestly told him she had no idea where to locate him, other than perhaps in the caves. Guards scoured the tunnels and caves daily, but had turned up no sign of him anywhere.

What had happened? What could he possibly have heard that she hadn't already told him about?

Gillian groaned as she felt the lump in her throat tighten.

She'd done far more than given him a piece of her heart, she'd given him all of it. And he'd tossed her aside before he'd even left Rockskill. Dear Lord, if she started crying, she wouldn't be able to stop. She buried her face in her pillow, trying to muffle the sound of her distress.

Rory leaned his forehead against the chamber door. He reached for the latch to go back inside, then paused. She was crying. He felt horrible…guilty for treating her the way he had when she'd said she needed him, but he knew she would never understand his reasoning.

He turned away and walked to the nearly empty storage chamber on the floor above that he used as a makeshift bed-chamber. His pallet was directly above their bed and when he stretched out, he could hear her sobs.

What was he to do? She couldn't have frightened him so badly at the caves if he didn't care for her. The trouble was that he cared for her far too much. He hadn't realised just how much until he'd overheard the older woman talking about love.

Why would she fall in love with him? He had done nothing to make her think this was anything but a temporary marriage. She knew he was leaving and not coming back. He had no choice. He couldn't stay. He wouldn't stay and mark her with his treachery.

But if it were true and Gillian had become…attached, he greatly feared her feelings were returned in full.

And the only way he knew to spare her further pain later was to push her away now. Unfortunately, destroying what had become a budding relationship wasn't hurting only her.

He was miserable. He wanted to hear her laugh—that deep, throaty, seductive laugh reserved only for him. He wanted to taste her kiss, to hold her close and hear her sighs. Wanted to take her into the village and have her work beside him, just so that he could spend the day with her. He wanted to be the one who was challenging her with a sword—instead, he'd given that task over to Daniel. From what he'd witnessed in the cave, she needed to be trained better, harder and if he wasn't going to do it, Daniel was the best choice—even though it left him burning with a jealousy that threatened to choke him.

His only solace was in knowing that her cousin Albert should be arriving soon. Once that man was dealt with, put in chains to be carted to King David with the other two—three, if he could find Jonathon—he could leave since all else had been handled.

Her men were being trained and most of them had made good progress. The cottages in the village were being repaired, while most of the able-bodied men spent their days fishing or carting the catch to the market for trade and coin.

He'd made the rounds of the neighbouring lords without her knowledge and smoothed the way forward in peace. She should have no trouble from them any more.

As for the King's assigned tasks, Hell's door had been sealed off. The gold and weapons meant for Normandy were waiting in loaded carts to be returned to King David. The intentional shipwrecks had ceased. Two of the five culprits in charge of the happenings here at Rockskill were confined, one was dead. He had only to wait for Albert and somehow find Jonathon.

Then, not only would the tasks for the King be completed, his duty to Gillian and Rockskill would be fulfilled. He would be free to leave.

Except for one small detail—was his wife truly barren, or had his lapse in judgement created a child?

He rolled over on to his side with a groan of disgust at himself and these womanly worries, then reached out and tightly gripped the hilt of his sword. He was a warrior, trained from an early age to fight—and kill. There was no place in his life for these unfamiliar, useless emotions that did nothing more than distract him from his tasks at hand.

Yes, he was a warrior who would face death once this mission for the King was finished. He would face it gladly, embrace it willingly if it meant this endless dull pain in his soul would cease.

When Gillian woke the moon's light flooded into the chamber and across the chair by the window, letting her know she was still alone, that he hadn't returned while she slept.

She couldn't go on like this. *They* couldn't go on like this. It had to end. One way or another, it *had* to end. He would leave soon and she couldn't let their marriage end like this, not with them so at odds with each other.

She rose and retrieved her clothing from the top of the chest where she had placed them earlier.

She had no idea where to find him, but he had to be in a chamber nearby. He wouldn't sleep below in the hall with the men—that would have given lie to their marriage and she knew he'd not do that.

After pulling on her soft-soled shoes, she left the chamber. Taking a lit torch with her, she checked the chambers along the corridor and those on the floor above, finding them all empty. That left her mother's storage room, the one directly above their bedchamber.

She paused to press her ear against the door and frowned. He was mumbling…to himself? She jumped back at a ragged shout, then cautiously opened the door.

She stared in speechless shock at the sight before her. Rory sat straight up on his pallet, his sword in hand as if ready to fend off some unseen enemy. His overlong, untrimmed hair in wild disarray made him look like the wolf he was called. He was pleading with someone to kill him, not to kill him, apologising for the blood he'd shed, the lives he'd taken.

But it was his wide, unblinking stare devoid of any recognition that let her know he was caught fast in the arms of a nightmare.

Was this why he slept alone? He hadn't wanted her to know he had nightmares like any other person.

The sudden swinging of his sword wiped away that question. No. He slept alone not just because of the nightmares, but because he feared harming anyone within his reach.

'Rory.' She softly called his name as she closed the door behind her and stuck the torch in the wall sconce.

He turned his head in her direction and once again swung his weapon. It was obvious from his blank stare that he was still asleep and didn't know who she was. She offered up a brief prayer for her safety, 'Please, Lord, do not let him kill me.'

He might be angry with her for whatever unknown reason, but she knew if he took her life, he wouldn't be able to live with himself.

She circled around him, debating her best move. How was she going to get close without being injured?

He spread both his arms wide, then repeatedly pounded a fist against his chest. 'Do it, just do it. Let this be done.'

She raced forward and threw herself at him, wrapping her arms around his neck and knocking him down on to the pallet. 'Rory. Rory. Wake up.'

She pressed her face against his to whisper, 'Rory, love, wake up. You are safe. All is well.'

His cheek was hot and covered with sweat, as was his forehead. She brushed his damp hair from his face. How long had he been trapped in this horrible dream? 'Rory. Please, wake up.'

His sword bounced off the floor a heartbeat before his arms came around her. He reached up to thread his fingers through her hair, caressing the back of her head and coaxing her up so he could claim her lips in a kiss that seemed an act of desperation.

She didn't try to dissuade him, as she'd so missed his kisses. Instead, she tried to match his intensity.

When he broke their kiss to roll her over, she cupped his cheek and stared up at him. Rory rested his forehead against hers. 'Yes, I am awake.'

The rough hoarseness of his voice concerned her. She stroked a finger down his neck. 'What troubles you so?'

'No.' He shook his head. 'We can't do this.'

'Do what?'

With a heavy groan, he rolled off her. 'You know that once I have your cousin secured, I am still leaving.'

Gillian fought to swallow back a cry of denial. How could she give way to her pain when his was so obvious? He needed her right this moment, whether he would acknowledge that or not. It was her turn to urge him to talk, to listen to him, to somehow help him lessen his burden.

She'd once thought that she'd chosen a good man to take as husband. She'd been wrong. He might be infuriating at times, but he was more than simply good. This man was more honourable than any man she'd ever known. He was kind, understanding, giving and helpful, and she would hold him close to her heart until her dying day. She had offered him little help in his time here, but right now the King's wolf could use her assistance. Help she'd not deny him. 'I know you are leaving. But you are here now and I still need you. If all we have left are a few days, must we spend them at odds with each other?'

'I thought…'

When he let his words trail off, she gently stroked his arm. 'Tell me. What did you think?'

'That hurting you now would be more fair, less cruel. But I have only harmed us both.'

She smiled at the knowledge that he obviously cared for her, too. 'Yes, I hurt, but I am not some fair, weak flower that will wither and die from it. You, on the other hand, I am not so sure…it seems between the two of us you have shouldered the brunt of the pain from your actions.'

He laughed softly and drew her close. 'Ah, yes, I am well known for my tender heart.'

His heart was far more tender than he would ever care to admit. But she would take that secret to her grave. She slung an arm across his chest. 'So, was it your tender heart, or perhaps guilt for what you've done to have caused such horrible nightmares? Didn't you once tell me that if I felt guilty, perhaps I shouldn't have gone through with my plan to capture you?'

'No, it isn't my tender heart that causes my distress. What I am guilty of is far more evil and disgusting than capturing and forcing a man into a marriage.'

As a warrior, he'd have seen many battles that ended with lives lost. He was a wolf for King David, so she was sure he'd been tasked with many things that would be considered evil had they not been ordered. 'Rory, what could you have done that is so terrible?'

He flung his other arm over his eyes and shook his head.

Frowning, she wondered if she truly wanted to know. That wasn't fair. How many times had he listened to her? How many times had he eased her worries, her fears? Didn't she owe him the same in return? 'Rory, love, we are alone. It is just the two of us here. I would never, ever betray you by sharing what you have told me in private. I swear it, never.'

He uncovered his eyes and captured her hand in his. 'Gillian, you have wed a traitor—a deserter. A coward who walked off the field of battle.'

Coward? Never would she believe that of him. 'I am sure you did so for a reason.'

'I could not bear the slaughter any more.' His voice broke, but he cleared his throat and continued, 'Many of them were little more than boys. I couldn't look upon the lifeless bodies of the ones I could not save any longer. I couldn't sleep. They were everywhere. They haunt me still. Every time I close my eyes I see them, I hear their cries. I wake up drenched in sweat, with my sword in hand.'

Everything suddenly fell into place. That was why he would not kill Blackshore that first day. It was why he slept alone. And why he had to have proof, first-hand witnesses to the things that had happened here at Rockskill. He refused to kill just for the sake of killing.

'That makes you a man with a soul. One who was pushed too far, for too long. It does not make you a traitor, or a coward.'

'You don't understand.'

No, she didn't. How could she? She had never killed anyone—the closest she had ever come was her unsuccessful attempt at stabbing Smithfield. She had never been on a field of battle. Her life had been spent here at Rockskill, a woman doing a woman's tasks. Gillian tightened her fingers around his. 'Help me to understand.'

For a few moments she wasn't certain he would continue, but after heaving a deep sigh, he began to speak. 'My father joined with a group set on overthrowing King David. They considered him an outsider and did not want him on the throne. They were caught and most of them put to death for their acts of treason.'

He released her hand and rested his on her shoulder. 'My two older brothers grovelled at King David's feet to beg for our sire's life.'

She had a pretty good idea where this was going. 'And is that how the King's wolves were formed?'

He nodded, adding, 'They promised not just their lives in exchange, but also mine and Edan's when we came of age.'

'And your father?'

'Died an old man in his own bed. He died branded a traitor.'

'What has that to do with you? You and your brothers have surely more than paid that debt.'

'My father was traitor to his King and spent the remainder of his days wallowing in guilt of his own making. I was traitor to my brother, the man who essentially raised me, taught me everything I know, everything I am. He provided for me and provided well. I owe Elrik my life and I walked away from his orders while on a field of battle. I let him down, I turned my back on him as only a coward would. How am I to live with that?'

His voice rose in anger, a happening that occurred so rarely it brought her need to defend him racing to the fore. 'Rory, stop this. If he cared for you so well in your father's absence, do you not think he would understand why you did what you did? Do you honestly believe the brother who taught you to be a man in the only way he could wouldn't understand the honour, or the heart he'd helped form in you?'

'He has no choice other than to mete out the punishment required. It matters not who I am, or who he is to me. He is a newly made count and cannot afford to lose face before his peers, or his liege.'

Even she knew the penalty for deserting the field of battle. 'So, you believe your own brother will kill you in cold blood?' Now she understood him beating his fist on his chest while requesting whomever he spoke to in his nightmare to just do it, to let it be done. The expectation of what was to come might not frighten him, although it did her, she knew he would face this battle as he did any other one—bravely, head held high, a half smirking smile on his lips and with honour. His angst was caused by the waiting and it settled heavy on his mind and heart. She ached for him and wished she could find a way to ease his burden.

'Yes. Yes, I do.'

She pulled out of his embrace to rise and straddle his waist. Cupping his cheeks in her hands, she asked, 'Have you spoken to him since this happened? Have any words been exchanged?'

'No. I went straight from the battlefield to King David's court to beg for a task, anything to regain any measure of honour before facing Elrik.'

'And here you are.'

He covered one of her hands with his own. 'Yes, and here I am. Drugged, captured and wed by force.'

She laughed. 'Your complaints are pitiful. I for one am grateful for this task set upon you by King David.'

'You won't be so grateful when my sins fall on you. Which is what will happen if the King does not grant my request to nullify this marriage before I pay for my treachery. How will you go on then? What man in their right mind will wed the widow of a traitor?'

'It matters little, since I will never accept another as my husband.' Gillian straightened her back and hardened her stare to a glare. 'You think to make that choice for me? How dare you. No. It is not up to you, Husband. It is *my* life. *Mine*. I will follow you into hell if I must.'

She stroked his cheek, then threaded her fingers through his hair and tugged. 'You, Rory, are far from being a coward. I care not what you say, or what you might think.'

'You are my wife, of course you would say that.'

'Your men still follow you without question, they obviously think no less of you.'

'They understand loyalty.' He shrugged. 'They will not shirk their duty in the way I have mine. Soon it will be time for you to do your duty for Rockskill and to live up to your word to let me go.'

'I am not a man serving some liege lord. Duty be damned. You are my life. You are the man I have waited for my entire life. Do you think I will not fight you to my last breath on this? Do you believe for one heartbeat that I will sit idly by while you spew lies to the King simply to give me a freedom I do not want, one I will never accept?'

'That is what I fear. Why do you think I have tried so hard to push you away? We have an agreement, Gillian. Do not go back on it.'

'I already have.' She grabbed his hand and placed it over her heart. 'This beats for you. It is yours and will never belong to another no matter what happens in the weeks or months ahead.'

He drew his hand away to wrap it around her neck and pull her down against him. 'Everything may happen much sooner than that I fear.'

'How so?'

'Edan has taken far too long to arrive. I have a feeling he went to get Elrik to bring him here.'

Gillian froze for an instant. The Count of Roul coming

to Rockskill? The thought made her shiver. 'Why would he do so?'

'It is Edan's way to stick his nose into things that are not his affairs—especially when it comes to those he cares about. Someone must have got word to him about what I did, likely King David, and so now he thinks his most important task in life is to see the matter settled.'

She realised that in truth this could be a good thing for all involved. The Count and Rory could settle their current trouble. With another brother present to act as a buffer, hopefully they could do so in a peaceful manner. Better yet, they could do it here at Rockskill away from the court and the Count's peers, allowing him to consider his heart, to act on his feelings, their shared past, and their relationship to each other, without any outside influence or expectations. Just as importantly, she would have the chance to show Rory's brothers he was well and truly married—something that might help dissuade the King from doing anything to end their union.

'What are you plotting, Gillian?'

His easy assumption made her smile against his shoulder. 'Me? Plotting? Why, nothing. How could you even think such a thing?'

'Uh huh. I am now tempted to leave in the morning to take my prisoners to King David. It would save trouble on many fronts.'

His tone was different. Not as hoarse or rough. She tried to rise, to see his face, to assure herself that he wasn't serious, but he held her firmly in place against his chest. She reminded him, 'You still need to find Jonathon.'

'I can leave enough men here to continue the search. I am sure Daniel and Thomas can see to the men guarding the Keep and the village, while also setting patrols to look for Jonathon.'

Seeking to goad him, she asked, 'And who will you set the task of watching over me until I fall asleep at night?'

She squeaked in mock surprise when he flipped her over on to her back. He rested over her, propped up on his forearms, his hands on either side of her head and that endearing half-smile cocking his mouth. She placed her hands on his shoulders. 'You are too far away.'

He leaned closer. 'I am wondering, would you prefer someone younger? Or perhaps someone a little older with more experience would suit you better.'

She shrugged. 'Since neither would be you, it doesn't matter. You choose.'

'I think younger. The question is how much younger. Even a boy could do that small task.'

Gillian nodded. 'So be it. I request only one thing of you first.'

'I nearly fear to ask. What might that be?'

She drew her hand beneath his shirt, then along his chest. 'I would share one more night with you before you leave. I still need you, Rory.'

'I desire you, too. More than you will ever know. But, Gillian, we cannot take the chance again.'

She had no intention of telling him what she already feared. It seems Robert could have been wrong. Her monthly time had already come and gone without a trace of any flow. While there could be other reasons for that lack, she had a feeling she was with child. But she was not going to use the slight possibility of a babe to keep him at her side. If she stooped that low, she would always wonder why he had stayed. She wanted him here because of his feelings for her, not because of any sense of responsibility.

Although she wanted him desperately and wasn't above being as brazen as she could at this moment. Before he could guess her intention, she slid her hand further down his chest, then pushed beneath his braies to wrap her hand around his obvious erection.

He groaned. 'Gillian, stop.'

When she ignored him, Rory grasped her wrist and moved off her. 'I said stop. I am not a saint, but neither am I a trained animal who will perform at your command.'

She gasped and sat up. 'I never—'

He pulled her back down and wrapped his arms tightly around her stiff body. 'It is obvious that I want you just as much as you want me. But, Gillian, we cannot do this. The risk is too great.'

'Risk? We have already taken that risk. How can it be any greater now?'

'I know exactly what it's like to bear the sins of a father. I will not leave behind a child who will suffer because of what I did. Ask anything of me but that.'

'I hate you.'

'That was the overall intention, but you didn't feel that way a moment ago.'

She turned on to her side, with her back against him and huffed. 'You succeeded.'

'At what?'

'Ruining my life.'

Rory rolled on to his side and draped an arm over her. 'Because you cannot have something you want, I have ruined your life?'

'Yes. Had you not proven that sex with a man was neither boring, nor unfulfilling, I would not be in this constant state of…need. You are all I think about, night and day. Your touch, your kiss is all I desire. So, yes. Yes, you have ruined my life. You gave me something I didn't even know I wanted, but now tell me I can never have it again. So, I hate you, Rory. I despise you for that.'

'You will have every opportunity to find another man when I am gone. I hope, for your sake, that you do.'

She snorted. 'Who do you suggest? Which man will treat me as fairly? Which one will make my heart flutter with a half-cocked smile? Who will steal my mind with a kiss and claim my soul with a touch? Who? Do you suggest one of my guards? One of yours? Daniel? Adam? Which one can replace you in my bed, Rory? Which one will give me what I want, what I need?'

His hushed growl told her that she was winning this argument. Whether she would enjoy the outcome was yet to be seen.

He tore at the laces on the side of her gown, but when she moved to roll back, he held her in place with a hand on her hip. 'Stay there. Do. Not. Move.'

Gillian sucked in a breath at his tone. Yes, she might be winning this argument, but he wasn't the least bit happy about losing.

After loosening the neck of her chemise, he rolled her on to her back and knelt over her to grasp the hem of her skirts. In one fluid tug he pulled them over her head, leaving her arms trapped in the sleeves. From the glint in his eyes and the devilish smirk, she was certain that had been his intent.

She lifted her arms. 'I cannot move like this.'

'Good.' He batted her arms down with the flick of his fingers. 'That is the idea.'

The toad was enjoying her imprisonment.

Leaning over her, he brushed her lips with his. 'Is this the kiss you want? The one that steals your mind?'

Gillian groaned. He was going to make her pay for her

words. She feared to even imagine the how of it. She shook her head. 'No, not like that.'

Just before claiming her lips once again, he whispered, 'Trust me, Gillian.'

The stroke of his tongue drew a sigh from her. Yes, this was the kiss she wanted. The one that effortlessly coaxed her to think only of the beating of her heart, the feel of his warmth. She wanted nothing more than to draw him closer.

He cupped a breast to roll the hardening nipple between his fingers. Gillian moaned and arched towards his touch. He lifted his head. When she opened her eyes to stare up at him, he gave her that half-smile she found so irresistible.

'I am certain I have the half-cocked smile right because I can feel the fluttering of your heart.' He barely moved his fingers. 'But I am not sure about the touch. You do not have the look of a woman who has had her soul touched.' He ran the flat of his palm down her belly, stopping when his hand was between her legs. 'Maybe this is closer.'

She closed her eyes and held her breath, waiting…wanting…

'No. I think perhaps…' His words trailed off as he rose to settle between her legs.

Gillian opened her eyes, lifted her head, but before she could say anything, or even think of what to say, she found herself captured in a kiss so intimate she had never dared to imagine.

Her head fell back on to the pallet as her eyes closed. Colours grew behind her eyelids and then burst into countless tiny stars that glistened. She curled her fingers tightly into the fabric of her chemise, seeking something solid to hang on to as she rose and fell with the sparkling stars.

His hand flat on her belly kept her steady as a cry of release tore from her throat. 'Rory.'

She didn't know whether to laugh or cry when he rose

and came over her to stare down at her. 'Ah, yes, that's the look I wanted to see.' He freed her hands from the confining fabric. 'Come, let me hold you. Stay with me this night.'

She wrapped her arms around him. 'I am going nowhere.'

Just before she fell asleep, he whispered against her ear. 'While I draw breath, nobody will take my place in your bed. Nobody.'

Chapter Seventeen

Rory awoke with a groan at the weight pinning him to the floor. He swiped at the wispy irritation tickling his nose and opened his eyes. The torch had gone out, so it was dark in the chamber. It was just before dawn—the moon's light no longer shimmered through the window, but the sun had yet to rise.

He didn't need light to tell that the weight pressing him into the floor was Gillian sprawled on top of him. He didn't remember rolling on to his back, or her clambering over him to use his body as a mattress.

Rory lifted his arm to brush her hair from his face and groaned again. Every muscle in his body ached. Perhaps he would reconsider using the bed in their chamber to sleep on, or even the large, cushioned chair. Either would be better than a hard, wood-planked floor.

He eased his sleeping wife off his chest. Since she didn't wake up, he assumed she was exhausted.

After taking a lit torch from the corridor, he dressed, draped a blanket over her, tucked it around her shoulders, then headed below to find something to quiet his growling stomach.

An odd prickling at the back of his neck made him pause at the top of the stairs. He'd learned long ago not to ignore any warning—real or imagined—and returned to the chamber to retrieve his sword belt from a wall hook and his weapon from the floor where he'd dropped it earlier.

'You are leaving?'

He buckled his belt and sheathed his sword, then knelt beside her. 'Only for a few moments, Gillian. I need something to eat. Do you want anything?'

'Something to drink would be welcome.'

Rory nodded. 'I'll see what I can find. Go back to sleep.'

When she rolled over on to her side, he left the chamber. Uncertain what caused his unease, he descended to the hall, keeping a close eye before and behind him. At the bottom of the stairs, he greeted Thomas. 'Has anything been amiss this night?'

'No. Not thus far.'

'Anyone in the kitchens?'

Daniel, standing nearby answered, 'The cook's daughters came in a short time ago to start the day's prep work. Not sure if the cook arrived yet or not.'

Nearing the corridor that connected the kitchens to the hall, Rory heard a cry of fear, followed by a man's menacing growl. He quietly drew his sword and pressed his back to the wall as he moved closer.

'Do as I tell you and you may live another day.'

Rory peered around the corner to see Blackshore holding a dagger to the cook's youngest daughter's throat. He had already torn her gown and was fondling the girl's breasts. At the other end of the corridor, the cook muffled her cries with her hands over her mouth as her older daughters huddled behind her.

Too many questions slammed into him. How had Blackshore escaped his cell? Someone had released him. Who?

Rory knew that if he gave any warning, Blackshore would slit the girl's throat—in front of her mother and sisters. As hard as it was to listen to the scum tell the girl what he was going to do to her, he waited and gritted his teeth to keep from making any sound. For Blackshore to achieve his objective, at some point he would have to lower his guard.

At the instant Blackshore fumbled with the tie to his braies, Rory lunged, knowing he had one chance to rid the world of this walking piece of evil.

His sword found a home through Blackshore's side. With a stroke of luck, the blade slid clean between rib bones. From the way the man instantly hit the floor, Rory knew he'd found the cur's blackened heart.

He caught the cook's daughter as she fell towards the floor and carried her to her mother. Handing her off, he paused, frowning. 'Where is your son?'

She shook her head. 'I don't know.'

'Woman, I have neither the time, nor the patience, for your lies. Either tell me where he is, or you can be gone from here.'

She pleaded, 'My Lord... I...he is my son.'

Rory didn't even try to keep the growl from his tone. 'I won't ask again.'

Tears streaked down her cheeks, she stared at the floor and said, 'He was here earlier, right after the evening meal, to take some food and leave without any word.'

It didn't require much thought to realise who had released Blackshore. Rory spun around, barely paused to free his weapon, motioned to Daniel as he quickly crossed the hall and mounted the stairs two at a time.

Light flooded the corridor outside his makeshift chamber. But he'd closed the door behind him when he left. His heart thudded in his chest as he tightened his grip on the hilt of his sword.

He heard her scream and then what sounded like a body hitting the floor. 'No!'

Rory came to a rocking halt just inside the chamber door. The body on the floor was Jonathon's. His naked wife knelt alongside him, rocking back and forth on her knees, a bloody dagger gripped tightly in her hands. Her keening cries sounded like that of a wounded animal and they tore at his heart.

He knew there'd been trouble afoot. How could he have been foolish enough to leave her alone?

Slowly approaching her, so as not to frighten her any more than she already appeared, he waved at Daniel. 'Hand me my cloak.'

He spared a glance towards Jonathon. It appeared that he'd been stabbed repeatedly in the throat. From a warrior's standpoint it was impressive. But his wife was no warrior and she didn't need a pat on the back, she needed him to gather her close and chase away the demons that would soon buffet her.

He draped the cloak around her shoulders before the others gathered in the doorway. 'Gillian, love. Come with me.'

She turned towards him and it was all he could do not to gasp in dismay. Her lip was split open, she had a black eye and a handprint on her cheek that would bruise by morning. There were scratches on her chest and she was covered in blood—thankfully, from what he could discern it was Jonathon's and not her own.

'He said he would kill me once he had used me fully and then come for you.'

Rory bit back a groan at the tone of her voice. She sounded like a lost child who didn't understand what had just happened.

'Shh, sweeting, we can talk later. For now, just come with me.' He wanted, needed to get her out of this chamber and away from the gruesome sight on the floor.

He helped her to her feet and she followed him like a defeated submissive dog who had been beaten one too many times. With a soft growl, Rory lifted her in his arms and pressed her head to his shoulder. The men gathered in the doorway parted to let him through with his bundle. He paused in front of Thomas. 'Get someone to clean this up. And get some water sent to my chamber. Warm water.'

He kicked open the door to their bedchamber and crossed the room to sit on the chair by the window. Still holding her, he tucked the thick cloak around her shivering body and just held her. Certain she was in shock, he didn't know what to say to soothe her, so he remained silent and she soon fell asleep on his lap. Right now, that was probably for the best.

Catherine rushed into the chamber, took one look at Gillian and with a hand to her mouth cried aloud.

'If you can't contain yourself, leave.' He knew the woman was horrified by her Lady's appearance, but he didn't want Gillian upset more than she already was. However, the older woman might prove useful.

Catherine sat on the edge of the bed and softly asked, 'What happened?'

Rory shook his head. 'She was attacked and defended herself.'

'Where were you?'

'In the hall dealing with Blackshore.'

'So, who…?' She waved towards Gillian.

'Jonathon.'

'Oh, my Lord, the boy has been sick a while now.'

'Was sick.'

Her only response at first was, 'Oh.' Then, as what he'd said registered, she stared at Gillian, her eyes widened and she nodded. 'She was trained well.'

'That she was.' He owed Daniel much.

However, she hadn't been told how to handle the aftermath. It was a little late for that now. All he could do now was keep a close eye on her and make certain she was safe in the days and nights ahead.

Gillian slid a hand through the opening of the cloak to stroke his cheek. 'Rory?'

'Yes?'

'I don't feel so well.'

'No, my love, I am sure you don't. Once we get you into a warm tub, you'll feel much better. I promise.'

Her hand slid off his cheek as she closed her eyes and fell back to sleep.

He turned his attention back to Catherine. 'Any idea how he might have gained entry to these chambers?'

She looked away.

Now he knew where Gillian had learned her avoidance techniques. 'Please, I have no patience for games. I need to know.'

'The kitchens. A tunnel runs from the kitchens to the Lady's bedchamber.'

He nodded. 'Thank you.'

How long had Jonathon been coming and going? He wondered if the cook knew. Of course she knew—nothing happened in her kitchens without her knowledge. What was he going to do about that? Especially now.

'Rory!' Gillian bolted upright on his lap, her eyes wide and filled with fear.

He stroked her hair and eased her back against his chest. 'I am here. I am right here.'

She plucked at his shirt. 'I thought you left.'

This was not a conversation he wanted her maid to overhear. He looked at her and asked, 'Could you see what's keeping the water? I want to get her into a tub and then to bed so she can try to rest.'

Once Catherine left the chamber, he asked Gillian, 'Where did you think I had gone?'

'To the King. I thought you left for good.'

'Sweeting, be easy, I will stay as long as you need me. I swear it.'

'At least he didn't hurt the baby.'

Rory froze. An overwhelming warmth washed over him, only to be replaced with a sudden chill. Could this night get any worse? He should be elated. Instead, he wanted to rage at the unfairness. How long had she known? It couldn't have been long—a few days, a week at the most. Why hadn't she said anything? If she was so adamant about him staying, why had she remained silent about the one thing she knew would keep him here? He swallowed his curse. He could berate her later. Right now, he closed his eyes and rested his forehead against her head. 'No, my love, he didn't harm the baby.'

He was uncertain she'd heard him because she'd fallen asleep again. He lifted her hand to his lips and dropped a kiss on an unbloodied spot atop. 'Oh, Gillian, I am sorry, so very sorry. For everything.'

Catherine returned followed by four lads, each carrying two steaming buckets of water. She directed them to dump the water into the tub and then set about gathering items needed for Gillian's bath.

She held up two vials and asked, 'Lavender or rose?'

'I don't care.' It wasn't as if he could tell one from the other. 'Whatever will soothe her more. Make sure the water isn't too hot.' He had no idea if the heat would matter to the babe. But he'd already placed her in harm's way, he was not taking any more chances with her well-being and safety.

The maid nodded. 'It is just right.'

He wanted to ask if she knew, but doing so would only confirm Gillian's belief. And he wasn't yet ready for that.

'The bath is ready. Do you wish me to leave?'

'No. I could use your help.' He rose with Gillian still sleeping in his arms. 'I want to get her bathed as quickly as possible and into bed. But I warn you, she is covered in blood. She is not harmed. Most of the blood is not hers. But I will stand for no outburst that might distress her more.'

Catherine nodded. 'Let's be at it, then.'

He let the cloak fall on to the floor, stepped over it to cross to the alcove and lowered her into the water. Gillian did nothing more than sigh.

Catherine worked on her hair while Rory ran the soapy cloth slowly over her belly. What would she look like a few months from now when she was obviously full with his child? He sucked in a deep breath. Was there a way he could be here to see it for himself? To be here as the child was born and grew from a baby to a child to a young adult. A way for him to help shape the adult it would one day become?

He shook his head. It was useless to waste his time wishing for things that would never happen. Not when what he needed to do was find her a husband—one who would raise this child as his own.

Rory bit his lip. He had to find a way to make these thoughts and wonderings go away. Otherwise, he would go mad. He wanted to face his death not as a confused man with little rational thought, but one who knew exactly what was happening and why.

Perhaps…and it was a huge if…maybe Elrik, or Edan, perhaps even King David, could help him in this. He glanced at Gillian. She didn't need to know. Some day, when he was gone, what if a stranger simply showed up at her gates and swept her off her feet? Would it matter if he'd arranged it in advance? No. Not if this stranger made her feel safe and wanted, it wouldn't matter in the least.

Although in the meantime, it would eat at him.

But his feelings and wants were of little concern. The only thing that mattered was that this woman he'd lost his heart to and their child would be cared for, loved and safe after he was gone.

A soft sniffle drew him away from his thoughts. He looked at Gillian only to see that she still slept. Lifting his gaze to Catherine, he saw her swipe at her cheek. The older woman's chin trembled. He placed a hand on her arm. 'I can finish this.'

'No.' She shook her head. 'No, I am fine. I cannot believe that of all the people at Rockskill *he* did this to her. She loved him like a brother, always had.'

Since she'd kept her voice soft and it didn't seem to cause Gillian any distress, he let her ramble on. If nothing else, it took his mind off his own bothersome worries.

'I knew he had grown sick of late, but I had not known just how sick he'd become.' Her words shook. 'Had I known...' She turned her face towards him. Tears dripped from her eyes. 'I am sorry, my Lord. I failed her.'

'No.' He patted her cheek. 'You have never failed her.' Rory swallowed hard. If anyone had failed her it was him. He had left her alone and unprotected after he knew something was amiss. How would he ever make that up to her?

Once Gillian was clean and dry, Rory carried her to the bed where Catherine dropped a soft, clean chemise over her head. The maid returned to the bedside with a comb, which he took from her. 'I can do this.'

'Then I will take my leave.'

He nodded. 'Would you see to it that her confessor be here first thing in the morning? She'll have need of him.'

'Yes. I am certain Father Bartles will make the time.'

After the chamber door closed behind the departing maid, Rory sat up against the headboard and pulled Gillian to sit between his legs, with her back against his chest. He worked the wide-toothed comb through her hair slowly to remove the tangles.

She sighed and leaned her head against his shoulder. 'What are you doing?'

'I believe it is called combing your hair.'

She reached up. 'I can do that.'

He held the comb away from her. 'So can I.'

Gillian lowered her hand to his leg and drew circles on his thigh. 'Is he...? Did I...?'

He waited, silently, wanting her to ask the question.

She took a shuddering breath, then asked in a rush, 'Did I kill Jonathon?'

Rory ran the comb slowly through a lock of semi-dry hair, searching for the right words. He watched it curl around his wrist as he released it. Still bereft of words, he leaned closer to softly answer her question. 'Yes.'

When she stiffened against his chest, he wrapped his arms about her and held her tightly. This was where he would tell a soldier that he'd done good work, had performed his duty well. He would urge him to hold his head high and be proud of following orders so well. He would thank him for his service to his liege and to his King.

She wasn't one of his men.

She'd had no duty to perform, no orders to blindly follow.

She would never be proud of what she'd done to the man she'd always considered her friend.

She was not in service to a liege, or their King.

He was at a complete loss over what to do, what to say. How was he to handle this correctly?

'So, it wasn't a dream, a nightmare?'

Her soft, barely discernible voice shook. He silently cursed himself for being a witless fool. Why could he not find the comforting words he so needed, the ones she needed, at this moment?

'No, I am sorry, it was not a dream.'

When she burst into the tears he'd expected, he turned her around in his arms and pressed her face to his shoulder. If he couldn't find the words, he could let her cry and hold her close while she did so.

A sharp rap on the door distracted him. 'Come.'

Catherine entered the chamber nervously, waving an arm as she explained, 'He would not wait until morning, my Lord.'

Father Bartles followed her in. Rory had never been so relieved to see a man of God before in his life.

Gillian untangled herself from his embrace to throw herself on her knees at the priest's feet. 'Father, help me. I have sinned gravely.'

The man took her hands in his and pulled her to her feet. 'Hush, Gillian. Come, let us talk.'

Then he sat her in the large chair and dragged the other chair over so he could sit in front of her. Once he took his seat, he looked at Rory.

Knowing when to take a hint and certain she was now in good hands, Rory stood up, saying, 'I am going.' He grabbed his boots, sword belt and weapon and followed Catherine out of the door.

Before the maid could take her leave, he lightly grasped her arm. 'Show me this tunnel.'

Once she showed him the sliding panel in the small chamber, he dismissed her. Pulling on his boots and buckling his belt, Rory drew his weapon and entered the narrow tunnel, following it carefully in the dark, down to another door.

He shoved the door open, sword at the ready.

And stepped back at the loud screams of the cook and her daughters.

Daniel, Adam and Thomas raced through the door at the other side of the kitchen, armed and ready to defend the women from whatever threatened them.

'Hold, Roul!'

Certain his men heard him, Rory stepped into the room and sheathed his weapon. He looked at Daniel. 'It seems this tunnel was missed.'

Chapter Eighteen

Sunlight streamed through the narrow windows of the bed-chamber. Rory pulled the woman in his arms closer and kissed her forehead. 'Time to get up.'

Gillian snuggled closer to his side and patted his chest before sliding her arm across him. 'Not yet.'

He yawned, then asked, 'How are you feeling?'

'Better now that I actually slept well.'

He completely understood since he'd spent the last seven nights with her in their bed. He'd watched over her and had little sleep himself, but it had proven much more comfortable than a lonely pallet on the floor. Each night she'd been pulled awake by multiple nightmares. Until last night when she'd slept through the night.

He laced his fingers through hers and stared up at the ceiling. 'The cook returns today, are you ready for that?'

She nodded against his shoulder. 'I don't blame her for anything. It wasn't her fault that her son lost his wits.'

It wasn't as if Gillian had easily put all that had happened behind her, she hadn't. Besides the nightmares she still had moments where her hands would shake uncontrollably, she was easily startled and on occasion would burst into tears that she tried hard to hide.

He just made certain he was right there to grasp her suddenly shaking hands, rest a steadying hand on her shoulder when she jumped as someone came up behind her and gather her close when she needed him to do so.

'What are we going to do today?'

For the last week they hadn't done anything. They had simply existed—eating, sleeping, stealing kisses, talking of little things, but nothing else. It was time she returned to life. Rory tightened his hold on her hand. 'I think it is time to return to the practice field.'

She tensed, but said nothing.

'Gillian, at some point it must be done. I think you are ready. But I will not force you.'

'You will be there?'

'Yes.' He wasn't leaving her to Daniel's care, *he* wasn't ready for that yet.

'I will try.'

'That is all I ask.' He released her hand and started to sit up.

She leaned over him, keeping him in place. 'In a few moments.'

Rory winged a brow and stared up at her. 'Something on your mind?'

Was she going to tell him about the baby? It was obvious to him that she had no recollection of telling him Jonathon hadn't harmed the baby, she seemed to remember little of that night. So as far as she was concerned, he didn't yet know. She'd had every opportunity this last week, but had said nothing.

'I—'

Daniel burst into the chamber unannounced, shouting, 'Rory!'

Rory pulled Gillian down on to his chest and jerked the covers up over them, then looked at his man. 'Yes?'

Daniel, looking everywhere but at the two of them, said, 'We have company', and left the chamber.

With a curse, Rory flung back the covers, kissed her forehead and moved out from beneath her to rise. 'I guess our day has been planned for us.'

'Do you think it is Albert?'

'It's either your cousin, or my brothers. Take your pick on which would be worse.'

Grumbling, she rose and rushed over to her clothes chest. Only to be stopped short when he wrapped an arm about her waist and pulled her close.

'Either way, they can wait.' He lifted her from the floor with one arm and carted her back to the bed. 'What were you going to say?'

She drew lazy circles on his chest, then teased his flat nipples.

Rory grasped her hand. 'We can spend all day in this bed if you'd like. I would have no complaints.'

'Tempting.' Gillian sighed. 'But what if it's your brothers?'

'They can camp outside the gates for all I care.' He stroked her hip. 'I doubt if any man would question my decision if given the choice of being in bed with a warm, lovely, very naked woman, or conversing with visiting family.'

'And if it's my cousin, he will not wait.'

Rory rolled her on to her back and threaded his fingers through her hair. Lowering his lips almost to hers, he chuckled. 'If he is locked in a cell, he will wait as long as I say he will.'

'Rory?'

'Hmm?'

She cupped his cheeks and urged him closer, to whisper against his lips, 'Stop talking.'

Later, once they were dressed, and groomed for whatever company awaited them, Rory opened the chamber door to find Daniel standing outside with his arm raised as if he'd been ready to pound on the door.

He lowered his arm and shook his head. 'The two of you have the appearance of just having climbed out of bed.'

Gillian ran her gaze down Rory's body, then looked at her gown. 'What is wrong with the way we are dressed?'

Daniel snorted. 'I didn't mean you'd been there sleeping.'

Gillian's cheeks reddened. Rory's fist caught the man by surprise. He staggered backwards from the blow to his chest. Once Daniel caught his footing, he bowed his head to Gillian. 'Forgive me, my Lady. I spoke out of turn. My crude comment was uncalled for. You look lovely as always.'

Satisfied with the oaf's response, Rory asked, 'Who is below?'

'The Lady's cousin. He has a priest with a marriage order from King Stephen.'

Both men ignored Gillian's gasp. 'Thankfully we aren't on Stephen's land.' Rory took her hand. 'Shall we go correct their mistaken assumption?'

She tugged free and went back inside, asking, 'Do you have a tabard like Daniel's?'

He glanced at his man. Daniel was wearing the single standing wolf, a replica of Rory's standard over his armour. Rory followed her, frowning. 'Of course. Why do you ask?'

She stretched out her hand, palm up. 'Let me borrow it.'

He reached into his saddle bag and dug out his tabard. 'Here.'

She dropped the black garment trimmed in silver over her head and fumbled with the side buckles. Realising what she was doing—purposely, openly announcing her relationship to Roul—he secured the tabard for her. 'You don't have to do this.'

'Yes, I do.'

Daniel removed his tabard and handed it to Rory. 'Perhaps if you both display a united front?'

Rory freed his sword belt from his waist, dropped the tabard into place and re-secured his belt. 'Now can we get on with this?'

Gillian slid her hand into the crook of his arm. 'Yes, let's do.'

They followed Daniel out of the chamber and down the stairs to the hall. Her heart raced. She hadn't seen Albert in months and had hoped never to do so again. She should have known better. Of course, he wasn't going to walk away from Rockskill.

Rory stopped on the bottom step as Daniel joined the men in the hall. Gillian blinked at the gathering and smiled as her racing heart eased to a steady beat. Never had she seen so many armed men in one place before. Thankfully most of them—even her guards—wore Roul's colours of black and silver.

Her husband nodded to his man. Daniel unsheathed his sword and swept the blade seemingly at nothing. All their men immediately moved to form a circle around the perimeter of the hall and then stepped forward in unison, closing the circle. They all stepped forward again, forcing Albert, his men and companions into the middle of the hall surrounded by the combined armed force of Rockskill and Roul.

The look of shock on her cousin's face widened her smile. It was about time something, or someone, intimidated him.

Daniel shouted, 'Hold!' And then he stepped back making a single opening in the circle.

Rory looked down at her. 'Ready?'

She leaned closer so nobody would hear her. 'They've all worked so hard and are so impressive, how could I disappoint them now?'

He smiled, straightened, then waved her forward.

Gillian forced the smile from her face and headed towards the opening Daniel had made for them. She paused only a heartbeat, long enough for Rory to put a reassuring hand on the small of her back, before stepping into the circle of men with her husband at her back. She heard Daniel's booted feet step back to close the circle again.

'What is the meaning of this?' her cousin asked before he even bothered to turn to look at her. When he finally did make the effort, his face turned red.

He was livid and, God forgive her, that knowledge gave her great satisfaction. 'What is the meaning of what, Albert?'

He waved wildly at the force surrounding him. 'I did not expect to be threatened in my own Keep.'

'It is not your Keep. Rockskill is mine. It always has been and always will be. You are no longer welcome here.'

'You talk nonsense. Your father gave me the rights to Rockskill.'

'You are either mistaken or lying. My father did not possess that power. Rockskill was my mother's, by the King's decree. When she died it became mine, again by the King's decree. Did he forget to tell you that, Cousin dear?'

Albert reached for the sword hanging at his side.

Gillian reached behind her towards Daniel. Her husband's man instantly slapped the hilt of his sword in her palm. Rory stepped back, giving her room. She swung the weapon around, grasped it in both hands, spread her feet, turned slightly, raised her arms and warned, 'You don't want to do that, Albert. I have already killed one man. I will not hesitate to use this weapon.'

Rory cleared his throat. The sight of his little wife, dressed in his colours, brandishing a sword, using the stance he had drilled into her while threatening her cousin in a calm, steady, tone worthy of any wolf, had to be the most seductive thing he'd seen in his entire life. He would carry this memory with him into eternity.

Albert laughed at her. 'You don't frighten me, Gillian. I know how much of a coward you truly are. Put that away before you hurt yourself.'

Her cousin's complete lack of wits amazed him. Rory held his breath as his wife squared her shoulders and lunged.

The tip of Daniel's sword pierced Albert's tunic directly over the man's heart, then stopped.

Albert screeched and jumped back.

Rory released his held breath, stepped forward and wrapped a hand around Gillian's. 'Enough.'

She relinquished the weapon and moved away as he returned the sword to Daniel.

He turned his attention to Albert. 'What do you want?'

'Who are you to ask me that?'

Rory sighed and then recited his qualifications. 'I am Rory of Roul, here at the behest of King David.' He lifted his chin. 'I am the Lord of Rockskill through my marriage to its Lady.' He extended his hand towards Gillian and drew her to his side.

Flustered, Albert whined, 'I gave her no permission to wed anyone. Especially not one of David's wolves.'

'That's *King* David and we didn't need your permission.'

From outside the circle Father Bartles waved a single piece of parchment overhead and shouted, 'The King's permission is right here.'

Rory swallowed his surprise. When had King David sent that?

Albert's priest stepped forward and extended a scroll to Rory. 'These are King Stephen's orders.'

'What do I care about Stephen's wishes? He is not the King here. Rockskill is on King David's land.'

Albert nearly shouted, 'Where is Blackshore? She is to wed him or Smithfield immediately.'

Gillian gasped and stepped closer.

Rory laughed. 'That is going to be a little difficult considering both are dead.'

Her cousin lowered his voice to ask, 'Cranwell?'

That man stepped forward. 'I am here.' He tossed his weapon towards Rory's feet. 'And I am giving myself up to Roul.'

Rory raised an arm and pointed towards Cranwell, ordering, 'Take him.'

Two guards stepped out of the circle to escort the man back to his cell. The others moved in to keep the circle intact.

Her cousin's shoulders slumped. In a weak quivering voice he asked, 'Jonathon?'

Rory opened his mouth, only to feel Gillian's hand on his arm. She raised her chin, took a breath and stated, 'I killed Jonathon.'

Rory took her hand in his and squeezed gently. She was going to be fine. Of that he had no doubts.

He glared at Albert and nodded towards Daniel. 'Take him.'

Albert must have realised what was coming, because he spun around, but before he could make any move to escape Daniel and Thomas grabbed his arms. Neither the priest nor the other men in Albert's company did anything to protect the man. In fact, they meekly let the guards escort them all to the cells below.

Once the hall was cleared of Albert and his companions, Rory turned towards Gillian. 'Woman, I have never been prouder of another person than I am of you.'

She batted her eyelashes at him. 'You enjoyed that sword-play, did you?'

He grabbed her to pull her close. 'You think to mock me after I've paid you a compliment?'

She collapsed against his chest and looped her hands behind his neck. 'Never, my love. Never would I mock you.'

He laughed at her outrageous lie.

A commotion behind him drew them apart. One of Rock-skill's guards yelled as he raced towards them. 'My Lord! My Lord! There are visitors at the gate. They appear armed.'

Rory cursed. He knew who it was. His brother's timing was legendary. He grabbed Gillian's hand. 'Come. It's time for you to meet the family.'

'Today? Now?'

'Apparently.'

She followed him out into the bailey and up on to the wall near the gatehouse.

If she'd thought the sight inside the hall had been impressive, this one was...extraordinary. Leading all the way back to the wooded area between the Keep and village were armoured men on horseback. She stared at the three men leading the force behind them.

Her gaze flew to Rory, then back to the men. These were his brothers. Of that there was little doubt. The only thing that appeared to vary was their size. Two, Rory and the one in the middle, seemed taller than the others. But all were still larger than most men she'd known. Rory and the one she assumed was Edan were clean-shaven...mostly. The other two, the older ones perhaps, had full beards. All four had the same dark, silver-streaked hair that needed a serious trim.

Obviously unimpressed, he casually leaned over the wall and shouted, 'What do you want?'

The one in the middle, the largest of the three, urged his horse forward. 'I seem to be missing a standard.'

Four foot soldiers stepped forward. One was empty-handed and walked behind the others—the other three each carried a pennant. The one in the middle was of four standing, snarling wolves. The one on the left was of three wolves. And the one on the right contained two. She glanced at Rory's tabard. His was a single wolf. Apparently, they went in reverse order—Rory, the youngest, was the single wolf, working up to the oldest brother having four.

Daniel joined them on the wall and whistled. 'Looks as though Edan made anchor at Warehaven, too. With Gregor along that makes for quite the family reunion.'

Rory snorted. 'Get me a flag.'

Daniel pulled one off the side of the gatehouse and handed it to him.

Rory tossed it over the wall. It fluttered to land at the hooves of his brother's horse. 'Here's your standard, Elrik, now go away.'

Gillian saw the flash of teeth right before his brother ordered, 'Open the damn gate, Rory.'

Rory sighed and flicked an imaginary speck off his chest with his fingers.

'You need to open the gate, Rory. You can't just let them stand out there,' Gillian urged.

'Maybe tomorrow.'

She tugged at his arm. 'Rory.'

Daniel laughed. 'This is typical of them, my Lady. Do not let it bother you.'

When Daniel waved at the men and then walked away, she turned to her husband and in a hushed voice asked, 'Is this the man who holds your life in his hands?'

He glared down at her. 'Do not.'

'Do not what?'

'Do not presume to tell me how to treat my brothers.'

She wasn't trying to tell him how to treat his brothers, she was trying to get him to fight for his life. And leaving them standing outside was not the way to gain any measure of mercy or leniency. Did he not want to live? 'Rory, please.'

He waved a hand at her and turned away. As he headed for the ladder, he said harshly, 'If you want them to come in so badly, be my guest.'

Shocked, she watched him descend the ladder, take three steps towards the Keep, then turn and walk back to the gate, where he did nothing more than stare out at his brothers.

Finally, the oldest one, Elrik, dismounted to approach on foot.

Gillian moved closer to the gatehouse to hear what they said.

'Open the gate, Rory. This has gone on long enough. Let us be done with this. Just you and me.'

Rory silently motioned to the guard in the tower. Gillian heard the groan of chains as the gate was lifted. Elrik strode into Rockskill and walked at Rory's side as they headed towards the Keep.

She grabbed the skirt of her gown and headed below. Only to be stopped at the bottom of the ladder by Daniel and Adam. 'No, Lady Gillian, leave them be. This is between them. There is nothing you, or anyone else, can do.'

Daniel gently grasped her arm and turned her towards the approaching force, saying, 'Come, let me introduce you to your family.'

Chapter Nineteen

Rory turned to face his brother once they stepped into the hall. Elrik clasped his shoulder and glanced at the people milling about. 'Not here. Somewhere private.'

Rory shook off his brother's hand, then led him to a small unused chamber at the rear of the hall. He opened the door, waved Elrik inside, then followed and closed the door behind them. He took the time to lock the door.

'Why are you here, Elrik? I would have come to you.'

'I am sure you would have. Once you had driven yourself mad.' Elrik peeled off his mailed gloves and tossed them on to a small wooden table. 'I know you, Rory. As well as I know myself.'

'Then why?'

'Because our King asked me to when he sent me a copy of your marriage agreement. Then our brother showed up unannounced and begged me to because he was convinced something was dreadfully amiss. Imagine my surprise to learn that not only did my youngest brother think I considered him a traitor, a deserter worthy of death at my hands, but that the same brother had gifted me with the responsibility of a Keep and a wife I knew nothing about.'

Before Rory could guess his next move, Elrik's fist made contact with his jaw. The blow sent him reeling backwards, but before he could stumble to the floor, Elrik grabbed his arms and kept him upright long enough to hit him again. This time Rory tasted blood—his own. And this time he had to pick himself up off the floor.

The urge to fight back nearly overwhelmed him, but knowing he deserved this and more kept him from striking back. He simply stood there with his hands fisted at his sides.

'This is what I taught you? To stand there and be beaten to death? Defend yourself.'

Rory shook his head.

Elrik took a deep breath and hit him again.

The man could still land a punch. Rory shook his head to clear his vision and stayed down on his knees.

The locked door splintered behind him. Gregor and Edan both cursed as they entered the chamber. Gregor grasped Rory and lifted him to his feet.

Rory saw the pity in his brother's eyes and shoved him away. 'Leave me be.'

Elrik shook off Edan's hand from his arm. He stood before Rory and shouted, 'What is wrong with you?'

When Rory said nothing, Elrik grabbed him and pulled him close. 'Rory. Talk to me. Tell me what happened.'

'I can't speak of it.'

'Yes, you can.' Elrik softened his tone. 'I am truly sorry, Brother, but you must. Tell me what happened on that field.'

The nightmares he thought he had so recently left behind suddenly became real once again. The screams and cries of mere boys rang in his ears as they were cut down one by one in what seemed a never-ending line of death. He shivered like an old woman and tried to push away, tried to escape the horrors, but Elrik held him tightly, refusing to let him go, forcing him to relive the nightmare.

Their faces, twisted masks of agony and fear—so much

fear—raced through his mind until he cried out on a choked broken sob, 'They were children. My God, we were slaughtering children.'

Edan gasped and looked at Gregor, who seemed equally shocked. 'What the hell?'

Rory's legs gave out and Elrik dropped to his knees still holding him. He clutched Rory's head to his shoulder and hoarsely said, 'I know. I know, Rory. I saw. I knew then why you had left. But there was something you did not know. The fires had been salted with henbane. What you saw had been enhanced by the smoke. Did none of your men get sick afterwards? Did none of you see things that you knew were impossible?'

Rory nodded.

'I saw the aftermath and, yes, it was horrible. But, Rory, it was nowhere near a slaughter. My God, Brother, I love you. I have always made certain to be there for you. Why did you not come to me? You have always been the strongest, the most stubborn, the most fearless and I knew that even you could not have left that battlefield unscathed. I feared for your well-being and for your soul. King David did you a great service by sending you to complete a mission.

'But once this task is done you are finished, Rory. No more. Unless you must fight to protect your wife, your Keep or yourself, you are not killing another man. I have already discussed this with King David. We agree, no more. I need you whole, not broken. You are useless to me, to yourself, to everyone if you are not whole. I am heartily sorry for having asked so much of you. It was too much to ask of any man.'

As the long-held tears fell, Elrik waved the other two men from the room. When Rory's sobs started to lessen, Elrik said, 'I do not know how you have borne this alone.'

'I haven't been alone.'

'Ah, yes, that wife I know nothing about. Tell me about her.'

Rory eased out of his brother's embrace and sat back on his heels. 'She drugged me, captured me, chained me to a wall and forced me to wed her.'

'That little thing who was up on the wall with you?' At Rory's nod Elrik burst out laughing. 'Just the sort of wild woman you need. If nothing else, she should keep you on your toes.'

'That *little thing* ripped out a man's throat with a dagger. She has done more than keep me on my toes.'

'Ah, so the wolf cub found his mate. Do you care for her?'

'Care for her?' Rory stared at the floor, then lifted his gaze to meet his brother's searching one. 'She was born for me. I love her with every fibre of my being.'

'And have you told her this?'

He shook his head.

'Of course not.' Elrik clasped his shoulder. 'You have prisoners to escort to King David?'

'Yes, two prisoners and a shipload of gold and weapons.'

'We have three ships anchored at the harbour south of here. Use them.'

'No. I would rather travel over land.'

'Take a ship, bring your wife along.'

'No. I will go alone, over land.'

Elrik lowered his arm and frowned. 'What is going on?'

'We have an agreement that once my task for the King is completed, I would leave and ask the King to nullify the marriage.'

'So that is why you left her, and this Keep, in my tender loving care?'

'Yes, she needs to be protected. Who better to do so than Roul?'

'Of course, she realises that I am Roul?'

'Well, not exactly. I'm sure she thinks I mean all of you.'

'Oh, as if that's any better. Do you really think she wants three brothers underfoot?'

Rory squinted and turned his face away. 'She's going to need a husband. Soon.'

'I fear Avelyn might not approve of me taking another wife and I know Beatrice certainly isn't going to let Gregor do so. That leaves only Edan and you know as well as I that he gave his heart away years ago. So, exactly what are you suggesting?'

'I had hoped that perhaps you might know someone who would make her a good husband.'

'Why does she need a husband soon? Have you slept with her?'

'I haven't been a monk. And I fear she is carrying my child.'

'Rory.'

'Elrik, please help me with this. She needs someone with a steady hand, someone who will not let her run amok, but who will not seek to break her. She deserves to be loved and cherished. I cannot leave her alone. She is not meant to be alone. And I need to leave. I must leave.'

'Why?'

'I left my honour on that battlefield and I must find it, somehow. I cannot do so here. I do not sleep with her for fear of killing her. And now that she is possibly with child… I cannot take that risk. I would rather take my own life than harm her.'

'I do not agree that you will find what you seek away from here, but go. Do what you must. Take your prisoners and the goods to the King. Then take yourself off to discover whatever it is you need to find so you can once again be whole. I will see to your wife and your child if there is one. But I will not wed her to another unless that is her wish.'

Rory paused to consider his brother's offer. Perhaps once they were granted an annulment, Elrik would see things differently. He nodded. 'I leave today.'

'So be it.' Elrik reached up to wipe at the blood on Rory's split lip. 'Are we in agreement here?'

'We are.'

'Go, Rory. Be safe. Be well, little Brother.'

Rory left the chamber and motioned for Daniel to join him. As they crossed the hall towards the door, he said, 'I am leaving.'

'Your brothers just arrived.'

'They will be staying. At least Elrik will be.'

'Where are you going?'

'I need to take Albert and Cranwell to King David along with his goods. After that, I am not sure.'

'When do we leave?'

'As you are the Captain of the Guard at Rockskill this is now your post. You might want to send for your sons, because you are staying. I am leaving as soon as I can get the men and prisoners ready.'

'She is not going to be happy.'

'I know. Let Elrik handle it. You are responsible only for the guards and the safety of Rockskill.'

'Rory.' Daniel reached out to put a hand on his shoulder. 'What are you doing?'

'Don't. Just don't.' He moved away from Daniel's touch. 'You know I care for her.'

'This is not how you show a wife that you care.'

Rory nodded towards a quiet corner. 'Except for the last few nights when I watched over her, I have slept alone since we arrived. I fear killing her in my sleep. What sort of marriage is that? What sort of husband fears doing that?'

'You think you are the only one who still has nightmares?'

Daniel waved his arm towards the men gathered in groups throughout the hall. 'Ask any of them what they dream about. Ask them what awakens them screaming in the middle of the night.'

'I cannot go on like this.'

'Go.' Daniel raised his hands and backed away. 'I have known you all my life and I never once thought you a selfish man. Go. Just go.'

Rory stepped closer and lowered his voice. 'She is pregnant, Daniel. Pregnant. She carries my child. It would not be just her life I take. After what we have seen, what we have done, I cannot, I will not take that risk.'

Without waiting for Daniel's response, he left the Keep.

Gillian's heart drummed loudly in her ears. The noise in the crowded bailey was deafening. Guards packing up to leave Rockskill. Their families bidding tearful farewells tore at her heart.

But not as much as the task ahead of her tore at her soul. How was she to calmly tell Rory goodbye? She hadn't told him about the coming baby and now was not the time to use it against him to change his mind. She couldn't do that to him. She wouldn't force him in that manner.

Oh, but how she wanted to do so.

A hand fell lightly upon her shoulder. She would know his touch anywhere and turned to lean against his chest.

'I did not expect to find you here.' He wrapped her in his arms and held her close.

'I know. But I had to be here.'

'Gillian, please…'

'Hush.' She silenced him with a finger against his lip. 'I am not here to argue with you, or to beg you to stay. I want only to hold you a moment, to kiss you farewell and to tell

you that I will always love you, Rory of Roul. I will carry
you in my heart for ever.'

She leaned back to look up at him and shook her head
at his split lip and bruised face. 'Obviously the two of you
fought.'

'Not exactly.'

'You will take care of yourself?'

'Of course I will.'

'Maybe once in a while you might consider sending me
a missive?'

'Perhaps.' He graced her with his crooked half-smile. 'If
you will send me one in return.'

Knowing he would never send her a missive, she replied,
'I promise I will.'

He rested his forehead against hers. 'We will never write
to each other.'

She tightened her embrace around him. 'I know.'

'Gillian, I...'

He wasn't going to say the words, she knew that, yet she
smiled against his chest, because she didn't need to hear his
words to know in her heart how he felt. 'I know that, too,
my love.'

'You know I have to go.'

'I have known that since the day we wed. You made it
perfectly clear you would not stay.' She stroked his whisker-
stubbled cheek with a fingertip. 'Rory, you have given me so
much in your short time here, how can I now go back on my
word? I vowed not to hold you here, I will not break my word
to you, no matter how much I long to do so. I will miss you
sorely, but I will never regret one moment we have shared.'

'Gillian, I do so love you.'

His unexpected admission made her stare up at him in

open-mouthed shock. He covered her lips with his, giving her a kiss so sweet and heartfelt that it brought tears to her eyes.

He broke their kiss and slowly released her. 'I leave Daniel as Captain of your guard. Elrik will see to whatever you need. Trust him as you would trust me. Be safe, Gillian. Be well.' He reached out to brush a tear from her cheek. 'But most of all, find happiness.'

Unable to speak, she could only nod while wondering how she was to do that as he was riding out of her life.

Chapter Twenty

Gillian rolled over and groaned as another wave of sickness overtook her. Catherine had given her dry crackers to eat before she rose from her bed in the morning, but they didn't help. Nothing helped ease this morning sickness that had bedevilled her for the last two months. The thought that this could last for her entire pregnancy made her want to cry. She was so tired, so sick and so tired of being sick.

She hardly did anything any more. She hadn't trained with Daniel in weeks now. The first time she'd shown up too weak to hold her weapon, let alone train, he'd ordered her from the training grounds. When she refused to leave, he'd sent Elrik to bodily remove her and forbid her from returning.

The women, Catherine, Avelyn and Beatrice, had all repeatedly assured her that it would get better. She didn't believe them. Not when she felt worse by the day.

Edan had returned to Roul a few days after Rory's departure. Gregor and Elrik and their wives had remained, swearing it would only be until she gave birth. She didn't believe that either.

Gillian took a large drink of water and swished it in her mouth before spitting it out into the bowl she kept beside her bed. It took a few more times to wipe the bitterness away. She set down the goblet, rolled on to her side and groaned again.

She felt the tears build in her eyes and cursed softly. She was sick of this weepiness, too. But, knowing she would soon fall back to sleep, she tried to ignore it. Just something else the women claimed was normal. And just something else she didn't believe.

She closed her eyes and sighed.

An added weight dipped the mattress, and she froze. Who… she forced herself to remain calm and listened carefully.

An arm snaked around her waist. A large, strong hand rested over the slight mound of her belly.

She rolled on to her back with her arms already reaching to draw him close. 'Rory.'

He pushed himself up on to his hands, stiffened his arms and refused to come into her embrace. 'I understand this pregnancy of ours is not going so well.'

'You know.' She didn't care who had told him. The only thing that mattered was that he was here. Why did he look so angry?

'Woman, I have known since the night Jonathon died when you told me that he didn't harm the baby.'

She frowned. 'I don't remember saying that.'

'Well, you did and you had every opportunity afterwards to explain that statement, but you never bothered.'

'I never bothered? Me? I didn't? You knew, never said anything and you still left?' She smacked his arm. 'You left! You broke your word to me.'

He shook his head. 'You thought I left here without knowing and you were fine with that. You let me leave thinking I didn't know we were going to have a child. Had you planned on raising him or her alone?'

'If I don't want him or her to be as dense as the father, then, yes, I will raise the child alone.' She shoved at his chest. 'Go back to where you came from! We don't need you.'

When she tried to turn away from the sheepish look on his face, he grasped her arms and held her in place. 'I had to go, Gillian.'

She knew he was seeking to distract her from being angry. It wasn't going to work this time. 'Go away. I hate you.'

'Of course you do. What else is new?'

'I...' She choked back a sob and silently cursed herself. 'I...'

'Go on. You what?'

She knew she would forgive him anything. Surrendering, she whispered, 'I have missed you.'

'I have missed you, too. But beating your husband doesn't quite lend truth to your claim. I thought we'd got beyond the keeping of secrets.'

Now her tears fell in earnest. 'I didn't want you to stay because of the baby. I wanted you to stay because you wanted to be with me, because you loved me.'

'How could you not have known how much I loved you?'

'You never said it until right before you rode away.'

He knelt over her and placed his palm back atop her belly. 'This happened because I loved you. I would never have used you in such a manner had I not cared deeply for you. Gillian, how could you not know that? What sort of man do you think I am?'

The door to the chamber opened, 'Lady Gillian? Who are you talking—?' Catherine's question came to an instant halt.

Rory growled, then shouted, 'Get out!'

Before leaving, the maid laughed and said, 'Welcome back, my Lord.'

Gillian reached up to clasp her hands around his neck. 'Rory?'

'What?'

'Kiss me.'

'No. I am waiting for an answer.'

She stroked the outline of his ear, then cupped his cheek. 'What sort of man do I think you are? An honourable and brave one. A strong one. A loyal one. An extremely handsome one. A man who treats me fairly. One who makes my heart flutter with a half-cocked smile. One who can steal my mind with a kiss and claim my soul with a touch. The only man I will ever love.'

He stretched out alongside her and pulled her gently against him. 'Ah, Gillian, my love, you make me weak with your flattery.'

'Weak is one thing you could never be. Tender of heart, perhaps, but never weak. Now that you have your answer, do I get my kiss?'

He dropped a kiss on her forehead.

'That isn't what I meant.'

'I know that. I need to tell you something first and I need you to hear me, to understand what I say because I will never say it often enough.'

She nodded. 'I am listening.'

'I love you, Gillian, with all my heart. It took leaving you to know just how much I wanted and needed you. I adore the sound of your laughter. I long for your touch. You will never be rid of me from this day forward. I left to find the honour I thought I had lost and all I found was emptiness and loneliness. You bring me honour. You fill my soul with light. You are the beating of my heart.'

She sighed. 'Rory, I love you so. Please—'

He covered her lips and gave her the kiss she had so desperately missed.

* * * * *

If you enjoyed this story,
then you're going to love
Denise Lynn's other captivating romances

The Warrior's Runaway Wife
At the Warrior's Mercy
The Warrior's Winter Bride
Pregnant by the Warrior

HARLEQUIN
Reader Service

Enjoyed your book?

Try the perfect subscription for Romance readers and get more great books like this delivered right to your door.

See why over 10+ million readers have tried Harlequin Reader Service.

Start with a Free Welcome Collection with free books and a gift—valued over $20.

Choose any series in print or ebook.
See website for details and order today:

TryReaderService.com/subscriptions